Awkward Streak

Year of the Hamster

by

Martin Wilkes

WINTER

Chapter 1: NINE-NINE-NINERS

Distant memories are often triggered by smells. The slightest whiff of creosote, blended with a smidge of hamster, whisks my mind instantly back to 1963 - to a time when my dad had just bought a new shed.

"Show me a boy of seven and I'll show you the man!" my dad would quote, whenever my age became the topic of conversation. In 1963, I was that boy of seven. Half-a-century later, with the merest olfactory stimulus, my memories surge straight back to those formative years.

My family lived at the top end of Bladon Circle, on the posh side of Sutton Green. Everyone knew this to be the classiest council estate in Staffordshire. British council houses were a post-war experiment, designed to lift the impoverished from the clutches of the slum-lords. To qualify for the low-rent homes, all you needed was a breadline income or a large family. We squeaked in on both counts.

"A bun-in-the-oven's like a foot-in-the-door," dad would joke, about the council house waiting list. Needless-to-say, the estate had its fair share of feckless adults and scruffy, malnourished children. In contrast, there were a significant number of social climbers grappling for betterment. My family had a foot in both camps.

Outsiders saw Sutton Green as a characterless monotony of semi-detached, orange-bricked clones. If you were not paying attention you could easily find yourself in the wrong house, even on the wrong street. Dad always referred to it as "Chairman Mao's dream come true!"

Some houses had three bedrooms but the Wells family settled for two. Mum and dad shared the smaller one, whilst my two brothers and I bunked down in the master bedroom.

Having a new shed made us the envy of the whole neighbourhood. Indeed, this miniature cedar playhouse spawned serious cause for jealousy. Dad had mollycoddled it, with lavish coatings of top-grade wood preservative, which most Sutton Greeners considered to be an audacious luxury.

"A bloody waste of money!" next door's Reg Johnson articulated, whenever we were in earshot.

Reg was a short, thickset neighbour from the attached side, who wore his flat cap with pride. He was never seen without a cigarette dangling from the corner of his lower lip and he used smoke inhalations to punctuate his statements. He spouted bigoted, Woodbine-flavoured opinions about anything and everything. In Reginald's eyes, anyone trying to better himself was betraying his working class. His attitude was not atypical.

The eight by six-foot shed was our gang headquarters. Mum would not actually let us call ourselves a gang - that was far too thuggish. So, we officially classified ourselves as a club - the 999ers. We considered this to be edgy and sophisticated. Nine-nine-nine, was the phone number for emergency services – hence, the edginess. The sophistication was lost on my seven-year-old brain but Andrew, my nine-year-old big brother, assured me that the number had some pretty mystical connotations.

Andrew was the club leader and his word was law. Andrew was a mine of information, which he acquired from everywhere and remembered forever. He loved to learn, and everything that he read, or his teachers told him, or he heard on the television seemed to just stick. As well as being a brain-box, he also had a way of making calm, rational decisions which were particularly appreciated by teachers and parents. Neighbours would stop us just to comment on his big brown eyes.

"Oh Beryl, he's going to break a few girls' hearts," was a common comment, amongst the women who would stop to gossip. Mum would always bristle with pride whenever the attributes of her firstborn came under scrutiny.

Andrew devised most of the gang's dares, which we called buckers and doffers. He also invented 999er passwords and rules. The password was 666.

"Brilliant in its simplicity," we all agreed, long before we knew of the number's connection with the Antichrist. Andrew reserved the right to sporadically change our password, if he so wished. He invoked this privilege with frustrating frequency, whenever he wanted to flex the old sibling muscles of rivalry. Many a time, I was reduced to a sobbing mass of tears outside the den, randomly guessing number sequences.

"007," I chanced, remembering the code number of Andrew's favourite spy, James Bond.

"Not quite, Miss Moneypenny," he taunted in a bastardized Sean Connery accent.

"I'm telling mum that you called me a girl!" I sniffled, hoping my bluff would gain some leverage. 'Telling mum' was always a last resort gamble, which could backfire if the grievance was considered too trivial to report. In which case, the victim may be further victimized with a triple cuff to the head, punctuating the words, "Don't! Tell! Tales!"

"I never called you a girl, Moneypenny. It's only a saying," was Andrew's defence, "come on, you nearly got the password."

"So, I am close?" reasoned my inner dialogue. Then, for a split second we were two brothers in psychic harmony. It was the name of an American soap opera that was sweeping the nation; the catchy theme tune was being sung daily on every school playground in England.

"77 Sunset Strip!" I cried, enjoying my eureka moment.

His eyes widened in shock, flummoxed as to how I had managed to read his mind. After all, he was the genius and I was a mere minion. Everything about his body language told me that I was right. He instinctively started to open the shed door but my gloating face must have been too much for him to bear.

He suddenly decreed, "Actually, it was '76 trombones' but its close enough." I knew that he was lying because he was struggling to look me in the eye, but I had no way of proving it.

On another equally frustrating occasion, I found that Andrew had totally strayed from the presumed numerical parameters. The secret entry code turned out to be 'Brylcream.' Another time it was 'Nitram' – my own name spelled backwards. How fiendish was that?

It was also Drew, as us club members were could call him, who came up with the famous wolf-cry, reserved only for our inner circle. Although I was two years younger than Drew, I perfected the howl better than any of the other shed-dwellers: Barry Pratt, from across the way; Tony Boswell, the next street down; and Jimmy Drinkwater, were the only other humans in the clan. Whiskey the hamster made the sixth team member, despite his limited wolf crying abilities. We saw ourselves as a loose hybrid of Enid Blyton's 'Secret Seven' and her 'Famous Five,' although they were admittedly classier.

Mum kept us presentable, with well-darned socks, re-attached shirt buttons and nicely ironed school trousers. However, our home attire could hardly be defined as classy. Comfort and warmth were our main non-school priorities. From one Monday wash day to the next, my maroon tracksuit top over a T-shirt and shorts, concealed a conglomerate of blood, mud and snot. Andrew had the same tracksuit in blue. Mum tended to buy outfits in pairs, one size apart, but always in different colours to spare us the twin-look. Hand-me-downs were my fate, as the second-born; just as I was tiring of a fashion, it was resurrected in a faded, alternate colour. A duffel coat and Wellington boots were standard winter issue for all children and we were no exception. Mum was also a wizard with the knitting needles, so Andrew and I also sported unique speckled jumpers and cardigans that could be found in no shop. However, while Andrew's jumpers hung from him like the models on the front of knitting patterns, mine always rendered me a shapeless blob.

Each member of the 999ers brought his own unique set of skills to the table. Andrew was obviously the mastermind of the operation. He invented invisible ink, using a combination of lemon and onion juice, loaded into an old fountain pen. All you had to do to reveal the secret message was hold the paper over a fire for a minute. Of course, some of the best secrets accidentally went up the chimney in flames, leaving nothing but an oddly pungent after-smell. He later went on to modify the formula, with a secret ingredient, to manufacture ink eradicator. The mystery solution had a fragrance suspiciously similar to that of domestic bleach.

Andrew was a unique storyteller. We would sit transfixed, as he described in detail how a Boa Constrictor would slowly tighten its vice-like grip around a victim's chest, each time they exhaled, making it impossible to breathe in again. His yarn was so captivating that we found ourselves gasping, to test whether our own rib-cages were still functioning. He told us that Jack-the-Ripper was secretly the King of England's crazy bastard son, who was let out on foggy nights to slaughter prostitutes. Apparently, he was never caught because he was under the protection of the crown. Andrew taught us about Japanese torture techniques, where the victims were pinned down in bamboo fields and the unstoppable shoots would grow slowly through their bodies. We never questioned his sources; he spoke with complete authority.

I was the daredevil of the group. I could climb any tree or building and 'run like buggery,' as my dad would brag. Also, my long-distance vision was astonishingly good - I could read the destination on the front of any bus long before others could even see the bus. However, my proudest boast was that I could jump off anything! Garage roofs, climbing frames, giant walls and bridges offered little challenge to my fearlessness. It was extraordinary how often Andrew's plans seemed to exploit my gift.

"Here's how it works," he would decide, "Martin will climb along the branch of that tree and tie a rope, using a Staffordshire knot, then drop down onto the escarpment below." No sooner was it said than done.

The whole of Sutton Green was in an idyllic setting for gang of ruffians, looking for buckers (straight dares) and doffers (challenger goes first), to hone their athletic skills. We had fields, with valleys and hillocks, streams, rivers and canals, instantly accessible via our back fence. There were railway tracks, smoldering slag heaps and fenced-off underground air-raid shelters constantly beckoning exploration. Two streets away was the 'spare ground,' with a play area of swings, slides and climbing frames in one corner, and an equally alluring unofficial dumping area in the other. Treasures, such as discarded prams, mattresses, bald lorry tires, mangles, dolly tubs, and old bikes magically appeared in the night. The rule was simple: if you could not play with it, you could always burn it. We often did both!

Jimmy Drinkwater had a namesake who was a famous Native American wrestler. Whenever we played 'Cowboys and Indians,' Jimmy got the bow and arrow, which was never a match for our spud guns. This suited Jimmy because he loved to take a fictitious bullet to the gut and then drag out his show-stopping death.

Every male in Jimmy's family had an identical pre-Raphaelite nose and greasy, gassed-back blond hair. Being third-in-line to his brothers' hand-me-down clothes, Jimmy epitomized the word ragamuffin. Luckily, he had no pride. Where many choose to hide their light under a bushel, Jimmy's talent involved hiding in bushes. He was basically a peeping tom. He insisted on teaching the skill to me, which I had to concede proved far trickier than I had ever imagined.

One day, we hid in some brambles on Paxton Lane, a quiet country road that ran parallel to the canal, for going-on five hours. We simply watched oblivious people stroll past. Sometimes, they would be singing or talking to themselves. At one point, as an old lady was passing, Jimmy swore that he heard her fart. I was convinced that he made it up because, in my seven long years, I'd never heard a woman do that. We nearly blew our cover trying to stifle the ensuing fit of giggles. Jimmy did not help the situation when he made a nose-pinching gesture, accompanied by a motion of fake air-wafting. Later in the day, our domain was invaded by a slobbery black Labrador and we had to let it lick our faces, while a middle-aged couple kept calling him:

"Bruce, Bruce, what are you doing in there boy?" the woman asked.

"I bet he's got a rat!" said the husband.

"Have you got a rat, Bruce?" his wife inquired of the dog.

Bruce had no answer, although the mention of the rodent seemed to trigger a Pavlovian dog response to his overly active salivary glands.

"Bugger off, Bruce," whispered Jimmy, pushing the canine face away.

"Yeah, sod off slobber-chops," I added.

This tickled both of us and Jimmy snorted so loudly that we seemed certain to be exposed.

"I reckon Brucie has got himself a rabbit. Bring it out, boy! Bring it out!" said the man.

In a split second, Bruce lost all free will. His master's voice was commanding him to 'bring it out' and he was compelled to obey. He had no choice but to try and drag me from my hide-away. Indeed, Bruce was about to lock his sloppy wet jaws onto the neck of my hand-knitted speckled cardigan, when Jimmy had a brainwave. The Drinkwater family knew about dogs and Jimmy took off his shoe and made as though he was going to throw it, whispering "Fetch!"

At this, Bruce darted out of the brambles, involuntarily chasing the imaginary projectile. Once he saw his owners, Bruce was too distracted to remember that he was just about to 'bring it out,' and the trio continued on their 'walkies.'

Barry Pratt had the most vivid imagination that I have ever known and he had natural comedic timing, for a nine-year-old. He could make you laugh by simply scratching his blond brush-cut, or rolling his enormous green eyes. Bazzer had this amazing ability to lower people's inhibitions. After a few minutes in his presence, our whole gang felt comfortable saying whatever nonsense came into their heads. Barry was the most fashion-conscious member of our clan and his parents invested heavily in keeping him trendy. He was the first person on the estate to wear a polo-necked sweater. Sutton Green had several recluses, who never seemed to enter or leave their houses, and Barry was full of sinister stories about what went on behind their dark curtains. If Barry's tales were to be believed, beatnik predators were ten-a-penny on our estate.

Luckily, our school friends never saw Barry and me engrossed in one of our make-believe escapades. Otherwise, we would surely have been the laughing stocks of Marston Road Primary School. Barry would borrow Drew's old teddy bear and I would take charge of the panda that I'd had from birth.

"Teddy and Panda are in the jungle being hunted by cannibals," Barry started.

"We have to hide!" I responded. A uniquely familiar feeling surged through my entire body as the adventure began. It was more than adrenaline; it was like a powerful hallucinogenic drug. I know that Barry was also experiencing the same transformation. Barry and I figuratively 'became' the stuffed animals. We raced to conceal ourselves behind a privet bush at the bottom of the garden. Doodle, the family cat, came to check what we were up to, as Panda and Teddy whispered a constant running commentary.

"There's a dangerous beast!" I whispered urgently, as if the looming savages were not enough of a challenge. In reality, Doodle was the most passive of creatures; he would only bare claws if seriously provoked – like, if you tried to lever him off your lap.

"We'll have to run for it!" insisted the Barry/Teddy amalgam. I could tell that his heart was pounding as fast as mine. We ran at full pelt, holding Teddy and Panda at arms-length in front of us.

"The head-hunters are gaining on us," I injected, as we tried to escape.

"We need high ground," insisted Barry. We could feel the man-eating natives closing in on us, so we began to climb to safety.

"Eh! Get off my bloody shed roof, you little buggers!" yelled my dad, through the kitchen window.

"Don't swear at the kids Peter, they're just playing a game," my mum's voice jumped to our defence.

"That's fine dear," dad added with bitterness, "I'll just let them destroy the water-proofing; the shed will start leaking; the damn hamster will probably be drowned or catch pneumonia; all your garden tools will rust." Dad was a catastrophist, which somewhat diluted his credibility.

However, the trance was almost impenetrable and dad's attempt to jolt us back down to earth was a fleeting distraction. Barry and I scampered off the roof and were soon swimming up the Orinoco River of Bladon Circle, evading piranhas and crocodiles. Mum and dad's perennial arguing disappeared once more into the distance of reality, as Ted and Panda re-entered oblivion. These fantasy escapades would sometimes last for two hours before the spell was finally broken, usually by one of us being called in for dinner.

Tony Boswell was the gentle giant of our group. He had the luxury of never having to prove his hardness because of his height. His crushing handshake was the only proof anyone ever needed. Tony seemed to know everyone, including the toughest of roughnecks from the legendary lower end of Sutton Green. He was eternally practical for a ten-year-old. He could rebuild motorbikes, play guitar, build canoes, catch fish and find birds eggs. You name it, Tony could do it. If Andrew named it, it was as good as done! He was a definite asset to the Nine-nine-niners.

One day, Tony saved my life, after playing a big part in nearly ending it. Barry and Tony dared me to squeeze my supple body into a dolly tub. This corrugated metal barrel, about the size of a dustbin, had been used for washing clothes, during its previous incarnation; no doubt, agitated with a wooden three-pronged pole, called a dolly peg. When people acquired washing machines, dolly tubs were often transformed into rainwater collectors or compost bins. This relic was currently empty. The challenge was a straight bucker. They were so impressed by my ability to compact myself into this small drum that they decided to seal the deal, by adding a dustbin lid. It fitted well. In fact, it fitted so well that it stayed on, even when Barry decided to roll me around. It was fun at first but after a couple of rotations every little bump seemed to intensify. After twice cracking my head against the side, I shouted, "Let me out!"

I was relieved to regain orientation, when Tony stood the container upright.

"It won't come off," I heard Barry laughing; "I suppose you're stuck in there forever."

It seemed funny to me initially, as I was still enjoying pleasure of having re-established my bearings.

"I'll push from the inside, while you pull," I yelled.

"What?" came their muffled replies.

I could tell from the echo when I shouted, that my voice was not escaping the vessel - the lid was tightly sealed. Moreover, I could not move my arms to help push because they were pinned firmly at my side by the corrugations. I started to panic, especially when I felt my friends lift the tub about a foot off the ground and then drop me.

I screamed, "Ouch!" as I bashed my chin against my knees.

Barry was not laughing any more. He was crying. He must have been loud too, because I could distinctly hear him in my soundproof sarcophagus. I started to cry in empathy which quickly turned to self-pity. My head felt like it was bruised and bleeding but worse still my whole body was aching from the contortions it was suffering. My nose was running but I could not get my sleeve near enough to relieve the sensation. I tried to sniff and swallow but that precipitated a new problem. All of a sudden I was having trouble breathing. I drew in breath but it was not satisfying.

"Get me out, I can't breathe!" I cried. I listened for a response but my plea was met with silence. My fellow Nine-nine-niners had abandoned me, leaving me to inspire my own stale air. The mouldy smell of dolly tub was to be my last sensation, as I felt myself slipping in and out of consciousness. With what felt to be my final lungful of carbon dioxide I mustered up an involuntary wolf-cry, "Oh...Oh....Ohhhh.........Bang!"

I opened my eyes, half expecting to see God in heaven. Instead, there stood my dad clutching a broken shovel handle, with Tony, Barry and my mum at his side.

"Peter, he's blue" mum yelped.

Dad moved toward me and I cowered, anticipating a hiding. However, he scooped me up in his arms and kissed me on the forehead.

"You're okay son," he assured me.

"He's going to be okay, Beryl," he told my mum, in a kind but commanding voice that instantly diffused her hysteria.

Then he turned to the sheepish-looking Tony Boswell and said, "Quick thinking kid! You did the right thing coming to fetch me."

Barry came over to me and put apologetic arm on my shoulder, looking over for similar forgiveness from my parents. Dad slowly looked him up and down and said, "Bloody idiot Pratt, you're as daft as your dad."

Barry took no offence. His dad was not known for his common-sense. Instead, as an act of appeasement, Barry tried to launch a Ted and Panda game but the magic wasn't there. ur adrenaline was spent. On that particular day, reality had presented more drama than our imaginations could possibly conceive.

I went and spent some time with Whiskey the hamster. He knew just what to say in these circumstances: Nothing.

Chapter 2: 1963 – The Best Winter ever!

The distinct odour of the Evening Sentinel triggers three memories. Ironically, none of these involve reading the newspaper. Firstly, it reminds me of the way dad used to place the paper over his face to fall asleep in his armchair. I often wondered whether he was faking it because, whenever I tried to simulate this, the tickling, rustling and stench of ink made sleep impossible. Perhaps the ink solvents had a hypnotic effect on dad because he could be snoring within five seconds, even if my mum was talking to him at the time.

Mum and dad met at Loggerheads - literally! They had both been nurses at Loggerheads Sanatorium, when cupid chose to shackle their fates together. It was easy to see the appeal: Dad was tall and athletic, with a great sense of honour and a worldly wisdom, forged from a childhood of neglect. He had a wicked sense of humour and a hairstyle that boasted just the right amount of teddy-boy rebellion. With his James Dean swagger, the only tempering to his film star looks was the gold-rimmed spectacles that never left his face.

Speaking of film stars, my mother had allegedly been compared to Elizabeth Taylor, the classy English actress. Mum's dark brown, naturally curly mop was admired by many; no need for perm or hair dye. Birthing three sons had taken its toll but, according to dad, she still had a 'decent figure,' which was as close as he ever got to a compliment. Indeed, mum and dad made a handsome couple and both were known for their generosity and kind heartedness. Unfortunately, their kindness rarely extended to each other, for it was all-to-often eclipsed by mutual resentments.

The second memory activated by the local newspaper is of Fish 'n Chips shops. Their delicacies were always wrapped in newspaper and everyone swore that it enhanced their flavour. To this day, a tinge of vinegar, added to an old Sentinel, can turn me into Bruce the slobbering dog.

My third, and most vivid olfactory association with the local newspaper, must be that of home-made firelighters. Every winter evening, Andrew and I would make long tubes from the paper and then roll them around our hands, tucking in the ends, to look like giant Catherine Wheels. Mum confided that she viewed me as the most talented in this area. There was a definite technique: If it was too tight then there would not be enough trapped oxygen for the flames to penetrate the inner folds; too loose and the fire would flare up before the coals could catch.

1963 was turning out to be the coldest winter ever. The house was freezing and everyone was grumpy until the fire was lit. Mum was a slave to the origami firelighter technique but dad was less patient and would resort to throwing a cup of sugar on the flames with spectacular effects. Being on the poverty line, mum could not bear such waste and so we always tried to get the fire established before dad got home from work.

The council architects had energy conservation in mind when they designed our houses. At the back of each fireplace, on the kitchen side of the wall, was a multi-purpose oven. This was sometimes used for baking, especially when the real oven's gas supply was running low; the gas meter invariably exhausted its weekly allotment of shillings prematurely. However, the main function of the fire back-oven was for drying clothes. Hanging from the ceiling, directly above it, was an indoor drying rack. This could be raised and lowered by a primitive pulley system. Ideally, mum would prefer to peg out her washing on the outside washing-line but the weather of 1963 kept 'the rack' in permanent demand.

Throughout my seven-long years of life I had heard tales of the famous winter of 1947, with alleged ten-foot snow drifts and lakes that were so frozen that you could skate on them. Now finally, we had our own legend - two foot icicles and all! One morning we opened the curtains, to find that it was still dark. Then we realized that snow was completely blocking the downstairs. I got a science lesson that day, learning that snow is only white when there is some light to illuminate it.

One television weather reporter suggested that this winter was 'turning out worse than 1947.' Mum and dad acted as though this was a personal affront. I could not see why they clung to their own memories, rather than embrace the new nostalgia that was happening before their very eyes.

My parents were always reminiscing about the past. They had a way of referring to it as the 'good old days' and yet persistently claimed that their lives were tougher and that children today 'did not know that they were born.' It put me in mind of a saying that my teacher, Mrs Forsythe, had recently taught me and I shared this analogy with Andrew.

"Mum and dad want to 'have their cake and eat it too!'" I told my brother, elaborating that they were constantly claiming that their lives were simultaneously better and worse than ours.

Andrew considered this paradox, at length, before ingeniously adapting the saying, "Actually, it's more that they want to **not** have their cake, and then **not** eat it, too!" We both found this hilarious. This was another psychic sibling-bonding moment for Andrew and me. We had devised a phrase that totally epitomized our parents. They were definitely comfortable in their misery. It was the first time that I remember consciously challenging the possibility that my parents might have imperfections.

One particularly cold evening, the fire routine had gone well and mum had fed us beef lobby - dad's favourite winter treat. I loved it too, so long as I didn't accidentally get a mouth full of grisly meat, or worse still, a fragment of the dreaded suet dumplings.

I came downstairs after successfully putting my two-year-old brother, Eric, to bed. I loved Eric more than Whisky, Panda and Doodle combined. Despite being a toddler, Eric already displayed positive genetic traits of each family member: Andrew's sharp-mindedness; mum's resilience; dad's handsomeness and charm (when dad was talking to anyone other than mum); and my sense of humor. Eric idolized me. I had even campaigned for him to join the 999ers but Andrew, quite rightly observed that he brought no skills to the club. Moreover, he was too young to be trusted with the password.

When I re-entered the living room I came upon, what started off as a pretty innocuous conversation.

"Kids didn't cheek their elders when I was young," my father would explain. Apparently, Andrew had misguidedly mentioned 'Martin's cake theory' during my brief absence. My parents did not share our view of the hilarity of the modified proverb; Andrew's punch-line delivery was not in the same league as Barry Pratt's.

"I definitely didn't cheek my mum," mother retorted, "she would have killed me!" My parents could never resist a good who-had-the-worst-parents pissing contest.

"My mum wouldn't even let us in the house till bedtime!" dad would brag, "And we didn't have the luxury of a shed to play in."

I glanced at the door which led to the outside, then to the other door, leading to the stairway to our bedroom. These seemed to be the options that dad was floating. Perhaps he was trying to warn me he was about to infuriate mum. In such circumstances, her wrath would inevitably end up turning on me. However, this winter was the coldest on record and the dark outside held no allure; shed or no shed. On the other hand, bedtime was even less appealing, especially since the six o'clock news had only just started. The BBC news was dreadfully boring but lately they had started having the odd clip of an upcoming phenomenon that Andrew had discovered - The Beatles. I was compelled to sit through inane stories about parliamentary sex scandals, whatever they were, just to catch a glimpse of my heroes: John, Paul, George and Ringo.

"At least your mum didn't tell you she hated you every day of your life!" mum blurted out.

"Here we go," dad competed, "we're going to hear about the coalhouse, in a minute."

"You don't even know how traumatic it was, Peter. She deliberately locked the door and pretended she didn't know I was in there; and I could hear my sister laughing. I thought I was going to die in that coalhouse!" yelled mum, spiralling into rage, as she relived the trauma.

It was undeniable, Beryl had been raised by a wicked alcoholic mother who seemed to single her out, as a middle child, for particularly sadistic treatment. Her dad worked away most of the time but, when he did return home, her mother's jealousy prevented him from making any public display of kindness.

"Yes, well I know all about dying, dear. My mother put me in a sanatorium for two years. I watched people die of TB everyday, every damn day! I used to lie on that ward wondering whether I'd be the next victim of consumption!"

He placed a plain-tipped Woodbine in his mouth, ripped a corner off the newspaper and acquired a light from the coal fire.

"Well, you might still die of lung disease. Those things can cause cancer, you know," she reminded him. He should know because he was a charge nurse at the General Hospital's Respiratory Physiology Department. "What do you think Doctor McDermott would say if he saw you smoking?"

Doctor McDermott was dad's boss. It was a dirty trick to invoke his name. The metaphorical gloves were off! Dad tried to draw me into the conversation.

"When you get married, son, take a good look at the mother. The apple never falls far from the tree," he jibed. The battle was on! This was about the cheapest shot that he could make. If there was one person Beryl was determined not to be like, it was her mother.

Drew sensed that this last comment had jeopardized my health and he jumped to my rescue. "Come on, Mart, let's go to bed and see if Jack Frost's been yet," he suggested.

"I want to see The Beatles," I protested.

Mum glared at me. I could not envisage that the legendary evil grandmother could have cast a more penetrating hateful stare.

"No Beatles tonight," my brother calmly added, "Goodnight mum and dad, love you."

"Love you," I echoed, chasing Andrew up to the bedroom.

"Don't run on the stairs!" Mum's maniacal voice screamed after us, creating the conflicting desires to simultaneously freeze to the spot, and sprint faster to escape the wrath.

We leapt into our freezing pyjamas then snuggled under the painfully cold sheets. The only comfort they offered was a false feeling of sanctuary. We marvelled at the latest artwork of Jack Frost on our windows, we listened to the muffled arguing intensify. It was always the same pattern -as mum got louder dad got quieter. I thought that this meant that mum always won the argument but Andrew, in his great wisdom, had a totally opposite theory.

"The one that makes the other the maddest is the winner," he tried to explain. He could tell from my expression of puzzlement that it was too deep or me. So he took out a poem by Rudyard Kipling that his teacher, Mr. Barton, had been reading to his class and quoted a line from it, "If you can keep your head when all around are losing theirs, then you'll be a man, my son!"

It took me a while to get it because mum was a woman but the magic of Jack Frost, Rudyard Kipling and filial-bonding, brought an insight that became an unexpected defining moment in my life. I realized that the ability to turn 'psycho' at the drop of a hat was not actually a gift - it was a curse! This held true for parents, teachers, bullies and victims alike. Strength lies in controlling your temper, not losing it.

1963 was indeed officially the coldest winter on record despite both my parents continued assertions that 1947 had been snowier. I found that hard to believe because one morning we opened the front door to a wall of snow. Instantly, there was a four-foot pile of fresh snow on the linoleum of the entrance hall. It was not a mistake that could be rectified. There was simply no space for the snow to be pushed back out again. Luckily, Andrew's problem solving skills went into overdrive. We managed to close the front door but we still had to get rid of a giant snowman at the foot of the stairs.

"There's no way we can get it past dad in the living room," Andrew deduced, even though dad's face was covered with Evening Sentinel in his typical sleeping pose, "not to mention mum in the kitchen."

"We're doomed," I admitted, "Mum will kill us!" She had specifically told us to, 'under no circumstance open the front door.'

Then it hit Andrew. "We'll take it upstairs and melt it in the bath," he insisted. He devised a masterly way of transporting copious balls of snow, by cradling it in our sweaters.

"Brilliant in its simplicity!" we described the plan, which may have worked except for three serious miscalculations:

Firstly, the combination of weight and moistness left our hand-knitted wool sweaters with spherical frontal bulges, usually reserved for the severely pregnant.

Secondly, the persistent traipsing up and down the stairwell, with dripping snow, made such a filthy set of footprints that it would take hours of scrubbing to restore the linoleum to an acceptable standard.

The third misjudgement was the most serious. The temperature upstairs was not much different from that outside and the bath full of snow was in no mood to thaw. We tried to turn on the tap, but the pipes were frozen solid. Andrew tried to open the bathroom window to the throw out the snow but it was ice-welded shut. Doodle, who had been snoozing on one of the beds, came to check what we were doing. He carefully walked around the rim of the bath, looking at the snow as if to say, "What have you bloody idiots done now?"

We were seriously worried, at this point, because there was no solution. Then help came from the most unexpected of sources. Our constant stamping up and down stairs had obviously aroused my dad from his ink-induced hypnotic state and we were caught red-handed.

"What have you bloody idiots done now?" he laughed, as though he had just read the cat's mind. But instead of being angry, it all seemed like a big joke. It was an event that evolved into an epic tale, that would go on to repeatedly entertain Ted and Bertha - mum and dad's best friends.

Ted, who was funny in his own right, saw humour in absolutely everything that dad said. Moreover, he was a catalyst, who never failed to spark my father's inner-comedian. On first prompt, dad would launch into one of his hilarious stories and Ted's wheezing hysterical laughter would commence. Furthermore, Bertha's raucous screeches would kick in, right on cue. They were the perfect audience. Here is how the story was eventually retold at family gatherings:

"I'm not kidding, the buggers had filled the bath with snow," dad recalled.

"Ha, tell 'em about the cat, Pete," insisted Ted.

"Yeah, Doodle was prancing around the tub with his nose in the air," said dad.

"Ha, Doodle, great name, great name!" added Ted.

"It's a great name, Doodle," Bertha confirmed.

"I sneaked this massive brass jam kettle up the stairs and the kids filled it with snow," dad explained.

"Ha, those things are really heavy," Ted added, trying to add a little foreshadowing to the story.

"I wouldn't dare lift one of those things with my lumbago," added Bertha. Ted cast a glance to let his wife know that she was destroying the momentum of the tale.

"Really heavy," injected Ted, getting the story back on track.

"You're not kidding," said dad, "anyway, I got three kettles past Beryl in the kitchen without her noticing."

"I knew something was happening," added mum, claiming her part in the story.

"She knew nothing," said dad.

"Ha! Knew nothing" laughed Ted, incessantly tickled by the snipes that Peter and Beryl made to each other.

Bertha and mum smiled at each other sharing a men-think-they-know-everything look.

"Anyway, we've just filled the final jam kettle with snow, and Beryl doesn't know a thing about it. The kids are heading down the stairs,"

"Ha!" added Ted in anticipation.

"Anyway, Doodle decides he's going to rub up against my leg - one of those tail-in-the-air rubs that cats do. Next thing I know, I'm going arse-over-tit and nearly fell down the bloody stairs. The cat screams, 'Me....ooow,' and leaps for his life! The brass kettle goes sailing past the kids' heads and crashes down the stairs sounding like a bloody Caribbean Calypso band."

"Ha! I bet Beryl knew something by now," suggested Ted.

"I said 'What the hell's going on?'" mum finally got herself into the story, "and do you know what Peter said?"

"Ha! What did he say?" asked Ted, knowing the punch-line.

"Nothing dear!" she delivered monotonically, then added, "I mean, I could have opened that door and discovered three dead humans and a dead cat covered with a pile of snow and a bloody jam kettle."

"Ha! Let's see Scotland Yard work that one out," laughed Ted, "Hello, hello, hello, what been going on here then? Ha! 'Nothing dear!' Ha!"

So here was a nostalgic winter story from 1963, as opposed to 1947. We had finally joined the history books. At the time it occurred, it seemed decidedly unfunny but the further we got from the incident the funnier the memory grew. That, too, was an eye-opener for me.

During the winter months, the two-and-a-half mile walk home from school took so much longer than usual. We had to stop regularly for snowball fights and impromptu slide-making. Mum always encouraged me to keep up with one of the walking groups, who made the epic journey, from Beechwood Heights to Sutton Green. Most of my home friends went to a different school, Sutton Street, along with the scary ruffians from the lower end. Mum had selected Marston Road Primary School on its merits rather than proximity.

One January afternoon, we bombarded a red double-decker bus with a pelt of snowballs. It was transporting some of our richer counterparts, back home in style. Actually, they weren't particularly richer, just more namby-pamby - softened by their more 'caring' parents.

"How are my over-protected peers ever going to learn to say 'No' to perverts?" I puzzled, *"If they are never given the opportunity?"* Believe me, the route home was lined with 'funny men' dying to offer us sweets and liquorices for who-knows-what? We were well-drilled to make a loud noise and run for our lives. I often wondered whether the perverts would have a higher success rate if they targeted the mollycoddled bus kids.

The next afternoon, I had dawdled and found myself walking home alone, when I saw the bus approaching. The previous day had been such fun, with at least twenty dollops of snow ending up stuck to the bus windows. The bus driver had seemed to be enjoying it as much as anybody. I decided to recreate the event, although this time it was an overcrowded single-decker.

Twenty-four hours is an eternity in terms of 'snow hours.' I molded some snow into a suitable ball. The consistency was icier than the previous day. I flung the missile and hit the window of the closed swing door, at the front of the bus. Instead, of the clinging to the glass, like its predecessors, this ball made a cracking noise. The bus skidded to a halt and, with a terrifying whoosh of air, the door sprung open. Out jumped the livid driver. He had me by my shirt collar in a flash.

"What the bloody hell do you think you're doing, you bloody hooligan?" he demanded.

"Sorry," my instincts replied.

"Sorry?" he snapped, "You nearly broke the sodding window, you bloody vandal!"

"I d-d-didn't know," I stammered in terror.

"I want your name and address, you little bastard," he insisted.

I told him without hesitation. He finally loosened his grip on my collar, took a cigarette pack from his pocket to write on, and magically produced a short pencil from behind his ear. He wrote down my name and address and, to my horror he added, "There'll be a policeman coming to your house tonight!" I stood rooted to the spot, trembling and petrified, as he returned triumphantly to his bus, greeted by the rapturous applause of his passengers. The bus driver was a hero and I was the villain.

As a child, I was a worrier. However, my frets were usually restricted to everyday worries, like losing my dinner money, or whether Ivy Morrison and Sandra

Adams would try and make me blush in front of my friends, or whether Mrs Forsythe would make me read out loud. Now, I had a more serious worry. I was suddenly a criminal and the police were going to turn up at my house. It was too much to bare. I would be arrested and sent to Borstal - a special school for wayward children. My parents would be so ashamed of me and they would not love me anymore. Andrew would ban me from the 999 club. Worst of all, I would no longer be Eric's hero.

I cried all the way home and my face was red raw from the frozen snot and tears. I had an insoluble problem that I could share with nobody. Although, I did confide in Whiskey, as I was cleaning out his cage and replenishing his food supply.

"I just thought it would be funny," I told my hamster, "and everybody on the bus would laugh." Whiskey twitched his whiskers in sympathy.

As I relived my felonious moment, something started to haunt me: I remembered that there had been a split second, before I let go of the icy projectile, when I considered aborting the mission. I knew that I was doing wrong but I was momentarily consumed with devilment. Mum always referred to it as my *awkward streak.*

"The snowball seemed to hang in the air forever," I told my non-judgmental captive audience.

Whiskey listened for a second and then packed as many sunflower seeds into his pouches, as would fit. His little knobbly face usually amused me but on this evening I was inconsolable.

"I could have broken the bus window," I explained, as the tiny swollen-faced rodent tilted his head sideways, as though he was contemplating my dilemma.

"Maybe the driver was bluffing and just trying to scare me," I reasoned further. Whiskey lost interest at this point and went for a run in his wheel. He would never entertain self-pity for long.

This helped me gain some perspective. After all, it was already dark and the police had not yet arrived, at least not at my house. Who knew whether they had turned up at 12, Baggot Grove, the false address that I had given to the bus driver? Who could say whether they were currently brandishing handcuffs, at that address, ready to slap on the wrist of Martin Butcher - who did exist but not at that abode?

Being such a worrier, it took a couple of weeks of counselling sessions with my mentor-hamster, to accept that I may be out-of-the-woods. Even though I had given a semi-false name and totally false address, there was always the chance that someone on the bus might have recognized me and revealed my true identity. I was also worried that the bus driver would discover that he had been duped. Then he might turn up at Marston Road Primary School with policemen and they might have an identity parade. Or they might arrest the real Martin Butcher, which I know would have laid heavily on my conscience.

Also, whenever my mum took me on a bus, I wondered whether the driver would recognize me and make a citizen's arrest and drive us straight to the police station. For some reason, maybe shame, I had no memory of making eye contact with the driver and there was no image of his face in my memory banks. I hoped that he had a similar anonymous recollection of me. Maybe I was just another young tyke in a duffel coat?

3. A Hunting We Will Go!

Another odour that launches me back to the famous winter of '63 is a smell that no boy of seven-and-three-quarters should encounter. At least no council house-dwelling urchin, whose father should know the age-appropriate times to introduce life's uglier side to his children. This fragrance was that of a freshly-fired shotgun - no less!

One Saturday morning in February, dad was left in charge of me, while Andrew and Eric were being treated to an emergency shoe shopping expedition. For all of our ragamuffin clothes, mum always vowed that her children's feet would never be subjected to the torturous distortions that her sick mother made her suffer. Mum's feet had been truly 'gnarled up' by ill-fitting footwear.

Soon after my mum and brothers had caught the bus to town, a Land Rover screeched to a halt outside our house. It was driven by dad's work buddy, Carl Wagstaff.

"Come on Pete, the boss has invited us to go hunting!" Jim insisted.

"Damn it Carl, I've got the kid," dad replied.

Carl Wagstaff was the coolest of adults. He even had a Beatles hair-cut. Dad and Ted thought that it looked effeminate but they also acknowledged that Jim was a 'hit with the ladies.' Mum and Bertha would deliberately start conversations about him, to try and make their husbands jealous. Bertha attributed Carl's popularity to his kind face and mop-head, whereas mum thought that it was his muscular physique. This invariably provoked a comment from dad, such as, "Are you talking about Fat Arse Wagstaff?"

I think that he may have been jealous, but not necessarily of mum's affectionate tones. Wagstaff lived the existence that my father would have had, if only he had not opted for the 'joys' of married life and parenthood. Fat Arse was the same age as dad but he was far more relaxed and carefree; they had similar social backgrounds; and their career paths had matched, since they graduated from nursing school together. Yet, where dad's shoulders bore a world of responsibility, Carl had a Land Rover, a permanent grin on his face, and an answer for everything.

"Bring the boy with you; the boss' kids are going to be there," Carl reasoned. Dad needed no further convincing.

Before I knew what was happening, he was buttoning up the toggles on my duffel coat and pulling a hand-knitted balaclava over my head. Next, he was reclaiming last year's Wellington boots from the shed and hammered them onto my reluctant feet. They were unpleasantly tight and mum would certainly not have approved.

"You're okay with me shooting rabbits and wood-pigeons aren't you son?" he checked, sheepishly resisting eye-contact. "Actually, they're not rabbits; they're hares: real vermin!"

I was delighted to be doing something with just dad; it was a potential father-son bonding moment. I said, "We're really going hunting?"

"We're really going hunting!" he declared, lifting me up and tossing me into the back of Wagstaff's truck. Soon, our hunting party was speeding through the narrow lanes of Endon, often slamming on brakes to narrowly miss a variety of tractors and animals, domestic and wild.

In no time, we were arriving at Inglewood Hall, the country mansion of dad's ridiculously rich boss. The architect had obviously been given carte blanche on space constraints. Our entire house, plus Johnson's next door, could have comfortably fit in the banquet hall - which they humbly referred to as the living room. There were two stairwells, at least seven bedrooms, a study, library, workshop, several bathrooms. The huge kitchen had two pantries. All the rooms were linked by wide corridors. The grey stone exterior and dark oak panels everywhere gave a feeling of unabashed opulence.

On arrival, Dr McDermott's wife greeted each adult with a glass of sherry from a silver tray. She had a kind face and posh voice; she was not snooty, like my Nana Lena, just naturally classy. Her casual slacks and cashmere sweater reeked of wealth but in a non-bragging way. All the ruddy-faced farmers of Endon were gathered for the 'culling of the hare.' Apparently, these pests were at their most defenceless whilst there was snow on the ground.

As it turned out, Dr McDermott's boys were sixteen and fourteen years old. They had returned home from boarding school for the February half term. They were also there to enjoy a rare bonding opportunity with their dad. However, they were allowed to partake in the sherry, while I was only offered Dandelion and Burdock: my least favourite of pops. They wore stylish burberries and flat caps, while I was stood in my sad duffel coat, balaclava and increasingly painful wellies.

Once the formal drinks had been consumed the 'real stuff' came out. Dad and Jim had already made several surreptitious forages to the greeter's tray. They rarely moved in circles where the drinks were free and they were determined to get their money's worth. Now, the doc was cracking open firkins of real ale and offering generous five-star brandy chasers.

As dad became the life and soul of the party, I nursed my Dandelion and pigging Burdock! Added to this, I was left to make small talk with the other 'children.' Nobody else seemed to notice that they were twice my age and at least three levels above my social standing. I was half expecting them to be snobbish with me but they were very kind. They did not patronize me, at all.

"Are you on hols from school, then?" asked Alexander, the sixteen-year-old. His comfort with eye-contact was unnerving, at first. Mum was persistently nagging me to 'look at people when they were talking to you,' but my *awkward streak,* lazy eye and self-consciousness made it difficult. However, as this teenager's eyes locked onto mine like a hypnotic tractor beam, I had no choice but to reciprocate and soon I became more comfortable. Alexander seemed to be under the misconception that all kids were sent away for their education.

"Yes, winter hols are my favorite," I responded. The famous five talked in a similar way, so I was not totally out of my depth. I had also read several "Just William" books and these adventures always occurred in the dorms of boarding schools. I was ready to talk about 'tuck' and 'hampers,' if necessary.

"What's your housemaster's name?" Robert, the younger boy asked.

"Forsythe," I replied, suddenly ashamed to admit that my teacher was a woman.

"Sounds tough," stated Alexander, "I've got Chumley this term, he's a right bastard! You got a gun?"

"No," I responded. Alexander motioned for me to follow him. When we got to the gun cupboard there was already a crowd around the door. Dad was proudly clutching a double barrel shotgun and Carl looked as though he was checking his single barrel for straightness. Not that anyone could accurately see straight in their states of advanced inebriation.

Dr McDermott was identical to his two sons - if you removed thirty years and his pencil-lined moustache. His short-back-and-sides haircut was parted in the middle and held tight against his head with a dab of Brylcream. He would not have been out of place in a P.G. Woodhouse novel; Alexander and Robert were a couple of budding Bertie Woosters.

"Father," Alexander said to his dad, "I thought Martin could use the .22?"

Dad's boss, was obviously pleasantly tipsy, and he certainly considered the suggestion for a second but then he decided, "He's too young, son, and I don't think that he knows gun etiquette."

"Sorry Martin," responded Alexander, obviously well-bred enough to never question his father's decisions. Although, he seemed bewildered as to how anyone could 'not know gun etiquette.' I was both disappointed and relieved at the same time.

Next, there was a gathering in the huge kitchen where a plan of attack was announced. Three teams of drunken country-folk would each be secreted about three miles away, at strategic points north, east and south of the manor. They would slowly converge across the slush-covered fields, firing at the ambushed bunnies. A fourth gathering of gout-riddled grandfathers was grouped by their inability to walk. Their brief was to wait an hour, then venture outside and pick off the fleeing hares, just as the creatures thought they had escaped the onslaught. It did not seem very sporting but it was probably something to do with 'gun etiquette,' which we had already established, I knew nothing about.

I was offered the opportunity to stay back with the old fogies, and was tempted, since my Wellington boots were starting to give me some jip. Some empathy for the aged gout-sufferers was developing. However, much to dad's disappointment, I opted to 'cramp his style.' In no time, our north team was fanned out and trudging south-west, making silent hand signals, in a suddenly serious way.

"Stay behind me, son," dad whispered, at last sharing some hunting rules. I wanted to tell him how much my feet were starting to hurt. However, I was aware that he was having one of the best days of his life and I could not bring myself to be a killjoy. He was obviously experiencing the 'Teddy and Panda magical zone.' The aura was unmistakable, only this was not make-believe. It was real!

As the hunt got under way, we started to hear a few shots from Dr McDermott's east group. They were the first to be in position. Soon, the southern posse was also releasing regular booms. They were surely enjoying a bloodbath? Yet, we continued to plod on, without the slightest a sniff of a target. We were ever so vigilant but there was not so much as a wood-pigeon, at which to pop. Then, I finally got chance to exploit one of my superpowers, much to dad's delight.

"Are those hares, dad? I whispered. He tried to shush me at first but then he seemed to recollect my telescopic talents. Finally, I found a use for my gift.

"Where son?" he mouthed, avoiding alerting his fellow gunslingers. If dad could bag just one hare, it would be such a 'feather in his cap.' I pointed surreptitiously to the brow of the hill. We crept forward nonchalantly, and dad finally focused on the creatures that I had spotted thirty yards prior. They were playing peacefully, oblivious to their impending doom.

"He's in range, dad whispered, taking aim. He seemed to wait an eternity, "gently does it," he told himself. I think that his fathering instincts were also pursuing some role-modelling on my behalf.

Then Wagstaff's voice declared, "Pete's onto something!" The hares took less than a second to work out that it was probably them that Pete was onto!

They were up and zigzag running in a flash.

"Bang," the first discharge unleashed from dad's gun. Both hares leap instinctively in the air to avoid getting hit.

"Bang" echoed his second barrel and again the furry pests jumped. However, this time one landed in a heap.

"Got it!" exclaimed dad joyously. A cacophony of gunshots chased the other hare up the field. However, he managed to make good his escape, into a copse at the top of the hill.

I heard some blue words that a seven-year-old should not be hearing, as the failed marksmen cursed their bad luck. However, I also heard some words that brought me to the verge of tears.

"You did me proud, son!" dad told me, placing his hand on my shoulder. "Why don't you bring home the spoils?"

I hobbled up to the fallen bunny, temporarily immune to the painful boots and studied the body. A dribble of blood hung from the corner of its mouth but there was no visible sign of life. I pushed any sadness straight from my mind. This was a blissful moment that should not be marred by erroneous childish sentiment. I grabbed the back legs and tried to lift the animal.

"Urgh!" I cried, in disgust. Shocked by the warmth of the body, I quickly let go of it again.

"It's okay, son, it won't hurt you," dad reassured me from a distance. He was already refilling the barrels of his gun. I tried again to lift the tepid corpse but this time it was the weight that surprised me. I had expected to encounter the same heaviness that Panda or Teddy usually offered. I considered dragging it but instinct told me that this would be sacrilegious.

Suddenly, mayhem broke out. The 'safe' hare had re-emerged from the woods and was on a kamikaze mission back down the field. Maybe he felt guilty about abandoning his pal but more likely the east squad had arrived at the copse and chased him back through the woods. Whatever his reasoning, he was greeted by a barrage of gunshots.

"Bang! Bang! Bang!" went the shotguns, as the hare taunted them, with his intricate high speed dance. I was rooting for the animal, which was beating all the odds.

"Bang!" was the sound I heard, as I felt an agonizing stinging pain in my midriff and half a toggle whistled over my shoulder. At the same moment, some shards of ice kicked up from the ground and splattered my face. I dropped the dead hare, again. There was only one explanation – I'd been shot!

I looked down, half expecting to see my guts hanging out. I knew that a bullet to the stomach could kill you in a few seconds - or perhaps a couple of minutes if you were Jimmy Drinkwater. However, all I could see were seven little dots on my duffel coat, in the exact position that the pain had struck, and half a toggle.

"Mum will kill me!" I briefly told myself, then my thought moved to, *"This will ruin dad's day."* So, I picked up the hare and limped back to where he was standing.

"Good job, son!" dad announced, deliberately loud enough for the other empty-handed hunters to hear. "We make a great team, kid"

"I've just been shot," I told him discreetly.

This was obviously too embarrassing for him to even contemplate, so he mentally placed an Evening Sentinel over his face and pretended that he did not hear me. Before I had chance to repeat it, Dr. McDermott's group came out of the woods and merged with ours.

"Got one did you, Pete?" acknowledged dad's boss, who was carrying two guns.

"Yes sir, the boy spotted it," dad said, sharing the glory.

"Indeed?" he looked impressed. "I had to disarm Podmore's kid. Bloody idiot got a bit over-excited when he saw the vermin and forgot all about 'gun etiquette'. Bloody fool discharged his weapon, with you lot in the direct line of fire. Lucky you were out of range."

The mile long walk back to Inglewood Hall has to be the most traumatic experience I have ever had. Not only was I carrying a giant dead bunny at arms-length, to prevent blood splashing on my clothes, I was also nursing, what I assumed to be, a fatal wound. It was of little consolation to me that I had learned my assassin's name: Podmore! The urge to drop to the ground in a blubbering mass of tears was so strong. I was living on borrowed time. Worse still, my feet had swollen so tightly against the walls of my Wellingtons that the blood circulation was getting cut off. The cold was transferring through the rubber boots and nylon socks like they were no barrier at all. I was convinced that I was getting frostbite. Andrew had recently told me about instances when toes had come off, because of frostbite. Apparently, people just took their shoes and socks off and their toes dropped off!

Each pace brought a greater numbness to my outstretched arm, which eventually succumbed to the strain. I took to cradling the dead hare, as if it were baby in my arms. I briefly thought of Eric, and whether I would ever see him again, as I staggered step-by-step, like a war-torn soldier returning from the battle. The distant guns of the doddering old cripples back at the manor were an ironically welcome sound. They were 'tidying up' the ambushed prey. To think, I could have stayed with these old folk, listening to their boring war stories, as they drunk themselves into oblivion. They would probably make me play the guess-how-old-I-am game. Instead, I had chosen to prematurely join their cripple world and get myself shot.

I looked over to see Dr McDermott giving dad a snorter from his hip flask. Dad was still in his state of Nirvana and he had, obviously, no intention of letting my revelation anywhere near his conscious brain. I could not ruin dad's day – our day. But I was starting to feel light-headed. The mouldy dolly tub smell came to me –the smell of death. Then I heard a voice.

"You okay kid?" asked Carl Wagstaff. Without warning he hoisted me onto his shoulders and marched me the rest of the way back to the manor, all the time singing "For he's a jolly good fellow."

As soon as we arrived back, I jumped into the toilet closet, opened my coat and lifted my shirt. Sure enough, there were seven little red marks in the same pattern as the one on my coat. However, amazingly there was no blood. I was not going to die. Somehow my duffel coat toggle must have miraculously absorbed some of the shot's impact.

Now I had to tackle the other problem. I needed to get my boots off to see if my toes were still there. I approached Wagstaff again.

"I can't get my wellies off, can you help me?" I asked politely.

"Sure kid," responded my life-saving fat-arsed hero. After an agonizing tug-of-war, we finally managed to prize off the Wellingtons and, to my relief all ten toes were still in place. However, Jim suddenly used a word that strikes terror into all children every winter.

"Pete, I think your kids got chilblains!" he exclaimed.

"Chilblains?" I gasped in horror.

According to mum, there were two dangers that adults knew about but never cared to explain. Firstly, swimming within thirty minutes of eating will cause certain drowning. Secondly, the result of warming up freezing extremities too quickly will be chilblains: permanent damage so indescribably horrible that nobody ever tried to describe them! Chilblains were invariably self-inflicted - the natural consequences of impetuosity. I had been drilled all my life to let cold limbs acclimatize naturally. Now, out of the blue, I had given myself chilblains.

"Chilblains?" responded dad, as though Wagstaff had sighted the Loch Ness monster or some other mythical creature.

"Chilblains?" inquired Dr McDermott, switching from Bertie Wooster to Doctor Finlay mode, "Let me see."

"You shouldn't have to work today boss," dad apologized.

"Nonsense, Peter, I did take a Hippocratic Oath, you know," insisted the well-liquored doctor.

"Thank you, sir," dad grovelled.

The room hushed as the doctor scrutinized my freezing throbbing toes. The onlookers were probably impressed by the intensive inspection the wise doctor was affording my mortal feet. From my position, it looked like his eyes were drifting in and out of focus, battling his alcoholic haze.

After great deliberation, Dr McDermott declared, "Chilblains!" The audience cheered his diagnosis, insensitive to the terror in my eyes. Some edged forward, driven by morbid curiosity, to observe the mythical beings. Then the doctor got that 'it's a long shot, but it might just work' look in his eyes. He turned to his youngest son.

"Robert, we need thick dry woollen socks and slippers," he demanded, flicking his fingers like an impatient surgeon. The boy raced from the room and returned twenty seconds later.

"Sock," the doctor commanded, and his son handed one to him. He carefully fitted it over my bright red, bulbous toes. I winced and the captive audience gasped. He then repeated the operation with the other sock and then added the slippers.

"I think he's going to be okay, Peter," declared the proud doctor. The crowd cheered, as if they had just witnessed a miracle.

"You're going to be fine, son," added a relieved dad patting me on the shoulder. Soon my feet were feeling much better. I was a chilblain survivor!

By the time, Carl Wagstaff's Land Rover was dropping us back at Bladon Circle, I was walking comfortably in my new pure wool socks and slippers.

Dad and I were full of tales of hunting when we got back home and I could see that Andrew was a little envious. Shoe shopping with mum was a constant nightmare. She always insisted on Clark's double E width, which assured comfort at the expense of fashion.

"I can't believe you took our seven-year-old son hunting, Peter," mum nagged.

"Nonsense dear, he's a big boy now," he replied, tapping me on the back.

"What happened to your toggle?' mum asked.

"Dad shot a rabbit!" I blurted.

"Peter, you could have traumatized the boy," she replied in horror.

"It was a hare, dear," he deflected.

"I don't see the difference!" she sniped.

"No, you don't, do you dear," dad responded in a passive aggressive way. "One's a pet, one's a pest!"

I thought it unwise to report that he was drunk at the time, as I could sense an argument was evolving. I also decided to keep the chilblains a secret, in the interests of family harmony. I knew that she would disapprove of me getting myself shot.

Chapter 4: The Butchers' House

You only had to walk two streets away from our house to find a family who were living a parallel existence to our own. They were the Butchers. Steamed cabbage and stinky faecal smells always wafted from the backdoor of the Butchers' habitat. Their toilet door was situated just inside their outhouse and it was rarely out of use. I never had a desire to knock on the Butcher's door but my mum was always trying to get the families to mix. I sometimes ran out of excuses.

Andrew showed me a Superman comic which featured another planet, known as Htrae, where the Bizarro people lived. On this planet, there existed a freak counterpart to everyone on Earth. For instance, 'Bizarro Marilyn Munroe' was the ugliest person on Htrae. Andrew said that the Butchers were the 'Bizarro Wells' family; he was right! They lived on Bognor Drive. They had three children and the eldest, Ian, was in Andrew's class. The middle child was Martin. He had the same first name as me, as well as being my age, and he suffered from my hyper-sensitivity toward blushing. It was his name that had been scribbled on the bus driver's cigarette packet during the snowball incident. Also, they had a much younger two-year-old surprise baby, as was Eric; but this one was a girl. Except for Mother Butcher, they all had uncannily similar haircuts. I suspected that their mum was the family coiffure and her armoury of tools involved a pudding basin.

I should have had a natural empathy with Martin Butcher. Like me, he had a cleverer elder brother, who knew exactly how to push his buttons. However, where Andrew's teasing was sporadic, the jibes of Ian were relentless. I liked to think that I had learned a few strategies to alleviate the victim role. I mainly used humour and flattery to deflect my brother's attention away from the spells of taunting. Of course, I was still occasionally hooked and reeled in but I mainly managed to resist taking the bait. However, Rehctub Nitram (Bizarro name) had no impulse control and he was easy prey to the merciless verbal goading of the Butchers' firstborn.

It probably did not help his prestige that Andrew had once overheard a conversation between Mrs Butcher and my mum, about their middle child. Since mum was a trained nurse she was always giving the neighbours medical advice; wanted or not!

"Sounds like he's got undescended testicles," my mum advised Mrs Butcher.

"That's probably why he cries all the time," Andrew quipped, as he retold the conversation.

44

"What are testicles?" I asked Andrew.

"Your bollocks, you fool!" Andrew clarified. "Mum said that he might have to go to hospital and have an operation to drop them into his goolie-bag."

"Well, where are they now?" I asked. I was worried because, throughout these cold winter evenings, I was noticing a few scrotal anomalies of my own.

"They're still in his stomach, they never came down," Andrew explained, leaving me more confused than ever.

As Jack Frost's winter of '63 laid down one final burst of misery before passing the baton to spring, the Butchers ended up with an unforeseen spectacle outside their house. A thick deposit of ice had formed on Bognor Drive, which just happened to have the perfect slope for slide-making. A quick polishing, from our leather-soled shoes, created the most frictionless sheet of glass. As we adapted to the unique surface, Ian, Andrew and I began risking more and more daring speeds. With each run the slippery area would extend a little further and soon it must have been a hundred feet long. Other neighbourhood kids started to join in the fun, giving an impromptu street party atmosphere. I was on the fringe of entering the 'magical zone,' usually reserved for Panda, when a loud obnoxious wailing emanated from the Butchers' house. It was my namesake, screaming like he had just been shot, as he a negotiated with his mum. He was obviously unaware of the audience outside.

"I've told you mum, I'm not wearing wellies, they don't slide!" came the spoiled brat's rant. He had my sympathy there; my feet were only just returning to normal and the emotional fall-out from the rubber boot experience was still too raw to address.

"Martin, you'll slip in those shoes," Butcher's mum asserted, at matching volume.

"I want to slip!" he sobbed hysterically, "because that's what sliding is!" He had a point. However, as an impartial witness, I could clearly see that he could have addressed the issue without playing the 'tears card.' Perhaps, his lachrymal glands were over-compensating for his lack of testicles?

As the embarrassing outburst progressed, I saw Ian and Andrew share a knowing look, like they carried a common burden. I seriously resented such insinuation but could think of no response that would not reinforce their analogy. I briefly wondered if I did appear this bratty when I succumbed to frustrations. I had certainly thrown the odd fit before, but surely my lapses from grace were not to these proportions. I was finding my counterpart's antics more irritating than anyone. However, I rationalized that, as a boy who had recently been shot and kept it entirely to myself, I surely held the high ground, in terms of self-control.

"Well don't come crying to me, if you hurt yourself," Mrs Butcher was finally heard to yell. This seemed ironic, as he was already 'crying to her.' Applying Andrew's theory, Mrs Butcher was obviously the loser in this exchange because she was the last person to shout. This carried some credence because minutes later, the backdoor flew open and the 'mardy pants' emerged sporting a triumphant grin. I heaved as I caught a blast of poo-tainted cabbage fumes. Looking down to check what had replaced the demon Wellingtons, I noticed that he was wearing his shiny church shoes. I half-expected the boy to be humbled. After all, there were now twenty-five children who had obviously witnessed his outrageous tantrum. However, he came out with an inflated sense of entitlement.

"You've all had a go, it's my turn!" he insisted, moving straight to the front of the queue. You would think, at eight-years-old, he would have learned some social decorum - but apparently not. Some of the other kids were ready to take a stand over the brat's queue-jumping but his brother intervened.

"Let's let 'Cry Baby Bunting' have his turn," said Ian, partly as a disclaimer but more pragmatically to avoid further distraction from the momentum of fun.

For his own safety, my blushing Bizarro twin would have done well to watch a few others first, to get a read on the speed. He would also have been well-advised to try a half-pace run, for starters. Instead, he launched himself at full pelt toward the slide. He seriously underestimated the properties of frictionless motion. Perhaps, God was teaching him a lesson, for flippant use of gripless church shoes, but The Almighty certainly seemed to abandon him, as he took off at an unholy velocity. Possibly, it was the combined desires of the masses, willing his comeuppance. Maybe it was Karma. Whatever, the forces behind the resulting scenario, the consequences seemed to be self-inflicted.

At first, he held good balance, as the slope accelerated him out of his comfort zone. He was probably traveling at thirty miles per hour, when he followed his instinct to brake. He turned his front guiding foot sideways but, without any grip, his body over-rotated; so that he was now approaching forty miles an hour in reverse. His arms began flailing madly, as he endeavored to maintain equilibrium. The spectators had the pleasure of witnessing the full terror on 'Baby Bunting's' face, as he made the calculated decision to go to ground. The increase in contact area had a negligible effect, as he sped feet-first on the glassy surface. There was a communal wince as his face and stomach finally gained some traction on the icy road.

"Aaaaaa...........aargh," he screamed, as he got an unexpected science lesson, that ice can 'burn.' However, instead of slowing him down it just altered his direction. He spread his limbs instinctively, which was unfortunate because the next second he came to an instant halt with one leg either side of a lamp post. We all grimaced in unison.

A forty mile-an-hour collision between a silent concrete post and a loud simpering wimp only had one winner. It was not the noisy one!

For a split-second there was silence. However, this was broken by the familiar cries of Martin Butcher. I was relieved that he was alive and it was the first time that I was glad to hear his whiny voice, as he ran wailing back into his house.

The familiar voice of Barry Pratt behind me was heard to say, "Good job his testicles hadn't descended."

"They'd be up in his throat by now!" added Jimmy Drinkwater.

Suddenly, it seemed that half of Sutton Green had turned up to experience the Bognor Drive Olympic size bobsleigh run. Unfortunately, news had crossed the recreational ground to the lower end and some of the scary roughnecks were coming over to see how our world celebrated winter.

First, there was the legendary thirteen-year-old, Pablo - fresh back from Borstal. He was alleged to have gypsy blood. He had a confident smile and a definite presence. I had heard that he possessed a flick-knife but I believed that, whatever he had done to be placed in

Reform School, it must surely have been an act of self-defence. His ear-length black hair, leather-jacket and winkle-pickers made him as cool as The Beatles. Rumour had it that Pablo was able to tame wild animals and he had once had a red fox for a pet. As if to prove the point, when Pablo got to the front of the queue, on the runway, he reached into a pouch inside his jacket and pulled out a tiny Eurasian Pygmy Owl.

"Hold Titch, for me kid," he told me. Andrew and Barry's eyes widened almost as much as the owl's. I was honoured that Pablo had entrusted me to hold his rare pet. The tiny bird of prey was shuddering in my gloved hands. I held it tightly. Pablo was obviously unaware of my reputation for being accident-prone and I could not afford a mistake because I did not want to encounter the switch-blade.

"Let me hold it," declared Jimmy, grabbing out. Pablo turned and made a kind of hissing noise, which instantly checked Jimmy's action. Then Pablo gave me an empowering smile to let me know that I was the only one he trusted to handle his pet. Considering his uncomfortably fashionable pointed shoes, he took to the slide with impressive dexterity. Then he walked back up to me and held out his hand.

"Come on Titch," he said. The owl looked relieved as I handed him over, and so was I.

"What kind of owl is he?" I asked.

"Eurasian Pygmy," Pablo explained, "they don't usually come this far west but the bad winter's driven them over."

"What's he eat?" I asked.

"Beetles," he told me, and then he tucked the bird inside the lining of his jacket again. "Did you make this slide?"

"Yeah," I bragged, forgetting to acknowledge the labours of Ian Butcher and my brother. They both glared at me.

"Fab slide," Pablo said, lighting a cigarette.

Next another group of lower enders arrived to check out our slide. A teenager called Biffo decided that he was going to attempt the stunt, whilst giving a girl a piggy back. She seemed so annoyed when they both hit the ground unceremoniously, even though Biffo had tried to cushion her fall. In fact, she went on to straddle his mid-riff and started pounding on his chest. The funny thing was that she suddenly seemed to lose all of her anger and started kissing him, instead. I do not mean a gentle peck but more a full-fledged sloppy wet embrace. I was partly nauseated and yet, fleetingly began to imagine that it was me and Sally Doyle.

This thought did not stay with me for long because, out of nowhere, a face that struck terror into all children in Sutton Green had appeared amongst us. Doug Pitt had come to scrutinize our slide. Doug was hard and psychotic. He would fight anybody, at any time, just to prove how hard and psychotic he really was! Many suspected that it was Doug's red hair and freckles, that gave him a complex, which made him want to constantly prove himself. I knew that he was just a bully because he loved beating people up.

"Who made the slide?" Doug demanded. Andrew and Ian pointed straight at me, suddenly absolving themselves of any responsibility. Doug looked over at me. I was confused, like a hare trapped in the headlights.

"What are you bloody staring at?" Doug demanded. This was Doug Pitt's battle cry and he was directing it at me. The only logical thing was to avert my eyes but I could not move and I could not speak.

"I said, 'what are you looking at?'" he reiterated, giving me another chance to redeem myself. He was right, I was staring! It was the flurry of freckles. Never before had I seen a face so full of freckles. In some areas of his skin, they had joined together to make large brown patches.

If the Beaufort scale was for hardness, rather than wind speed, Doug Pitt would be a Ten, a hurricane. On the same scale, I would be a One, too weak to flutter the sheets on a washing line. Yet, still I could not divert my attention away from the freckles on the face of the boy that was about to end my life.

The tension needed to be broken. Suddenly, heroics came from the most cowardly of sources. Jimmy Drinkwater's shoe flew over from the back of the group behind me, narrowly missing Doug Pitt's head.

"Who the bloody hell threw that?" demanded the bully, picking up the errant shoe. It would not take the ginger Bizarro Prince Charming long to discover Jimmy was the shoeless 'Cinderella,' that he needed to mutilate. However, as he was perusing the group's feet, Andrew's new Clarks double E sailed past Doug's head, quickly followed by one of Barry Pratt's slip-ons.

"You crazy buggers, I'll bloody kill you all!" yelled Doug Pitt.

Then a couple of females' shoes entered the arena which was difficult because, everybody knew Doug Pitt never hit girls. This was not the direction his fights usually took.

"Upper side freaks!" he yelled. He was now the loud one, so according to Andrew's hypothesis, he was starting to be a loser.

Finally, a winkle-picker landed at Doug's feet. The bully dropped Jimmy's shoe and picked up the high fashion footwear. Then a welcome voice broke the silence.

"Like my beetle-crusher, Doug," said Pablo.

"Pablo, you old bastard! Where've you been?" Doug asked.

"Been back inside, learning a few new tricks," Pablo replied, "still smoke?" He distracted the bully with a cigarette. Then he handed him a lighter while retrieving his winkle-picker from Doug's other hand. It was a brilliantly subtle manoeuvre.

"Only like a bloody chimney!" Doug insisted, as he blew out the smoke.

"Have you met Titch?" said Pablo, pulling out his owl while simultaneously placing his hand on Doug's shoulder. He slowly diverted Sutton Green's most legendary bully away from our shoe party, back over the recreation ground, to his own neighbourhood on the lower end.

Meanwhile, my fellow 999ers, hopped around on the ice, retrieving their respective shoes. If we were ever a gang, we were this evening.

Chapter 5: Marston Road Primary School

There are so many perfumes ready to teleport me back through space and time to Class Three. Most haunting is the unmistakable stench of the red disinfectant sand that was used to neutralize vomit. Flu season of '63 saw a big demand for the sand bucket.

Mrs Forsythe was my big-framed, round-faced teacher. Her age lay somewhere between 25 and 55 and her only interest in fashion was to disguise her natural contours. Her loose-fitting blouses, with cardigans and strings of pearls could well have been worn by her own mother, a generation earlier, along with her shin-length skirts and clumpy shoes. Her lank hair hung formlessly to her shoulders, with an incongruous little-girl fringe, under which her eyebrows regularly disappeared, to register disapproval. Completing the schoolmarm image was a pair of unflattering brown spectacles which, I suspect, she even wore to bed.

"This is the month, children," Mrs Forsythe announced, "when we will finally say, 'Good-bye' to the most horrible winter ever," She wrote the date on the board; 1st March, 1963.

"I think it was the best winter," argued Gary Smith. He looked around for support but it was not wise to contradict this teacher. A simple glare melted him back into his place.

"Who said 'White rabbits' this morning?" Mrs Forsythe asked. Her ambiguous tones left us unsure whether it was a good or bad thing. Eventually, Barry Cooper raised his hand half-heartedly.

"I did Miss Forsythe," said Barry sheepishly.

"*Liar!*" I thought to myself.

"Good boy, Barry, but remember it's not Miss, its Mrs," said the teacher. It seemed very important for Mrs Forsythe to have us know that she was not a spinster, unlike Miss Elliot and Miss Heath.

I raised my hand and asked, "Please Mrs Forsythe, why did he say 'White rabbits?'"

"Good question, Martin," she said, happy that I had got her train of thought back on track. "Its traditional to say 'White rabbits' before saying anything else on the first day of March, then you will have good luck for the whole month."

I was wishing that I had known this earlier because I could have done with a change of fortune. After all, since the year had begun I had become a fugitive from the police, threatened by Doug Pitt, almost crippled by chilblains and shot by the heir of Podmore.

"Is it too late to say it now, Miss?" I inquired.

"Of course, it is, silly boy!" she snapped, obviously irritated by the accidental spinster inference. It seemed odd to me that she was so insistent of us correctly categorizing her marital status. She spoke of her mother and sister regularly but never mentioned her husband.

"Sorry, Mrs Forsythe," I corrected, hoping to repair the damage.

"Well luckily, children, I remembered to say it, so March should be a wonderful month for the whole of Class Three," she reasoned. I did not really follow her logic. Was it possible that a phrase, uttered by one adult, could control the fortunes of thirty-three children? It seemed unlikely but I was more than willing to accept it. Unfortunately, my secret dream girl did not seem to be protected by the umbrella of luck.

"Hoo.....arrgh!' went Sally Doyle as she projected her breakfast all over the floorboards.

"Urrr...rrgh!" screamed the rest of the class in unison.

"Martin, go and get the red sand bucket from outside the head-masters office," commanded the teacher.

"Yes Miss, I mean Mrs Forsythe," I self-corrected.

"Just go!" she exclaimed, causing me to use my high-speed superpowers. Then, as I thundered down the corridor I heard her shout, "Don't run! Walk!" I mused how truly difficult it was to fathom out adults, as I dragged the sand bucket and broom to the scene of the accident. In my short absence, Yvonne Clamp had 'sympathy vomited,' in response to the spew fumes, setting up a potential chain reaction. Luckily, Mrs Forsythe dispatched lavish helpings of the antidote sand, before the waves of nausea could mushroom out of control. Mrs Forsythe put us through the full range of disciplinary actions to regain control after the class's over-reaction to the Doyle and Clamp show.

First it was, "Fingers on lips!" Then it was, "Hands on heads!" Barry Cooper was made to stand on his chair, which served him right because he had laughed heartlessly at poor Sally Doyle's demise. To me this proved that he was lying about the "White rabbits" because he was already out-of-luck. At least he was not banished to the 'naughty corner.'

Eventually, when Mrs Forsythe had made us jump through enough punitive hoops, she started her lesson. Apparently, amongst other things, it was St David's day and Mrs Forsythe gave all the girls a yellow daffodil and the boys received a big fat onion-like thing, called a Leek. She read to us a story about the Patron Saint of Wales. When my teacher read to the class, her voice was angelic and captivating. There was no hint of the latent tyrant that could be evoked by misplaced titles or forgetful pupils. After she had seduced our auditory senses with her St. David tribute, we were asked to write about it. For once, I had paid close attention and knew exactly what I wanted to say but others had been less engrossed in the story.

Whilst we were writing, Mrs Forsythe took advantage of the structured time, by collecting everyone's dinner money. I was lucky because I had remembered mine, this particular week. Dinner money was the bane of my existence because I had had several episodes of turning up without it. Mrs Forsythe had a policy of merciless intimidation toward anyone that dared to forget their weekly lunch funds. Andrew said that she was being 'cruel to be kind' but I had my doubts. The whole concept that, by terrorizing a child suffering from attention deficits, you could somehow prevent future forgetfulness seemed ludicrous to me. Being fretful by nature, I found the extra pressure counter-productive. I had already failed twice since the New Year had begun.

Luckily, I had already completed the St David assignment when ADHD rewound my mind back to the first time that I left it my dinner money sitting on the kitchen table, despite a reminder from my mum.

I remembered that I had already endured torturous day of 'Forsythe wrath,' where she had threatened me with 'the pump.' Then, I arrived home to face another onslaught of abuse. Unfortunately, it coincided with one of mum's ill-tempered phases, which seemed to happen monthly. Andrew postulated that it was linked with the phases of the moon. He said that the word 'lunatic' meant moon maniac.

"How come Andrew never forgets his dinner money?" mum demanded. Andrew smiled smugly.

"I didn't do it on purpose!" I had foolishly defended myself.

"Nonsense!" mum countered. I heard her voice change, mid-word, into the manic tones that usually pre-empted a slap. The last thing I wanted was further conflict. Every synapse of my brain was urging me to remain silent.

Then that 'awkward' voice from my subconscious took the reins and blurted out, "It's not my fault, stupid cow!" I was as shocked as anyone. It was as if I had deliberately tried to expedite the inevitable conflict.

Time seemed to temporarily freeze, while the whole family recoiled at my outburst. We were all hares in the headlights. Andrew was the first to break free of the trance and he leaped behind the sofa, as if a Darlek, from Doctor Who, had just entered the room. The Evening Sentinel instinctively opened and slid itself over dad's face, and Eric started crying in anticipation.

"What did you say?" mother cackled. She was obviously now completely possessed by the demons of her own mother. I saw her hand swinging toward me and

I really could have ducked. For some reason, I denied my own reflexes and took the full force across my face.

"Stupid cow!" I screamed again. I felt tears welling up but I did not flinch, as mum's backhand brought an even greater sting to the other side of my face. Still I stood firm, fully expecting the next blow to release me from consciousness. However, Eric began to bellow loudly, which caused enough distraction for me to turn and head off upstairs. I thought that mum would follow but she did not. When I reached the bathroom, my nose was bleeding and I stood sobbing, deliberately letting the blood flow over the bath and toilet and linoleum floor. It took about ten minutes for the blood-flow to subside and by this time the bathroom was like a scene from "Psycho." I went to lie down on my bed and waited for the other shoe to drop. I still wanted to cry but my tear ducts were empty. The waiting was far more terrifying than the actual incident.

It was silent downstairs and I was starting to drift into sleep when I was stirred by the sound of footsteps coming up the stairs. Then I heard mum gasp as she came upon the scene of my bloodbath. I thought that she would come and start upon me again but the outcome of my passive/aggressive bleeding session was even more distressing. I listened as mum cried uncontrollably, whilst she tried to divert herself by mopping up the blood. I conjured up some fresh tears of empathy, as my guilt trip backfired. I had never known her to cry before and it was a harrowing sound.

Eventually mum came into the bedroom and I pretended to be asleep. She knew that I was awake.

"I'm sorry, Martin, you didn't deserve that," she said with complete sincerity.

I roused from my pretend sleep. "I'm sorry mum, I promise I won't forget my dinner money again," I told her, trying to give perspective to her outrageous over-reaction.

"You silly boy, that damn 'awkward streak' of yours! You know I love you, don't you?" she said, giving closure to the episode.

"I love you, too mum," I told her, trying to ease her conscience. These rages always ended in a similar way.

After such a traumatic experience, you would think that my absent-mindedness would have been cured, according to the Forsythe theory. It had certainly plagued my every waking moment for the next week. However, would you believe it, the very next Monday, as I delved frantically into my trouser pocket for the money, two shiny half-crowns sat proudly in their regular spot, back home on the kitchen table?

True to her word, Mrs Forsythe gave me 'the pump.' My first ever public flogging! I did not have to suffer alone as Kevin Dagworth was also lined up for the humiliation. Kevin was made to bend over first, as the sized-ten plimsoll pummelled his bottom. Kevin was used to the beatings and took it like a man. However, I was more sensitive and the hurt went deeper than the physical pain. As 'the pump' bruised my buttocks, there was a danger that the humiliation would scar my mind.

"Touch your toes, Martin," was Mrs Forsythe's command. For all my agility, this was one feat that I could not perform.

"I can't reach, Miss," I told her.

"Nonsense, boy," she insisted, "I said 'toes'- and its Mrs, not Miss!" This was not the time to be antagonizing the teacher. I stretched with all my willpower but still my fingers were four inches short of my shoes. Mrs Forsythe was losing patience, obviously itching to continue the blood lust that the beating of 'Daggers' had activated. Finally, she could wait no longer and she let loose with a particularly venomous swing with the plimsoll. The whole class grimaced at the level of violence. However, as I swallowed back the lachrymal juices, I caught a glimpse of Sally Doyle out of the corner of my eye. Her perfectly-groomed mousy hair pulled tightly into a pony tail gave maximum exposure to her delightfully shiny forehead. I thought that she would feel contemptuous toward me, as I joined the ranks of the naughty kids. However, her gorgeous brown eyes were viewing me with warmth and admiration. It seems that my refusal to touch my toes was interpreted as a brave act of rebellion. Her attention distracted my mind from the sting of the 'pump' and my walk back to my desk was quite dignified.

"Did it hurt?" the seemingly beguiled Sally Doyle whispered.

"Nair," I declared nonchalantly, forcing a grin. She returned my smile, displacing the agony with an inexplicable yearning. I was not in pain, I was in love. Andrew had once shared with me the expression '*Every cloud has a silver lining*' but I had never understood before that moment.

When I got home that evening, to my amazement, the whole of the day had passed without mum noticing the money. I managed to lift it without receiving a double punishment, on that occasion.

My reminiscing was suddenly jolted back to White Rabbit Day reality, by Mrs Forsythe's voice. She had obviously noticed my daydreaming and decided to try and catch me out.

"So, Martin, what's so special about today?" she quizzed.

"It's Saint David's day, Mrs Forsythe," I instinctively retorted.

"Have you finished writing about it?" she tried to trick me.

"Yes, Mrs Forsythe," I replied, turning my usual beetroot red.

"Perhaps you would like to read it to us?" she asked, mistaking my blushes for guilt. In reality, my embarrassment was related to fear that my lazy eye might start skipping words, which could, in turn trigger a stammering bout. Fortunately, my concerns turned out to be unfounded. I took a deep breath, and read my essay perfectly:

"St. David, whose real name was Dewi Sant, was the Holy Saint of Wales. He was a monk and he lived for a hundred years. He spent his life walking around Wales turning Pagans into Christians. His best miracle was to make the earth rise up so everyone in Wales could see him."

"Very good, Martin, you get a gold star," she announced, obviously sheepish about having doubted me. March was truly turning out to be a lucky month because, although I was in the lead in terms of overall stars, this was the first gold star to be awarded all year! She gave me the honour of licking the back of the star to activate the 'sticky' before placing it by my name on the star chart. Sally Doyle's mum turned up to take her flu-riddled daughter home, just as Mrs Forsythe was leading the applause to my success.

"That's Martin," Sally uttered from her semi-comatose state.

"Oh, a clever-clogs, is he?" her mum replied.

"*A perfect moment, if ever there was one,*" I thought to myself. Mrs Forsythe's 'White Rabbits' were working fast.

Furthermore, there were extra ginger button biscuits to go with our milk for break, since so many pupils were out sick, so we all got seven rather than the usual four.

After the recess, Mrs Clark, my drab-looking music teacher with a tight perm, arrived and escorted us to the Assembly Hall. She was always calm at the start of our music sessions but she never failed to lose her temper, at least three times, especially on instrument day. She was highly organized, and had placed all of the instruments under the chairs before we arrived. The rules were clearly posted on the wall, as well as being read to us each time before we entered the room:

1. Enter the room in order. (Not a mad dash!)
2. Do not touch the instrument under your chair until the teacher tells you.
3. No swapping of instruments.
4. Do not start playing the instrument until the teacher tells you.
5. STOP when the teacher says STOP!

These were simple rules but they were so hard to follow. Mrs Clark seemed particularly delighted when

Mrs Forsythe informed her that we only had twenty-four pupils.

"Wonderful," she said optimistically, "then everyone should be able to play an instrument." That was good news because usually there were about eight kids that were selected to be the 'clappers.' Mrs Clark told us that is was the most important job of all but we all knew that she was purely trying to manipulate us. It just did not add up because, invariably the punishment for breaking the five rules was banishment to the clapping section.

As we walked, in order, to our assigned seats, my heart began to flutter as a realization hit me. I was in line to be the drummer. I would have settled for anything that was not a triangle. The maracas and tambourine were highly acceptable in my mind but the drum was everyone's instrument of choice.

"Today, we are going to learn to play a waltz," said the excited music teacher, "and it will be a song that I can guarantee that you will all love." I was intrigued.

"1, 2, 3…1, 2, 3" she counted, waving her fingers to the rhythm. "Okay little drummer-boy, pick up your drumstick. Beat the drum on one." She nodded her head on the first beat of every bar and I soon picked it up.

"Bang 2, 3, bang 2, 3," said my snare.

Mrs Clark was also on a roll. "Very nice drumming, keep it up! Now tambourines, tap gently on 2, 3. Bang, tap tap, bang tap, tap. Triangles join the tambourines every fourth bar. Bang, tap tap, bang, tap tap, bang, tap tap, bang, ting-a-ling." It was magical because the whole class had just jumped right in with their parts and then Mrs Clark introduced the melody on the piano. It was only the number one hit of the moment. It was Cliff Richard's song, Bachelor Boy, from my favourite film, Summer Holiday:

"When I was young my daddy said,
Son I have something to say,
And what he told me I'll never forget
Until my dying day," she sang.

Spontaneously, everybody joined in the chorus:

Son, you are a bachelor boy
And that's the way to stay-ay-ay
Happy to be-ee a bachelor boy
Until your dying day.

For this short time, we were magnificent - a singing orchestra. We even swayed to the tune as we tapped out our beats and the class experienced a harmonic psychic link. It seemed a shame that Sally Doyle was missing this symbiosis. I saw Mrs Clark's face enter the 'magical zone' as if she was on a Teddy and Panda trip. Unfortunately, we never made it to the second verse. Anton Zeleski's tin-a-ling jumped in a bar early which threw Kevin Dagworth onto the off-beat. The deterioration was exponential as each pupil tried to rescue the tune and made it worse.

"Stop!" shouted Mrs Clark, as the cacophony of noise jolted her back from her short-lived ecstatic state. Gary Smith, on tambourine could not 'switch off' in time and Mrs Clark had to resort bashing the cymbal to gain his attention. Needless-to-say, Gary's instrument for the rest of the lesson was his own hands.

"Get to the clappers, boy!" insisted Mrs Clark, suddenly leaping to her zero-tolerance mode. She tried three more times to recapture the moment but each occasion was worse; the rhythmic glue that temporarily bound our minds was completely dissolved. Eventually, we all had to put the instruments back under our chairs and sit for the last ten minutes with our fingers on our lips.

"At least it's not 'hands on heads.'" I thought. It was always a little schizophrenic at Marston Road Primary; the adults would overexcite us one minute and then deliberately induce boredom to bring us back down to earth. Fluctuations between agony and ecstasy offered no constructive help to my scatterbrain.

Dinner time was the next part of, what was turning out to be an above average day. As soon as the dinner bell rang we raced to the queue. Not that we were fuelled by appetite. There was a far more important reason to be early to the canteen and every day the routine was the same. As usual, the canteen staff was not quite ready. In my opinion, there was no reason for this because they knew exactly what time we were coming. The main drive for an early lunch seat involved cutlery. On the back of each spoon there was one of three labels: '*Nixon*' meant that you were a boy, '*Bisby*' made you a girl and '*Nickel-Silver*' was completely asexual - you were not a boy but at least you were not a girl.

After waiting for about fifteen minutes the door was opened and a warm waft of cabbage gave us our first hint of lunch. My speed came in handy, as we all charged to our favourite tables. I flipped over my spoon in a flash and saw *Nickel-Silver*.

"A good start!" I thought. I turned over the three closest spoons, *Bisby, Bisby, Nickel-Silver*, and then one more, *Nixon*, I had hit the jackpot! I worked the switch and shuffled the disturbed spoons to cover my tracks. Then, as was the standard practice, I gave my *Nixon* spoon a lick, to protect it from further tampering. Now I could

relax and enjoy the spectacle of watching the other boys arrive at my table and scramble over the spoons. I knew for a fact that at least two of them would be forced to eat their puddings as girls. It was funny to watch Trevor Simkins settle opposite me, discover his *Bisby* and then blindly switch it with the unsuspecting adjacent Anton Zeleski. His face was a picture when he realized that he had made no gain and he was still a girl. Philip Whittaker and Ruth Parsons on the next table were wrestling over the same spoon, which made no sense; I could see no permutation that could not be peaceably resolved between opposite sexes. Rather like a poker player making an extra check of his hand before betting, I took a smug glance at my *Nixon* – except it was no longer a *Nixon*, it was a *Bisby*! I looked up just in time to see Simkins giving my spoon the 'Bruce the slobbering dog' treatment.

"I've already licked it, Simkins," I snapped, turning his temporary grin to disgust. A double-licked spoon had no appeal to anyone. My eyes scoured the other tables for a girl that might have an interest in my *Bisby* but I was out of luck. Then, Simkins decided to switch the double-licker back, and proceeded to lick the *Bisby*.

"*Unbelievable*," I thought. He had already licked my germs off the *Nixon* and now he was giving his bacteria-riddled saliva to me. It seemed hopeless and I had to devise an ultimate emergency plan. I brazenly ducked under the counter into the kitchen, where the dinner ladies were still rationing out the food.

"What are you doing in here?" said the kindly voice of the cook, who was in the process of putting the final touches to the chocolate sponge dessert.

Trevor Simkins has licked my spoon and he sits next to Sally Doyle and she's got flu," I explained, deliberately pitifully.

"Oh dear, we can't have that," said the kindly dinner lady, "let's give it a rinse."

"No pupils behind the counter!" yelled Mrs Forsythe.

"It's okay," the dinner lady covered for me, "he's doing a job for me." She quickly washed my *Nixon* and dried it on her apron and went back to her work without further fuss.

"Thank you," I remembered my manners. I gave my freshly-cleaned *Nixon* a lick and I could finally focus on the task ahead - eating dinner.

As a vegetarian, school dinners presented something of a problem. Nobody understood my refusal to eat meat. They always assumed that I had some wimpy abhorrence to eating animals but it was simply that I did not like the texture in my mouth. If I could not swallow it after two chews I would invariably begin to wretch. Vomit in the dining room presented the potential for a catastrophe that no amount of red sand would be able to rectify. My strategy had always been to leave the meat untouched and gain my nutrition through mashed potatoes, vegetables and gravy, followed by pudding and custard. Occasionally, some well-meaning teacher or hyper-vigilant dinner lady would notice my meat avoidance and try to cure me. There could be no good outcome from trying to make me eat animal flesh and these sessions never ended well. So, my mum eventually gave me a note to carry:

Dear Mrs Forsythe,

Please excuse Martin from eating meat or fish as he has my permission to be a vegetarian.

I know that this seems a bit awkward but Martin is likely
to be sick if you try and make him eat meat.
Thanking you in anticipation.
Yours sincerely,
Beryl Wells.

When I saw the particularly gnarly slice of fatty lamb on my plate I slipped my hand in my pocket to check for the note. I was already gagging in anticipation and was greatly relieved that was there. The luck was continuing. I ate my potato and cabbage and managed to scrape my unappetizing lamb into the pigswill bucket, without attracting unnecessary attention.

Then the puddings came out: chocolate sponge cake and custard, which was usually everybody's favourite. However, instead of the usual yummy sounds of delight, a wave of screams erupted around the whole canteen. Apparently, a distracted dinner lady, whilst adding a little finesse to the chocolate cake, had accidentally sprinkled Bicarbonate of Soda, rather than powdered icing sugar. Some bizarre reaction with the custard occurred resulting in fluorescent, bubbling green foam in everyone's dish. The teacher's table was the first to react.

"Bloody hell fire!" was Mr. Barton's unfiltered response. I saw Mrs Forsythe throw him one of her disapproving glances.

"Good God!" Miss. Heath blasphemed.

"Poison!" yelled Barry Cooper.

"It's the Blob!" I added, quoting a horror film that had recently been on the television. My intended humorous comment did nothing to quell the outbreak of hysteria.

"It's the Incredible Hulk," shouted Barry Pratt, trying to upstage my witticism. This made the screaming girls screech louder. Meanwhile, the verdant effervescence began to cascade over the sides of people's dishes and onto the table. Yvonne Clamp got some on her hand and her imagination determined it to be corrosive.

"It's burning me!" she declared, as she made a panicked dash out of the canteen, presumably toward the toilets. Three other girls tagged onto her, driven by a mixture of fear and morbid curiosity. The incident had hatched a riot which would surely make the Evening Sentinel. The sensation phenomenon that was occurring surely topped February's leading headlines:

CHRISTINE KEELER ROCKS GOVERNMENT.

This, in turn beat so many of the previous recent headlines:

BRRR…..RRR! IT'S A COLD ONE!

And:

BIG THAW! BURST WATERPIPE EMERGENCY!

Yes, I had no doubt that dad would soon be snoozing under a headline:

ATTACK OF THE GREEN SLIME IN PRIMARY SCHOOL!

The noise began to crescendo as excitement turned to terror. A communal fear seemed to ripple through the whole room as mass hysteria took a grip. We all needed a face-slapping to bring us back to earth. One glance at the livid expression on Mrs Forsythe's face told me that she would gladly administer this. However, it was Mr. Rice, the head teacher that finally injected some control into the room. He took out his whistle and blew with all his might. It silenced us so instantly that the whistle's echo seemed to reverberate uncannily for the longest time.

He announced, "Children of Marston Primary School, there is nothing to worry about. Someone accidentally sprinkled bicarbonate on your food. It's perfectly harmless. In fact, anybody that ate their cabbage has already ingested some b ecause that's what cooks use to keep our greens green. Now, it might taste a bit salty so you have a choice: You can scrape it off the sponge cake and still eat it –No Mr. Cooper, it is not poisoned; or you can leave it – I'm sure the pigs won't be so fussy." It was the perfect speech. Not so much for the content but more for the Churchillian confidence, with which it was delivered. His voice de-escalated everyone from crisis mode, back down to a calm baseline. I opted for the 'scrape and eat' option, especially as I did not want to waste my *Nixon*. Simkins followed suit except with a *Bisby*, as a girl.

Post-lunch playtime was shorter than usual and we hardly had time to set up a game of *rebounds* when the school bell called us back to class. Andrew invented the game of *rebounds* the previous summer. It had been months since it had been dry and warm enough to play outside and the game was in danger of extinction. However, this lunchtime I resurrected the game. All you needed was a tennis ball and designated section of wall. Each participant took turns to hit the wall with a single kick of the ball. The brilliance lay in the lack of rules. Hit the wall and you stayed in but miss it and you were knocked out. *Rebounds* had the right blend of luck and skill. The strategies were to either, stand near to the wall so that you could take the rebound quickly, or stand away from the wall, allowing the ball to slow down or stop before attempting a kick. It was speed versus accuracy. I tended to prefer the standoffish approach since my lazy-eye coordination did not match my distant vision skills.

Art class was great in the afternoon. Mrs Forsythe had us paint bright colours all over our paper.

"The wilder the better," she briefed us. I made some abstract swirling patterns which would have stood up as modern art in their its own right. However, once they had dried, we were all given black crayons and asked to completely cover the paint with a thick wax coating. We obeyed without question because Mrs Forsythe could always be trusted, when it came to arts and crafts. The third part of the project involved the use of a small chisel to etch off some of the black wax in the shape of a drawing. I made a horse for my dad because I knew that he was already thinking of the Grand National. Dad loved gambling and a brightly coloured engraved horse might inspire him to pick the winner that he was always threatening would change our lives.

I was pleased with my creation but when dad saw it he was absolutely elated. He regarded it as some kind of sign.

"Never look a gift horse in the mouth," he joked, quoting a proverb that I did not fully comprehend. He spent the evening scrutinizing the whole Grand National field for names like Painted Pony or Red Rum but no such horses existed.

Chapter 6: Birthdays.

Mum's strawberry trifle was indisputably the most delectable aroma to ever enter my nostrils. It was only ever unleashed on special family occasions. The wonderful thing about March was that it was birthday month and strawberries frequently filled the air. Mum, Eric and I would all become a year older this month. And Andrew had only missed it by a day. The anniversary of his birth was always the day before St. David's Day, except on leap years, when the time lords had slipped in an extra day. He had just turned ten; double figures, no less. My birthday fell on the Ides of March - most famous for being the day when Julius Caesar was stabbed in the back by all of his friends.

On the morning of March the fifteenth, I awakened just before dawn. At the end of my bed were a couple of parcels, as was the family tradition. The most intriguing was a large tubular packet - inside was a magnificent map of the whole world. Mum must have heard my stirrings because she came into the bedroom, readily armed with scotch tape and she helped me stick my new map on the wall directly over my bed. She pointed out a few exotic places, like Paris and Rome then some more obscure regions, like Ghana and Mozambique. The position of the map was perfect because I could study it before falling asleep each night. The next package contained a maroon propelling pencil, which I loved, and a giant pink erasure in the shape of a parallelogram. However, the best gift of all was a plastic template in the shape of Great Britain. I probably replicated it about fifty times, on various types of paper, with my propelling pencil. It was more than an outline because there were holes to poke the lead through, to mark the exact positions of places like London, Manchester and Bristol.

Mum's face looked almost apologetic when she saw the meagre size of the haul. However, I was delighted because I was bracing myself for a far more frugal affair. Our family seemed to be going through a particularly impoverished period. Apparently, the extra cold winter had created extra demands on the purse strings.

I knew that there would not be much money injected into my birthday because on the previous Friday evening mum had suddenly rushed in from filling the dustbin outside. Apparently, she had just spotted the man that emptied the electric meter two doors away.

"Everybody under the kitchen table," she whispered, quickly flicking the switches to throw us into virtual darkness. Dad grabbed Eric and slid across the orange tile floor to take up position under the table.

"What's going on?" I asked, excited by an unexpected hide-and-seek game.

"Sh…..hhhhh," was the joint reply of my parents.

Andrew and I tried to squeeze under the same corner of the table, which of course provoked me to insist, "I was here first!"

"Rubbish, you liar!" Andrew retorted in a whisper. We both turned sheepishly to mum, hoping she would select a winner. It was too dark to see her glare but we could both feel it. With no newspaper within reach, dad had nowhere to hide.

On this rare occasion, we were stunned when dad intervened. "Bloody hell, I'll bang your heads together if you don't shut up, right now!"

As our eyes began to acclimatize to the darkness I noticed that mum was not glaring at us at all, she was staring at dad with, what Enid Blyton would probably describe as a 'gaze of admiration.' Presumably, this was because he had finally stepped up, to shoulder the burden of discipline. She did not even chastise his bad language.

We sat silent for what seemed like an eternity, and were just about to assume that all was clear, when there was a knock on the back door. Mum placed a finger on her lips to reinforce the importance of silence. I could suddenly feel my heart pounding in my chest. In fact, I could sense that everyone under the table had the same adrenal response. He knocked again, louder this time. Surely, he would realize that we were 'out' and move on? It seemed for a minute that this was exactly what he had done, when suddenly, "Bang, bang, bang!" he was hammering the knocker of the front door. Surely our lack of response would convince him that we were out now?

"They're definitely in, duck," said the unmistakable voice of Sparky Ears Johnson next door."

"That bloody cow!" whispered Mum.

"Bitch!" agreed dad. Now it was the children's turn to shush the adults.

"Ducks, cows and bitches. It's like a farmyard out there," I quipped. Humour was my defence mechanism. Andrew laughed nervously in response but we were both instantly silenced, as dad delivered a simultaneous crack to the back of each of our heads. I saw mum reach for dad's hand and squeeze. I would like to have thought that she was trying to protect us from further onslaught, but I suspected that she was rewarding his aggression, with affection.

As the clock ticked on, we were once again being lulled into a false sense of security. I was just beginning to feel that the crisis had passed when all hell broke loose. The meter man was banging on the side kitchen window, and Sparky Ears was double-knuckling the back one.

"Peter, Beryl, are you in there?" her witch-like voice boomed, "the man's here to empty your meter." She was going for maximum humiliation, by making sure that the whole neighbourhood knew that we were not paying the electricity bill.

Apparently, our neighbour was possessed by jealousy. Her hair was always in curlers, obviously trying to simulate mum's natural hairstyle. And she always wore an apron, as if she was perpetually burdened with housework; keeping Reg happy was obviously no mean feat. She had never forgiven us for having a shed and I think mum had offended her, in a heated moment, by calling her a Nosey Parker. One day, when mum was loudly 'losing' an argument with dad, Mrs Johnson had banged on the wall, causing mum to scream, "Bugger off Sparky Ears!" The name tickled us so much we used it from that day on.

The meter man incident caused such a commotion that the Baggots,' on the other side, came out to investigate the source of the mayhem. Mrs Baggot was blind but her other senses were enhanced, so the racket probably sounded even worse to her. Mum often helped Mrs Baggot out, so she had a certain loyalty to us.

"What's going on?" asked Nancy Baggot, in a deliberately calming voice.

"The meter man's here and we can't get Peter and Beryl to answer the door. I wonder if we should call the police because they're always arguing, you know."

"I heard them all go out about twenty minutes ago," Nancy lied.

The meter man was probably feeling that he had already surpassed his duties because he said, "It's not a great problem, lady; I can call back next week."

Much to Sparky Ears' dismay, the meter man left, leaving her to look as though she was the unreasonable one. As quiet returned to the neighbourhood we all decided to remain under the table until we could be certain that the coast was clear.

"Why won't you let the meter man empty the meter?" dad asked in a hushed voice.

"Because I've been putting milk checks instead of shillings in the meter all week," mum explained. Blue plastic milk checks were provided by the welfare, for poor families with children. Theoretically, they could only be used for milk; whereas, cash might have been wasted on cigarettes or beer. However, an oversight by the designers made milk checks exactly the same size as shillings. "I meant to swap them when the meter was emptied but I had to give Martin and Andrew dinner money."

I knew that we would get some mention, when the blame was being assigned.

"So how have you been paying for the milk then," dad continued to inquire.

"Oh, the milkman's easy to pay," she told him, in a sort of playful tone. I knew from dad's response that there was a joke in there somewhere; dad was doing his 'Groucho Marx' eyebrow-raising routine and mum giggling like she was Sally Doyle. I looked toward Andrew for guidance. He had sensed it too but he shrugged to confirm that he was also at a loss. Our pulse rates were finally returning to normal. We realized that poverty had created a temporary family bond that the rich could never experience. Mum and dad seemed to suddenly be bonding extremely well.

"Well, children, we obviously can't make any sounds tonight, or have any lights on, so we'll have to try and get to bed in the dark," dad told us. Mum smiled at him in agreement. It sounded like the only logical plan. It would be fun to try and get up the stairs and into our pyjamas without a single sound, in near pitch black conditions. I had the extra challenge of putting Eric to bed, a duty that fell more and more on me. It was close enough to bedtime for us but it was at least a couple of hours away from mum and dad's time to retire. I felt a little sorry for them, having to lie there in the dark just waiting for sleep to come.

So, we crept ever so silently from under the table and stood up. Dad's bones cracked as he straightened out and proceeded to chivalrously help up mum. Her bones cracked too, which made Andrew snort, as he tried to silence a snicker. This, in turn, started me and Eric laughing. I was just about to launch into full-blown hysterics when I happened to glance at the kitchen window.

"Arr…gghhhh!" I screamed, as I saw the wide eyes of Sparky Ears Johnson staring straight at me!

"Bloody hell fire!" yelled dad.

77

"I knew it!" exclaimed Sparky Ears, finally vindicated.

Then it was silent, as if we were 'hares in the headlights.' The momentary pause summoned up the 'ghost of grandma' in my mum; for once she was not gunning for me. An instant later, the framed image of Mrs Johnson was joined in the window by an enraged mum.

"Who the hell do you think you are, trespassing on our property? You nosy bitch1" Mum asked. It was rhetorical but Sparky still floundered to try and answer.

"I was worried," she defended.

"Worried, my arse!" Mum attacked. "Well, you'd better be worried, nosy bugger!"

"Reg!" Mrs Johnson suddenly called for her husband. Having heard the tone of mum's voice, Reg was probably cowering under the Johnson kitchen table. There was no way that he was coming out.

"Get off my property now!" Mum screamed, as Sparky bolted, "and if you ever come within fifty feet of my house again I'm calling the police." This was the best example I had ever seen of Andrew's saying, 'the best form of defence is attack.'

After that, it seemed a little fruitless to continue the farce of us all sneaking to bed, in the dark. But having chased off our neighbour, mum's mood returned to 'nice' and she grabbed dad's hand and said, "So we all know the plan, so what are we waiting for?"

"So how did you pay the milkman?" was the last whispered question of the night.

Chapter 7: It's my Party and I'll kiss who I want to!

Only three days after my birthday, it was Eric's turn to celebrate with a fragrant trifle tribute. He was as delighted with his Toby Twirl colouring book and crayons, as I had been with my treats. My parents were lucky that we were such undemanding children. Obviously, they could not afford a party. Eric was just as happy to blow out two candles on a trifle, as he would have been a cake. However, what did seem unfair was that, out of the blue, we were all suddenly invited to Jane Dawson's party and it was not even her birthday.

Jane Dawson lived the other side of the Baggots. She was the same age as Andrew. She appeared to have something of a crush because she would go all cooie-gooie around him. Her big sister, Kate, was a seventeen-year-old apprentice hairdresser. Her own hairstyle was heavily back-combed, in the ultra-trendy Dusty Springfield tradition. This was obviously a perk of the job.

She used to come around to practice on my mum's hair every Thursday evening. Dad always made himself sparse on these occasions, going off to the hospital club with Carl Wagstaff. Kate never failed to bring us each a penny chocolate bar. Better still, she would put aside any American comics that ended up at her salon, knowing how much Andrew and I liked Superman and his contemporaries. Kate was well versed in all the skulduggery on the estate - the hairdresser's dryer was like a confessional. I suspect that mum enjoyed the gossip as much as her hair relished the teasing. I learned, by feigning engrossment in the comics, about some of the seedier 'goings on' in Sutton Green. Sometimes, after she had gone, I would have to clarify a few things with Andrew. For instance, apparently, Tina Carolla's mum, who lived on Wardle Street, was pregnant again.

"She isn't even sure who the father is," whispered Kate. The statement made no sense to me and Andrew's later explanation, involving more than one secret husband, did nothing to clarify things.

"Maybe its Horace Baggot?" mum sarcastically laughed.

"Which one?" Kate giggled back, "Podgy or Slimy?"

"I meant junior, you fool," mum clarified, obviously referring to the out-of shape nineteen-year-old son of our neighbour, as opposed to his cigar-smoking dad.

"Yuck," responded Kate, "even Carolla wouldn't stoop that low. Although, I've heard that three Babychams and she's anybody's!"

"Four and she's everybody's!" mum quipped in snickered whisper, checking that Andrew and I were still too pre-occupied to absorb the conversation. I obliged by turning a page of my Green Lantern comic. Maybe my response was too staged because mum suddenly looked suspicious.

"So, about Jane's party, I'll bring the boys at one o'clock?" asked mum, blatantly changing the subject.

"We're going to a party?" Andrew and I yelled in unison, abandoning all pretence of nonchalance.

"I knew you boys were listening," laughed mum.

In hindsight, we should have 'smelled a rat' because, the next day, it became apparent that this impromptu party was not linked to any celebration. Still, we did not care. Firstly, we played a variation of a game of Chinese whispers. Basically, we had to sit in a circle and pass around a bottle of Tizer. It was imperative to take a swig of the red pop and then whisper the given phrase into the ear of the person to the right.

"Bobby Charlton's got no hair," I dutifully repeated into Barry Pratt's ear, along with a Tizer shower, which seemed to come from my nose rather than my mouth. By the time every kid at the party had wrapped their larynx and salivary glands around the secret statement, it was Drew's job to reveal what he had heard.

"Bernie Winters loves Lionel Blair!" he insisted. Every one chuckled and then launched into Bernie Winters impressions.

"Who's my little choochy face?" was Jimmy Drinkwater's attempt, adding a dandelion and burdock lisp for effect. The party was becoming quite a sticky affair.

After some analysis, we discovered that the names had gone through many mutations, including Boris Karloff and Gina Lollobrigida. This inspired Tony Boswell to start staggering around like the Frankenstein monster. On the other hand, Tina Carolla began to adopt the persona of the Italian film star sex symbol. At this, I saw mum and Kate share a knowing glance, as if to say, 'like mother, like daughter.'

"Why don'tta we playa kissa chase?" came Tina's atrociously fake Italian accent. The girls all cheered, the boys groaned, and I blushed in anticipation. As it was Jane's party, she had the privilege of initiating proceedings. Of course, her eyes locked on Andrew and the hunt was on. It reminded me of one of the dramas that we watched at the Saturday morning picture shows, where the victim ran like crazy but the hunter still managed to close him down by relentless plodding. And so it came to pass that Andrew was trapped under the jelly and blancmange table with Jane moving in for the kill.

It was obvious that Jane had been unwell because she was sweating profusely. The exertions of the chase had also brought out a blotchy rash. However, the greatest indicator of her illness was two huge swellings behind her ears. She looked like Whiskey, after he had packed his pouches with sunflower seeds. I began to make some rationalizations. We were at an undesignated party for a host that was sick. The adults were blatantly encouraging germ sharing practices, such as drinking from the same bottle, and now kiss chase. It was a German measles party! A surge of altruism must have overtaken me, at this point, because I had an uncontrollable urge to save my brother.

"Dawson!" I yelled, grabbing her around the waist. The distraction worked and Andrew managed to dive past us, upsetting a few desserts on the table above. Adults leapt to stabilize the mayhem and suddenly I was boxed in by 'grown up' legs, with no hope of escape. Out of the blue, came my first kiss. It was not how I had imagined, pinned down under a jelly table with the hamster cheeks of Jane Dawson descended upon me. She licked her lips, giving maximum surface area to the rubella germs. In some weird sympathetic reflex, my tongue involuntarily moistened my own lips and my salivary glands acted as though I had just sucked a lemon. She secured my face with a hand on each temple and then our lips were locked. It probably did not last very long but it seemed an eternity as a myriad of thoughts rippled through my brain. *'If only it was Sally Doyle! At least Drew will thank me! I like this! I can taste Vimto! Maybe Drew didn't want saving! I really like this! I bet I'm blushing! German measles germs goose-stepping down my throat! My tongue feels weird in my mouth! My God it's not **my** tongue!'*

"Get off me, you bloody sex maniac!" I yelled, as I regained my senses and pushed her off. I scrambled from under the table. Everyone cheered, no doubt elevating my color to an even brighter shade of scarlet. I assumed my ordeal was over but Andrew, who may well have been harboring some envious thoughts announced that the 'kissee becomes the kisser.' I instantly realized that peer pressure made resistance useless, so I took on the mantle. After all, I was now experienced. Tina Carolla was an obvious target, deliberately running slowly and screaming loudly. However, a new plan quickly hatched.

Ivy Morrison and Sandra Adams had been having fun all year, making comments to deliberately make me blush. On one occasion, when my mum was picking me up from school, Ivy had dared Sandra to run up to me and say, "Oh darling Martin, I love you." Sandra had obliged, resulting in the desired effect of turning me into a human beetroot. I saw that, at the time, Sandra had felt some remorse, when she realized my degree of humiliation.

However, Ivy could not hide her glee at the awkwardness of the moment.

I threw in a few precursory red-herring runs, at the screaming girls. However, the truth was that I could catch any of them any time that I wished. I had Olympic speed and agility. Ivy Morrison was an emotional bully and she was not used to being the victim. Therefore, when it became apparent that she was my selected prey she became particularly defensive.

"Look he's blushing," she announced.

'A little predictable,' I thought, as I honed in.

"Oh darling, darling, I love you so much," she joked remembering how hurt I had been last time she had connived for this phrase to be used. I continued my pursuit without reaction.

"Bloody h.....," was all she managed to utter before my mouth was swallowing her "...ell." Having thrown all caution to the wind, I deliberately made this a kiss to remember. The Beatles 'Please, please me' was playing in the background. It was the strangest thing, Ivy was predictably putting up resistance at first and that was why I had used the element of surprise. I was also driven by motivations other than passion or desire. I had reasoned that, if I no longer showed any embarrassment, she might permanently leave me alone. It was also in my mind that, if I was already carrying the German measles bug, then Ivy Morrison was the person I would most like to share it with. We had a bond of contempt and I could not have imagined two people less likely to be locked in embrace.

However, it was as if the kiss took control of both of us. Our mutual abhorrence dissolved and I felt Ivy's resolve melt as she placed both of her hands around my neck. The crowd wolf-whistled and cheered, but we snogged on.

"Come on, come on, come on, come on," urged John Lennon, echoed by Paul, George, Drew and Kate Dawson.

"Look how red he is," remarked Sandra Adams, suddenly sounding a little jealous. While Sandra was usually Ivy's puppet, she was more familiar with the attentions of boys than her controller. However, neither Ivy nor I had free will any longer, as the all-possessing kiss pulled our strings. Her lips were thinner and less sloppy than Jane's and they tasted of Jusoda, which was far preferable to Vimto. It was a most delightful sensation and her tongue stayed firmly rooted in her mouth.

"Look how red **she** is!" shouted Barry Pratt, enjoying the moment vicariously through our empathetic mental pathway. Teddy and Panda had never had this type of adventure!

Ivy Morrison's mom was also delighted with the turn of events, for several reasons: Firstly, her bitchy daughter, who ran her mouth far too often, was getting a public comeuppance. Secondly, there was a certain pride that other prettier girls, such as Sandra Adams, had been shunned in favour of her own progeny. Mrs Morrison's third and most pragmatic reason was that her daughter was in direct line for a fully-fledged, undiluted dose of the Rubella virus.

The party was really for the girls because; apparently German measles could make females have deformed babies, if they encountered it when they were pregnant. So, mothers were delighted to expose their kids to it before they reached the age of conception. The boys were simply the carriers - mere pawns in their devilish scheme. Mumps parties, on the other hand, focused on the boys. They were aimed at preventing males acquiring over-sized sterile testicles, later in life. I remembered feeling really ill when I had had the mumps; the ache and swelling in my groin made my wish for Martin Butcher's handicap.

Toward the end of the embrace, The Beatles had stolen the attention of our audience. Everyone was trying to show off their knowledge by singing along to the middle eight:

"I don't wanna be complainin' but you know there's always rain in my heart" the fab four sang along with their fans, as we finally disentangled ourselves. It was true that Ivy was blushing as much, if not more, than me. We avoided eye contact for the rest of the party. However, the permutation of strawberry trifle, orange pop, adrenaline and Beatles still lay dormant, etched in our minds, ready to trigger the memories of an unpredictable magical kiss.

As we left the party, parents were no longer trying to hoodwink us, as to the purpose of the celebration. Of course, mum's nursing knowledge was suddenly in demand.

"So Beryl, how long will it be before she gets a rash?" asked Doris Adams about her daughter, Sandra.

"Fourteen to twenty-one days but she'll be contagious before then.

"How will I know its German measles, not normal measles," Ivy's mom asked. It seemed a perfectly sensible question.

"She'll break out in swastikas," laughed mum, uncharacteristically snubbing her. I got the impression that mum disapproved of Ivy's mum. Apparently, she had seen her smoking in the street once, which was not the place that a lady would smoke, unless she was a prostitute.

She was also none-too-plussed with me 'seducing the daughter,' as she later described it to my dad.

"Found yourself your own Christine Keeler, have you son?" joked dad with some pride.

"Peter, stop it he's a child for Christ's sake!" she nagged.

"Don't worry, he's not exactly up on 'current affairs' dear," he assured her. "Who's Christine Keeler, son?"

"Is she a prostitute who smokes in the street?" I said, pretending to know what a prostitute was and what they did.

"Well, I'll be buggered!" exclaimed dad.

The room fell silent. Soon after, Andrew, Eric and I were put to bed. Maybe mum felt a twinge of guilt. After all, she had just tricked us into contaminating ourselves with a potentially deadly disease. Whatever her reason, she was particularly adamant that we acknowledged her unconditional love for us.

"Good-night, God bless, see you tomorrow, I love you" was the nightly Wells mantra.

The incubation period had begun.

SPRING

Chapter 8: The Grand National

A warm wax crayon smell filled the living room. It was the eve of the Grand National and dad was still searching for clues as to where to place his bet. He taped my etching of the coloured horse onto the television screen, as he grappled for inspiration.

Clutching at straws, he finally said, "Tell me the story again. What compelled you to draw the horse, son?"

I loved his attention to my artwork but I suspected that he was accrediting it with too much significance.

"My teacher showed me how to do it." I told him.

"And what's her name?" he asked.

"Mrs Forsythe," I told him, a little offended that he did not know. His ears must have filtered out every conversation for the last seven months. He diligently wrote down the letters of her name the edge of his Sentinel then scrambled them, looking for clues.

"Ah ha!" he suddenly exclaimed, "MY FIT HORSES'S!"

"What are you on about? asked mum.

"MISS FORSYTHE is an anagram of MY FIT HORSES'S!"

"Aren't all the 'HORSES'S' in the Grand National fit?" asked mum, emphasizing the superfluous letter S's.

"Not at all, dear, half of them won't even make it around the course," dad replied, too excited to detect mum's ironic tones. "It's definitely a clue. All I have to do it pick the fittest horse," he concluded.

"Isn't that what everybody tries to do?" she pointed out, her voice dripping with sarcasm.

Even this could not dampen his excitement and he replied, "Not at all dear, sometimes it's the jockey, sometimes it's the firmness of the ground, some horses can't handle the Aintree race-track crowd; there's a hundred different factors. It's really complicated."

Mum seemed aggravated this patronizing comment and I cowered in anticipation.

Andrew, who also seemed annoyed took up mum's cause. He said, "Actually, its Mrs Forsythe, not Miss" Andrew explained," destroying dad's anagram theory.

"Are you sure?" has asked.

"Positive!" Andrew and I responded in unison.

"Sod it!" said dad.

"Peter, you're teaching the boys bad words."

"Sorry dear but a sod is a clump of turf," he tried to justify.

Drew piped in, "I thought it was short for sodomy."

"You see what you're teaching them, Peter?" mum added, somewhat vindicated.

"What does sodomy mean?" I asked in my naivety.

"I'm buggered if I know," joked dad.

"Peter!" mum scolded. Her face held firm for a couple of seconds but then she saw the funny side of whatever he had said, and cracked up, laughing.

"Yer daft bugger," she said, in a mocking northern dialect, abandoning her normal 'queen's English'

"Beryl, not in front of the children," he replied sardonically.

I loved it when dad's wittiness melted through mum's sternness. It all fitted with Andrew's theories. Quiet beats loud; funny wins over serious; bullies are insecure losers; stupidity triumphs over intelligence! The last deduction came from an old poem by Thomas Gray, that Mr. Barton had shared with Andrew: "*Where ignorance is bliss, 'tis folly to be wise.*" Funnily enough, mum's most common phrase of submission was, "*You can't argue with an idiot!*" which I believe captured the same sentiment.

"Oh, you can't argue with an idiot," delivered mum, perfectly in sync with my own thought pattern.

"You'd be a fool to try," added Andrew layering on the irony. Dad just looked confused, giving perfect credence to their mockery.

Then he said. "Let's get back to the story of why you drew the horse." His enthusiasm was rubbing off and I was beginning to feel that he was right, that I somehow held the secret to our fortune. I recounted Sally Doyle's throwing up incident and the double spoon-licking episode.

"Hold on, hold on! Why the hell was everybody licking spoons?" he asked, determined that fate had hidden the winner somewhere in my story.

"Peter, do you have to swear in front of your son?" mum reminded him.

"Sorry dear, just said 'Hell,' you know the opposite of Heaven," he foolishly retorted. Now he was scouring the newspaper for a horse with Heaven or Hell in its name.

"Well he's going to start saying H....E....double hockey sticks at school, if he hears you say it at home," she insisted.

Dad smiled at me and Eric, then he made a hockey gesture, making us giggle.

Eric started repeating "Double hockey sticks," over and over and the phrase seemed to tickle him more each time. Dad again checked the list of runners for secret meanings.

In frustration, he said, "Tell me about the spoon and the blobby green stuff again." He was like Perry Mason.

"Well, I had a Nickel-Silver but I wanted a Nixon because that makes you a boy and Bisby's a girl," I hurriedly explained.

"That's the sign!" he exclaimed, "*Nicholas Silver!* Good boy. I knew you could do it. Beryl, Martin's just picked the winner. It's the grey, *Nicholas Silver*. He won on it in 1961 and the conditions are the same. Why didn't I think of it?" I felt the same level of pride as when I'd spotted the hares in the field. I could see that Andrew was jealous of the attention that I was receiving.

"He didn't say *Nicholas Silver*," he told dad, "he said Nickel-Silver."

"Not what I heard," contradicted dad, dismissing Andrew's point as irrelevant. "It makes perfect sense; the horse knows the coarse, hell the bugger's won before. Yes, that's it, *Nicholas Silver* it is!"

Dad was so delighted with the breakthrough that he also let me and Andrew choose a horse for a bob-each-way flutter. I picked *Magic Tricks*, much to dad's dismay, because he saw it as a waste of money. Andrew picked *Ayala*, which also failed to impress dad.

When Saturday arrived, we waited all day for the race that was about to change our lives. Tedious horse-racing had suddenly become interesting. I was a little conflicted, as the horses were paraded. Obviously, *Magic Tricks* was my personal choice but dad had probably gambled the family budget on my 'premonition.' Even the pre-race banter was captivating. An American film star, Gary Peck, had come all the way from the USA to watch his own horse in the famous race.

Magic tricks fell at the first fence but that was OK because it removed all conflict and I could throw my weight fully behind *Nicholas Silver.*

"Don't worry, son. I never put the bet on that old nag, we've just saved a shilling," he assured me. I felt relieved and betrayed at the same time.

Of all the Saturdays that 'boring old horse-racing' had dominated the television, this was the first time I had seen the attraction. Dad's excitement was contagious. *Nicholas Silver* stayed with the pack, as horse after horse fell, during the gruelling steeplechase. She was easy to follow, being a dapple grey, and we began to cheer each time she cleared a fence, toward his predetermined victory.

By the time the horses were approaching the penultimate fence the TV commentator began to crank up his commentary. However, his change of motivation was nothing compared to that of dad.

"Come on *Nicholas Silver*! Come on you bugger!" he urged at the top of his lungs.

"Come on you bugger," echoed little brother Eric.

"Peter!" chastised mum instinctively, but as she started to sense that dad was about to win 'big time,' she joined in the shouting.

Somehow, fate (or God) had delivered inside information through me, via the name on the back of a spoon, about the winner of the great race. It certainly smacked of the 'mysterious ways' of God. It defied logic, but dad had 'put his shirt on it' and I was about to become immortalized as some kind of soothsayer.

"Come on!" we were all screaming in unison, as *Nicholas Silver* positioned himself for the final advance. We all 'became' the jockey, rocking involuntarily on the edge of our seats. Our combined willpower urged the attack and *Nicholas Silver* seemed to respond as if he had found another gear.

"He knows his way home from here. Come on baby!" yelled dad.

"Come on baby!" Eric copied. However, just as destiny seemed to be to be unfolding, the grey inexplicably began to fade. *Nicholas Silver* was spent. Suddenly a name that had hardly been mentioned throughout the entire race came blaring through the TV speaker.

"And its *Ayala*!" shouted the commentator, "*Ayala, Ayala, Ayala* wins!"

There were so many levels to this disaster that I could hardly breathe for a time. Dad had undoubtedly lost all of our money and it was my fault. To compound the problem, dad had persuaded several punters in the bookies to bet on *Nicholas Silver* making it embarrassing to face them. On a practical level, it would mean a week of jam butties and hiding under the table for the meter man's next visit. I would have no dinner money and Mrs Forsythe would be trying to stimulate my memory by pounding my bottom with her over-sized plimsoll. Maybe I would not be able to act so heroically in front of Sally Doyle and she would see me for the baby that I truly was. My freshly acquired kissing skills would never be put to the test.

Then there was the horse that did win, Andrew's horse, *Ayala.* Dad picked up the thirty shillings that Andrew had won and handed it to him.

"There you go, son. I'll have to pay more attention to you next time we need a horse picking," he remarked pointedly. A sideways glance at me confirmed that he still held resentments.

It seemed so unfair because I had never touted myself as a racing tipster and now I was being castigated for it. The attention had been nice at the time but Andrew was now firmly dad's favourite. I was fully expecting Andrew to gloat and tease for months to come, when he surprised me.

"Dad, I don't think it's fair to Martin, to give me this money."

"What do you mean?" dad responded, taken aback by Andrew's challenging tones.

"Because you didn't even put any money on *Magic Tricks,*" he reasoned, "so you shouldn't have put money on my horse."

"Don't be stupid!" dad said.

"I want you and mum to keep the money," said Andrew, noticing that mum had entered the room, just as he spoke. She was welling up at her firstborn's magnanimous gesture.

"Well, thank you, son," said mum, obviously touched by his sense of fairness, "you're a kind boy."

Dad swallowed, "You're a good boy," he said, taking back the money. He looked at his wallet, made eye contact with mum and then reluctantly handed it over to her.

Mum then turned to me and asked, "Martin, do you have anything you want to say to your brother?"

"Thank you, Andrew," I forced. That is what I said but it was not what I wanted to say. I could smell a rat. There was no way that my brother was protecting my interests when he rejected the money. In my mind, this was cold and calculated, if not decidedly sociopathic. He could easily have taken the money and bought himself a treat: the tent that he had always wanted; some Danny Blanchflower football boots; a record player and a Beatles record. However, he invested his money far more wisely, he consolidated his position as favourite child. To me, his angelic gesture smacked of devilment. However, I could not even hint at this, without pushing myself further down the family pecking order. How different it would have been if *Nicholas Silver* had won. A little cynicism grew in me that day, as I learned that willpower, prayer and fate were all meaningless fabrications.

Chapter 9: The School Bully

A hauntingly unpleasant smell is that of ink. I cannot imagine why Mrs Forsythe chose me to be the ink monitor because my mum had already identified me as accident prone - mum felt obliged to alert everyone to this personality flaw. However, every Tuesday morning, it was my job to fill up the porcelain inkwells. Each fitted neatly into a specially designed hole, in the front right corner of every desk.

I had to mix the ink powder with water in specific proportions, which was a task that Mrs Forsythe could only entrust to me. It took a full jug to top up all the inkwells. Spillage was an unforgivable sin. However, once the body of ink in the jug began to gain momentum it seemed to take on a life of its own. It took several serious stains to hone my skills; where was Andrew's secret ink eradicator when I needed it? However, perhaps Mrs Forsythe had method in her madness because I eventually gained mastery and was soon wielding the jug with the confidence of an accomplished waiter.

"Care for a drop of wine, Madam?" I joked with Sally Doyle, as I carefully took aim at the mouth of her porcelain well.

"I thank you, kind sir," she giggled, which invoked an unfavourable look from the teacher and a blushing episode from me.

However, the next desk housed a set of even more threatening eyes. Graham Parsons, reluctantly nicknamed Parsnips, was a thickset Australian kid. It was hard to work out whether he was a bully or a victim. He had been perpetually angry since he joined our class, a month prior. He did not seem to be able to accept the relentless mimicry of his irresistibly mockable accent. On the other hand, he was as hard as nails. Unfortunately, he was obviously smitten with Sally Doyle and our flirtatious banter had pushed him to the precipice of rage.

"I think I hate this stinky ink," I told him, trying to lighten the mood with a little alliteration. The plan instantly backfired because he obviously had no appreciation of my Oscar Wildish tongue. On the other hand, Sally Doyle started a fit of hysterical giggles and Penelope Evans accompanied her with an empathetic snort. However, the laughter dissolved as quickly as it had erupted, as pupils started to notice the deranged look on the Aussie guest's face.

"I only said the ink smells," I clarified, "I didn't mean you smell!" I instantly bit my lip because my intonation was completely wrong. Even as I heard the words leaving my mouth, I knew that I was sounding patronizing. Terror had impacted control of my vocal cords. Adrenaline prepared my body for fight or flight. Flight seemed the more prudent option but I was somehow rooted to the spot. Everyone awaited Parsnips' response. After what seemed like an eternity he finally responded with what could only be described as a weird displacement reaction. He started quoting the giant from the 'Jack and the Beanstalk' story that Mrs Forsythe had recently read to us.

"Fee, Fi, Fo, Fum, oi smeell the blad of an Eengleeshman!" he boomed in his strong Australian accent. The threatening tone should have provoked serious intervention from Mrs Forsythe. However, she totally missed the true intent of his declaration. I could taste blood, from the lip-biting, at this point.

"Well done Graham, that's exactly how the giant said it," she said, seemingly delighted that she had managed to get him to actually retain something.

"Theenks Mees Greeton," responded Parsnips' thick accent, as he was momentarily distracted by her kind words.

"Graham, its Meeses not Mees," corrected the teacher.

It was hard to determine whether this was just a slip of the tongue, or if the teacher had deliberately teased the boy. Either way, he was not happy.

"You're bloody Pommie bastards, all of you!" he screamed before he raced out of the room. It took Mr. Rice two hours to get him down off the roof, as a barrage abuse rained down on everyone.

"I was Perth Junior Boxing Champion, I'll fight any one of you Pommie bastards!" he screamed from above us, throughout our dinner break. There was something irresistible watching someone else driven to tantrum. Did he see himself as a winner or loser? He obviously thought that he was hurting our feelings calling us all "Pommie bastards" but he was only entertaining us, whilst humiliating himself. Andrew's theory was certainly correct on this occasion - the loudest was the loser! Yet, I could see how, on another day, in another mood, that could be me on that roof, beyond caring what the world thought of me. In fact, every kid in the school was probably nursing some emotional wounds just waiting to be opened. Martin Butcher and Kevin Dagworth were certainly potential rooftop yellers.

Mr. Rice had tried several different tactics.

"Don't make me come up there!" was the first threat to fail.

"Why don't you come up here, you Pommie bastard!" was the all-too-predictable reply. The headmaster quickly dropped that line of attack, as a chase across the school roof had no beneficial outcomes.

Then in a loud voice Mr. Rice addressed the audience. "He's just looking for attention, so I want all of you children to ignore him."

'*An interesting tactic,*' I thought to myself, '*but surely the plan would have a better chance of success if the victim had not just been informed of the strategy*. It would be like Batman broadcasting to Robin, "Let's pretend that we have not noticed The Joker sneaking up on us and then we'll suddenly release the Bat nets!" Added to this, there were 150 fascinated children, having difficulty ignoring an attention-seeking Aussie reigning abuse from above.

"You're all too scared to fight me!" Parsnips responded.

Eventually, the head teacher saw the flaw in his reason. Mr. Barton whispered something in Rice's ear, and yet another approach emerged.

"I hear that Mr. Barton is going to play you in the school football team," he coaxed, "why don't you come down and he will talk to you about it." Well this was news to me. I was vice-captain of the under-9's football team and Mr. Barton had always given me and Barry Cooper a say in the team selection. Introducing a thug like Parsnips would be a disaster. I don't think that he even understood the rules. Not only would he be giving away fouls all over the place, he'd probably pick the ball up and start running with it as soon as he became frustrated - which would happen instantly.

"Football's a stupid Pommie sport!" he yelled. This came as a relief but, in my mind, this was going too far.

Just when it seemed that the boy would remain up there forever, his dad arrived on a motorbike with a sidecar. Where all of the teachers' cajoling had only seemed to add resolve to Parsnips' defiance, his dad simply needed to say one monotone word.

"Down!" said daddy Parsnips. The boy obeyed without hesitation or dissent. He cowered, as the merest flick of his dad's hand knocked him four feet through the air.

Until that moment, I had enjoyed watching his suffering but seeing him abused by his dad conjured up instant empathy. I briefly wondered where my mother's allegiance would have lain. There were certainly times when she would have loved to project me through the air with such panache. On the other hand, there did not seem to be any warmth between father and son. At least, mum's almost schizophrenic attitude to me tended to dole out love and hate in equal amounts.

I caught a final glimpse of Parsnips' face through the window of the side-car as the Norton Commando zipped him away. His glare told me that he somehow blamed me for the whole incident. Luckily, he must surely have been expelled and so we were unlikely to ever cross paths again.

Chapter10: German measles invasion.

I am sure that mum was well-intentioned, when she chose to make shortbread, on the day that the rubella finally kicked in. The smell appeared to flip-over from *irresistibly delicious* to *nauseatingly repugnant*, as fever distorted my neural pathways. It seemed a cruel twist of fate that my brain was being reconditioned to identify my favourite food with a feeling of 'wanting to die.' If I remembered rightly, a jam kettle full of treacle toffee, during my mumps bout, had permanently alienated my pension for that treat. Ever since that day, the merest whiff of black treacle has triggered involuntary heaving, not to mention a sympathetic discomfort in my loins that the middle Butcher could only dream off!

My parents ought to have been fully prepared for the onset of the disease, as the fourteen-day incubation countdown was publicly launched at Jane Dawson's party. Therefore, it was strange to me that mum and dad were suddenly acting like I had imposed a great inconvenience on them. Mum obviously had plans for her Thursday. She had assumed that Andrew and I would be in the charge of our respective teachers.

"Why can't you ask your mother to nurse him, just this once?" I heard mum plead.

"She'll have the poor bugger in a sanatorium," dad retorted, reliving his own demons.

"Better than the coalhouse!" was mum's autonomic response.

I didn't like the sound of any of these three options but a day with Nana Lena was the least appetizing. It was not just because of the double bus ride on a showery April morning, while sporting a fever and rash. It was the thought of spending a day in the presence of 'Cruella Deville,' as Andrew called her. Her over-heated mansion always reeked of furniture polish and Grandpa Eric's cigars. Her snappy poodle, Ricky, and vindictive Siamese cat, Sookie, seemed to have both been trained to mutilate children, whenever adult backs were turned. Her endlessly ticking Grandfather clock had a way of emphasizing how slow time could actually go!

"No! Thank you!" I thought to myself.

Mum was going to start her new job, working Thursday and Friday nights at Bucknall Hospital. She was hoping to have the house to herself, so that she could get some pre-work rest. My German measles onset had really stymied these plans. So, mum decided to utilize the time wisely, by baking her special shortbread treats. She set up a bed for me, on the settee in the living room, so that she could keep an eye out, in case the fever became critical. Doodle settled on my chest, purring sardine-flavoured Kit-e-Kat fumes into my face. Little brother, Eric, loved having me at home and was 'taking care' of me by slapping a wet flannel on my head, each time I succumbed to the lure of sleep. We viewed "Watch with Mother," together, although I am not sure that mother was watching because she told Eric to look for Bill and Ben, the flowerpot men, when it was clearly "Rag, Tag and Bobtail." It was under these conditions that I drifted into a dreaded fever-dream. I remember my last coherent thought was a musing of whether Ivy Morrison had yet been stricken with Rubella.

Next, I was kissing Ivy, who evolved into Sandra Adams then Sally Doyle. In theory, it was a dream come true but it was not working out as I might have fantasized. Close up, her skin had a sickly, sweet stench of 'burned biscuits' which made me want to gag. Worse still, this was punctuated with rhythmic blasts of fish odour. The kiss was stifling and I needed to breathe. Then Bobtail, the puppet rabbit, was trying to pull us apart, and he turned out to be a real hare and dad was hunting him with a shotgun. Bobtail struggled to hang on, as I desperately tried to push him away, as dad pointed the gun at him. I was terrified that I would be shot again and began to squirm. Sally said that we should hide in the coal house but she smelled so strongly of burning sugar and kippers, I was fighting the urge to throw up. As she smothered me with fishy kisses, she began to make inexplicable squelching noises. All the time, a python was tightening its grip on my chest and I could not move. She kissed me so hard that I was gasping.

Then I jerked out of my dream to discover that Eric was holding a sopping wet flannel over my nose and mouth.

"Help me!" I gasped, before I had orientated myself. This drew Doodle from his own dream causing him to claw, screech and leap.

"Mee.....oowww!" cried the cat, as he took some of my rash-covered skin with him.

"Bloody Hell Fire!" I yelled uncontrollably, and started to scream, which in turn caused Eric to startle and cry. Mum raced in from the kitchen, furious that I was swearing and assuming I must have hurt my toddler brother. I received three smacks. The first was obviously for the cursing - that was a given. The second slap was for whatever I had done to make Eric cry, which seemed a little unfair. The injustice fuelled my own tears. I became so loud that I heard the all too familiar warning: "If you don't shut up I'll give you something to cry about!" I never understood the logic behind this specific battle cry. Mum never really allowed response time and the third smack was inevitable. The whole episode was probably over in less than a minute because Rag, Tag and Bobtail were still entrenched in their adventure when the dust finally settled. Of course, a minute later, mum was apologizing profusely and telling me how much I was loved.

Sometimes the best time to strike with mum was when she felt guilty. If beating a rash-encrusted, fever-struck eight-year-old did not induce guilt, then what? So, when she poured me a glass of Lucozade -the over-priced wonder tonic, I knew that she was on the road to making amends. Lucozade was the perfect follow up to a high temperature and mum's slap therapy and a short time after, I was feeling quite energized.

"Can I play with Whiskey?" I asked. Sure enough, my instincts were correct because she went and fetched my little rodent friend, sans cage, and plopped him on my blanket.

"Let's make him a tunnel," said mum, suddenly turning into a mother-beyond-envy. She took all the hardback books off the bookshelf and created a narrow tunnel by standing them up in pairs and making roofs with a third book. I had Eric put Whiskey in the tunnel at one end, while I waited six feet away at the other end.

Whiskey was reluctant at first and he kept turning around and exiting from the entry. However, with a few modifications to the width and a sickly shortbread lure at the other end, the hamster soon mastered the run.

Eric and I both giggled, as we redesigned the tunnel into a series of mazes, with five different exits and several blind alleys. It was hard to predict where Whiskey would emerge next. My pet seemed to enjoy the challenge, especially since the outcome was a pouchful of biscuit.

This game helped me forget about my illness and self-pity, as the frisky critter kept us entertained more than Rag, Tag or Bobtail. In fact, mum's initial investment of kindness paid off for her, too. She managed to get half-an-hour's shuteye, in the armchair, as Eric and I set progressively more ambitious challenges for Whiskey. At one point, the creature decided to take a little snooze himself, causing us to panic and dissemble the maze. However, a couple of minutes of mauling, by my little brother, seemed to make sleep the last thing on Whiskey's mind. The experience revitalized him so he was ready for our latest Pavlovian challenges. Eric seemed to have an instinct for the hamster's movements and could soon predict exactly where he would turn up next. This lured me into a false level of trust of the two-year-old. Indeed, I had such confidence that I allowed myself to succumb to the soporific atmosphere that had gripped the household. Again, the fever-dreams invaded my head.

Whiskey looked over his shoulder and the twitch of his whiskers revealed that he was ready to lead me into his world. I had to follow, as corridors of books turned into dark dripping wet tunnels, like Jack-the-Ripper's London. Andrew joined me, which was both reassuring and disturbing. I had always felt that my big brother had some jealousy toward my special bond with Whiskey and, in the powerful position of my dream, he did not even need to hide it.

"Whiskey's gone!" he coldly informed me.

"Where?" I found myself asking.

"In the roly poly pudding," he disclosed.

Now I was scared because I had been haunted for months by a story that Mrs Forsythe had once read to us, about some rats that lured a cat up a chimney, so they could bake him in a roly poly pudding. I hated rats, and to some extent chimneys, as both had featured in recent nightmares. As Andrew led me down the sinister cobbled alleyway, rats began to appear everywhere. A road sign told me that we were in Pudding Lane. They were plague-infested rats! I had done a school project on the Great Fire of London, which started in Pudding Lane in 1666, putting an end to the Great Plague by driving out the rats.

"Plague rats!" I yelled at Andrew.

"I know!" he replied, and I realized that Andrew was with the rats, not with me.

"Roly poly pudding time!" he said, as the rats gathered around my feet.

Terror took over, as I tried to cry, "It's not fair!" But no sound left my mouth because I was petrified. Then mum was there to help me, but it wasn't the kind, ' let's-build-a-hamster-maze mum ', it was the mean, ' let's-slap-some-sense-into-you mum.' I instantly knew that she was part of the conspiracy, too.

"You're an awkward boy, Martin," she told me.

At first I shuddered and tried to speak but my voice was still not working. My family was leading me to be cooked and eaten in a pudding made by rats. I was betrayed! I was doomed! I felt a surge of helplessness, which was paradoxically comforting. I had entered a zone where I no longer cared what happened to me. Andrew seemed to sense this and he became frustrated.

"Whiskey's gone!" he announced to mum, thinking it would add to my burden. But my burden had reached critical mass, and neither the rats, nor mum could bother me now.

"Whiskey's gone," Andrew goaded. I simply smiled back in my 'awkward' passivity.

"Whiskey's gone!" said Eric's cute little real-life voice.

"Whiskey's gone?" said mum's less cute tones.

And so, I was again awakened from a fever-dream into a crisis. Mum was lifting books and tossing them all over the place, looking for my hamster.

"How could you leave a two-year-old in charge of that vermin? You, stupid boy!" she asked. It seemed rhetorical, so I made no move to answer.

"Did you hear me, Martin?" she demanded. I was still in 'helpless mode' from my dream, which really seemed to be annoying real-life mum, even more than it did fever-dream Andrew. Suddenly, her priority shifted from hamster searching to chastising me. She took the scenario to a whole new level.

"Well, if you can't find him I bet Doodle will!" she told me. I could not afford to be helpless anymore. It was no longer about me - it was about Whiskey and Doodle. My two true friends set against one another. Now the tears flowed, as Eric and I frantically searched the whole ground floor. My little hamster could get quite inventive when it came to hiding. We had previously found him in the back of a drawer and inside the part of the washing machine, where the mangle was usually stored.

After an hour of searching, mum seemed to have calmed down enough to say, "Don't worry, I won't let Doodle get him. Why don't you tidy the books, back onto the shelves and he's bound to turn up," 'Nice mum' was back. Unfortunately, Whiskey was not back. Even, when Andrew and dad came home, and searched all the places we had already looked, my friend was still missing without trace.

Whiskey remained undiscovered for the next three days, as I cried myself to temperature-induced nightmare-riddled sleep. Mum was not even there to console me because she was still working her new graveyard shift at Bucknall Hospital.

"There, there," was dad's first attempt at comfort, accompanied with an awkward pat. This made me feel sorrier for myself and cry louder.

"Whiskey's probably dead by now," I told him, fishing for reassurance to the contrary.

"Well son, you can be proud that you gave him a good life," he told me philosophically. This was not what I wanted to hear. I began to sob again, like I was turning into Martin Butcher.

Andrew had once explained to me that parents only let their children have pets, so they could teach them to cope better with death. We had certainly gotten over the passing of Bluey the Budgerigar in record time, after finding him on his back one morning. In reality, the burial had been a fun ceremony. Goldie the Goldfish died twice. The first time, mum found him floating on the surface she performed some serious CPR and kidney massage which extended his life for another week, giving us ample time to mentally prepare for his end. I already had the hole dug for Goldie when he finally relinquished his grip on life. Speedie, the rabbit, was never officially certified as deceased because he had escaped before I could bond with him. However, everyone assured me that a pet rabbit, out in the wilds, was 'as good as dead.'

By Monday, my German Measles had subsided, and I returned to school, clutching my absence note and dinner money, I had a philosophical resolve to the fact that my cat had probably eaten my hamster. After all, Doodle was an expert hunter. Many a time he would proudly present me with a dead shrew, mouse or sparrow. Part of me wanted to believe Doodle had too much respect to harm Whiskey, but I knew this to be untrue. I had to accept that he was gone forever.

However, when I got home that evening, I was greeted by Eric shouting, "Whiskey's back! Whiskey's back!"

Andrew, off school with German Measles, had found him in his favorite hiding place - the mangle compartment of the washing machine. He had obviously worked a double bluff on us all, by waiting until we had searched it before nesting there. Whiskey was truly a genius amongst hamsters. He had made a sophisticated nest from a variety of materials, including half a Sentinel, a Superman comic, some parts of socks and the pom-pom off my Stoke City hat. Fortunately, he had overlooked the fact that Monday was washing day, and his master plan was destined to be foiled eventually.

Monday night was a happy time in the Wells household and we would all sleep well, except for a strange outburst from Andrew.

Suddenly, he sat bolt upright in bed and exclaimed, "Mon Dieu! J'ai chaud!" He was obviously experiencing a fever nightmare. The next day we learned that this was French for "My God, I'm hot!" It was mysterious because he had no explanation for how he would have learned this French phrase.

Mr. Barton had been teaching similes to Andrew's class, and my brother had come up with, what I thought was the most genius simile ever: "As Red Kryptonite is to Superman, fever is to dreams!"

Chapter 11: The Curse of the Gypsy

Anyone that romanticizes about gypsies has never smelled the sickly honeysuckle pong of their encampments. At least once a year, the gypsies would set up camp on the 'spare ground' separating the north and south sides of Sutton Green. For the three weeks that it took the council to 'move them on,' their temporary caravan sites would terrorize the whole neighbourhood. Ironically, the two halves of the estate would be temporarily united by their common loathing of these 'dirty, thieving scoundrels.' Several anti-gypsy vigilante groups sprung up and they would pay unexpected late night visits to intimidate the tinkers into shortening their stay.

Of course, rumours were rife that the gypsies would kidnap children and force them to make clothes pegs, which could be sold door-to-door. Packs of dogs always played freely around their trailers, protecting their spoils. Each day they would use a horse and cart to scavenge through the streets yelling, "Rag-bone! Rag-bone! Any old iron?" It was an irresistible cry, which we found impossible to avoid mimicking.

"Any old iron?" we echoed. They would take anything away, including children and pets. In fact, they would tie balloons to their cart-horse and give them out to the kids of anyone willing to donate scrap. Rotten old dolly tubs, broken bicycles, pre-war non-functioning radios, grubby worn out clothes, soiled mattresses and bald car tires would adorn their carts. Apparently, gypsy-law entitled them to scavenge people's backyards in search of scrap items. Mum said that they were also burglars, which I found particularly scary. Although no two carts had the same cargo they always had a smell identical to the insipid stench of their camps.

"Gypsy women are prostitutes," insisted Andrew. I knew this word to be rude but I was not sure why. Although, I suspected that their lush cleavages were part of the deal.

"Like Christine Keeler?" I asked, trying to pretend that I understood the word. I obviously did not fool him.

"Do you know what a prostitute does?" he taunted.

"Not really, except for smoking in the street," I had to confess.

"They go with men for money," he elucidated.

"How much?" was all I could think to ask. I was more confused than ever. *"Where do they go?"* I asked myself. It made no sense to me and I suspected that Andrew was not much better informed. So, that evening, when mum had gone to work, I put Eric to bed and caught dad as he was emerging from a sub-Sentinel snooze. I decided to feign naivety, which was not really pretence, and pose the question.

"Dad," I said, selecting a tone of innocence carefully.

"Yes, son?" he responded, taking the bait.

"What do prostitutes do?" I asked. This brought Andrew scampering from the kitchen to hear the answer. Dad obviously anticipating that, one day, such a question would arise. He sat us both down, lit a cigarette and began to talk to us in a very serious grown up voice.

"When a man and a woman get close to each other they become 'attracted,'" he explained, taking a long drag on his Woodbine. This gesture emphasized that he was talking to us man-to-man about a subject that was within his realm of expertise. I could relate to his theory of attraction because I had experienced a similar emotion when I was kissing Ivy Morrison, even though I had thought that I hated her. Unfortunately, everything he said, after that point, made no sense whatsoever. He kept talking about 'becoming intimate' and how it was dangerous. Andrew was nodding, as though he understood, which seemed to inspire dad to continue. Then the conversation took an even weirder turn. He started talking about babies and women 'trapping you, if you're not careful.' As if this was not irrelevant enough, he moved from the sublime to ridiculous. He went upstairs and returned with an odd little grey packet. He carefully opened it, to reveal a rolled up transparent balloon.

"You should always use these," he told us. He then proceeded to blow it up and tie the end. I was truly bewildered and the only connection I could make was that the rag-bone gypsies always gave out balloons. Ironically, dad left the conversation proud of his parenting skills; his sons had come for advice and he had addressed the issue with frankness, unfettered by mum's inhibitory filters.

I was hoping to clarify with Andrew what dad had been talking about but it was clear that the discussion had raised more questions than it had answered. We decided that the greasy rubber balloon that came from sterile packaging was something he used in the Respiratory Physiology Department, at his work. The maternity ward, where women with complicated pregnancies attended, was the next building to his department and that was what must have inspired the tangential comments about babies.

As for prostitutes, we were none the wiser. So we decided to go and check it out for ourselves. Under the pretext of a shed meeting, we went out and slipped down to reconnoitre the gypsy camp. The sickly honeysuckle wafts intensified as we crept closer. Amidst the broken washing machines and mangy dogs was a group of four male gypsies sitting around a camp fire. A pot of food was being cooked, hanging from a makeshift support. One man was hanging a streak of what looked like bacon over the fire, using a forked stick.

"They're cooking hedgehog," insisted Andrew. I was more than ready to accept this. The men were drinking beer and seemed to be in excellent spirits, clashing somewhat with the public perceptions. Another interesting thing was that all of them had their hands busy. One was hand-carving a piece of wood with his knife, another was stripping the plastic coatings off electrical wires and twisting the resulting copper into neat bundles. The third was using the fading remnants of sunlight to patiently examine the valves on a radio he was recycling. I had to reassess the stereotype that all gypsies are 'inherently lazy.'

"There's one!" I suddenly whispered, spotting a gypsy woman, cleavage and all, unpegging her washing from the makeshift line. As she returned to her caravan, we moved in closer. I could see how men might be attracted to her.

Suddenly, we were distracted by a vigilante who walked right past our crouched hiding place and approached the group of men. If the gypsies were frightened, they certainly played it cool. They hardly looked up from their tasks, even when his presence became undeniable. The conversation was inaudible, from our vantage point, but the vigilante seemed to show an interest in the object that the whittling gypsy was making. He even pulled out some money at one point, as though he wanted to buy it, but the Gypsy declined. Instead, he directed the man to the buxom woman's caravan. Obviously, the gypsies were a matriarchal community and she was in charge, not unlike my own household. The vigilante spent ten minutes in her caravan trying to persuade her that gypsy families were not welcome. She must have been a formidable negotiator because when the vigilante emerged from the caravan he looked decidedly flustered. He had obviously failed in his mission and the woman even blew him a mocking kiss, as he walked away.

Next, another member of the anti-gypsy syndicate arrived. Our mouths dropped simultaneously, as Andrew and I realized that we were looking at an inebriated Bill Pratt. We never pegged Barry's dad as possessing any bravery but here he was, bold as brass, stepping into the enemy camp. Admittedly, he was big and strong and he had intimidating tattoos. However, Bill surely had no hope of persuading the 'Gypsy Queen,' as Andrew labelled her, into a premature evacuation. All the same, we had to admire his willingness to try. He lasted longer than the previous man, before he emerged looking dishevelled but with an air of accomplishment.

Gypsy-watching was fascinating and just as we thought that the entertainment was waning, something happened to totally change our perspective. David Foot, the grossly overweight seventeen-year-old from across the street walked into the camp. David Foot was the local pervert, whatever that meant, and he was certainly too cowardly to be a vigilante. Perplexed, we watched, half-expecting him to suffer a similar fate to that of the roast hedgehog.

"They'll kill him," said Andrew in hushed voice.

"He's dead," I agreed, nonchalantly. We had no empathy with this freak; the world would be a better place without him.

But to our astonishment the men started laughing and one even slapped him on his flabby back, as he directed him to the Gypsy Queen's caravan. He was in there less than three minutes before he came back out, looking pink and exhausted. Behind him the woman emerged tucking a pound note into her cleavage. Then she did something which brought everything to complete clarity. She took out a cigarette and lit it; smoking, right there out in the open!

"She's a prostitute!" I exclaimed, in a screamed whisper.

"Didn't you know?" said Andrew, who was trying to maintain the upper hand by backdating his moment of realization. We still did not know what the Gypsy Queen was doing with the men behind the closed doors of her caravan but we had learned some facts. Firstly, she was definitely a fully-fledged, money-taking, outdoor-smoking, prostitute. Secondly, whatever she did, it only took a relatively short time and seemed to be lucrative. Thirdly, she was undiscerning about the cross-section of people with whom she was willing to spend time. Fourthly, the estate was riddled with hypocrites, who openly hated gypsies but were secretly willing to pay for their company. I had always been a little perplexed as to why the vigilantes employed individual visits rather than mob invasions. Now it made sense, they were not vigilantes at all; they had an entirely different agenda. We agreed that we should never tell anyone about Barry's dad because of the embarrassment it might bring to my best friend. On the other hand, nobody would be spared the story of 'Pervy' Foot and his three-minute visit.

We watched the gypsy evening winding down. This happened quite quickly, once David Long left the camp. The men responsibly put out the fire, tidied up the area, and retreated to their respective trailers. Andrew and I were about to call it a night ourselves, when he had a sudden urge to peak at the prostitute through a split in the curtain of her chalet window. So, we silently evolved into peeping toms. I am not sure what we were expecting to see, but we were both disappointed to observe that she was reading a 'Woman's Own' magazine, no different from the women in Kate Dawson's hairdressers.

Gypsies were starting to seem almost human. Unfortunately, their dogs were not! Out of the descending darkness, five snarling mongrels set upon us. Some kind of bull terrier wrapped its fore-limbs around Andrew's legs and started making determined pelvic thrusts.

"Bugger off!" exclaimed Andrew. He slapped it, which was a big mistake because it caused three others to leap to their buddy's defence.

"Get 'em off me!" my big brother yelled, as a whippet started snarling at him, baring its teeth, as if it were about to pounce.

"Get off!" I shouted trying to save him. Rumour had it that gypsy dogs had rabies, and this gum-baring mutt was doing nothing to disprove the theory. A Corgi fastened onto my jeans leg and I could feel its wet slobbery tongue and teeth grazing against my shin. Instinctively, I started to run dragging the beast along with me. The movement distracted the four dogs that were feasting on Andrew and they all let go of him. Unfortunately, they all turned their attention to me. I was suddenly being chased by a pack of potentially-rabid, wild gypsy dogs, one of which was swinging freely from my trouser leg. The whippet was soon ahead of me, despite my own lightning speed and I swear that it deliberately tripped me. I was on the ground with dog saliva splashing freely around my face as the mongrels worked themselves into a state of blood lust. The commotion had brought the gypsies back out of the traveling homes and the men were yelling commands to their respective hounds.

"Leave him, Rex!" the whittler screamed to the terrier. Rex ignored him.

The wire-stripper had no more luck in commanding his dog, "Heel Zeus!" Ironically, that was the very same part of my body at which Zeus was snapping.

"Ragbone!" called the radio-repair man, to the creature suspended from my jeans. It was hard to tell whether this dog was also being disobedient, or simply immune to his own name. However, this turned out to be an unimportant distinction because Andrew kicked it, at the exact same moment that his master called him. My

118

jeans ripped right up to the thigh, as Ragbone flew through the air, with a mouthful of denim in his jaws.

The situation was getting serious, even if the gypsies managed to regain control of their dogs enough to stop them killing us, they would probably kidnap us and subject us to a life of peg-making slavery. The options did not look good. Then, amidst the bedlam, a gong sound silenced all of the animals and humans instantaneously. We turned around to see that the Gypsy Queen prostitute was gripping a large metal dog bowl in one hand and a spoon in the other.

"Leave," she commanded in an almost hypnotic speaking voice. The dogs instantly desisted their attack and walked back to the camp.

She lit a cigarette and calmly said, "Go home boys, go home."

We obeyed.

Drew and I vowed not to ever go near the gypsies again. Natural consequences had taught us enough life lessons in that evening and we felt lucky to escape unscathed (if you discard the mental scarring of dad's sex talk). Andrew asked me to watch him for the signs of rabies; including a foaming mouth and irrational fear of water. We were confident that we would have no further interactions.

However, it was only three days later when there came a knock at the door and there stood the Gypsy Queen. She was selling lucky white heather. I was concerned that she might recognize me but I was not wearing the same clothes. The jeans were still in mum's repair bag and the maroon track suit top was in the wash. I quickly fetched mum who, instead of admitting to the gypsy that we had no money, opted for a proud answer.

"No thank you, I don't believe in luck," mum told her.

"Oh, you have to believe in luck, love," the gypsy replied in the same seductive voice that had so beguiled Bill Pratt and Pervy Foot and a pack of frenzied dogs, three nights earlier.

"So, what will this lucky white heather do for me?" mum goaded, unnecessarily laying down the gauntlet. She should have just told the Gypsy Queen that she was broke. I know that she would have understood.

"It'll improve your love life," said the gypsy, looking mum up and down, as if to insinuate that mum needed all the luck she could get in that department.

"I've been married for ten years," bragged mum.

"Sounds like you need some luck, then," the gypsy responded. The wedding ring offered little protection to the mystical ways of the gypsy. Then she took out a tipped cigarette and lit it and blew the perfect smoke ring, which floated almost magically over mum's shoulder and into the hallway. Andrew now came to the front door and the sight of us together seemed to trigger the Gypsy Queen's memory.

The combination of her cleavage, street-smoking and high pressure sales tactics were beginning to seriously annoy mum. Added to that was an underlying implication of frigidity. However, what was bothering mum the most was the way that the gypsy was looking at her children.

"Get off my property!" mum commanded, which was not a wise move.

"You should keep a closer eye on your children, lady," said the gypsy. Her controlled voice was certainly winning the battle, as measured by Andrew's argument rules.

"You can take your lucky heather and stick it where the sun doesn't shine, lady!" said mum, mistakenly thinking that the Gypsy Queen was openly threatening to abduct me and Andrew.

Eric joined the party at this moment and, the gypsies mothering instincts jumped in for a split-second. She smiled at Eric, which pushed mum over the top.

"Get your eyes off my baby, you gypsy whore bitch!" mum screamed so loud that the neighbours all came out of their houses.

"I'm putting a curse on you!" exclaimed the gypsy. We gasped and so did all the neighbours. At this, she ceremoniously dropped the cigarette on our doorstep and twisted it out with her foot. A gypsy curse was not to be taken lightly.

"The gypsy has cursed Beryl!" yelled Sparky Ears, almost gleefully, from the safety of her own garden. This seemed to inflame mum further.

"You put a curse on me? I'll put a curse on you! You, bloody fake gypsy!" she announced. "Yes, you heard me; you're not even real gypsies! I'll put a curse on you!" At this, she charged the Gypsy Queen who dropped her lucky white heather and fled. "Not so lucky now is it," she added, picking it up and throwing it. Then she turned to Mrs Johnson and calmly added, "I'll put a curse on you as well, Sparky Ears." Our neighbour scuttled back into her home.

The next day the gypsies moved on, a full three days before the mandated eviction date. However, the couple of weeks that they had been there had proved to be a true education. We had learned a little more about prostitutes but not enough to work out exactly what they did; we learned that dad had theories about attraction; we discovered that mum did not believe in luck. However,

Andrew and I felt that she had no right to risk the family's fate. Neither of us needed a gypsy curse added to our lives. I had already been shot, beaten up, wanted by the police and attacked by dogs. Andrew was just praying that he was not about turn insane and die a horrible mouth-foaming rabid death. We needed all the luck we could get!

Chapter 12: The fields

Sometimes adults forget to explain facts - like why cows smell like leather. It created a paradox because the waft of brand new football boots or a cased football triggered the sensation of everything good in life. However, every year, as the late April showers subsided, a herd of snorting bovines would make an appearance in the field directly behind our house, panting odoriferous fumes over the fence.

Just a squeeze through a broken strut in the fence led to a world of freedom. It was simply known as 'the field' to everyone in Bladon Circle. To the 999ers it was our field and we knew every inch of it. Directly at back of our house was an area of field, which we trampled so heavily, playing football, that it was considered 'the

123

pitch.' Occasionally, interlopers would turn up from other parts of Sutton Green to gate-crash our pitch. It led to several memorable 'international' matches but it was mainly just ours.

Unfortunately, as the May weather warmed enough to take full advantage of the field, the farmer had the cheek to turn out his cows. After a couple of days, the whole pitch was covered with cow dung patties, evenly spread three feet apart. Soccer balls seemed to be particularly drawn to the sloppy fresh ones! However, after a couple more days, the ever-resourceful, ever-disgusting Jimmy Drinkwater found a use for the drier cow excrement. He named them Shit Wizzers; if only he had known about patent laws, he could have sued the Frisbee inventors for a pretty penny.

Shit Wizz was a game with a single rule: you had to shout "Shit Wizz" between releasing the skimming disc and it hitting your human target. Andrew quickly came up with consequences - rule violators had to stand perfectly still, while the receiver became the thrower. To add to the grossness, as we gained mastery of the art of Shit Wizz, we learned that an extra flick of the wrist could cause a spray of maggots to centrifuge from the rotating missile as it approached.

As with so many of Jimmy Drinkwater's games, once he had taught us all how to play, he suffered the most. Jimmy was the only member of the gang to take a Shit Wizzer full on in the face, like a silent movie comic takes a custard pie. The first time we played was our only experience with viable cowpats. As most of our invented games, you could never quite recreate the spontaneity.

Directly across the field was our railway track, and past there was Cauldon Canal which ran parallel. Both were semi-obsolete transport systems were from times gone by. The canal used to be the best method of transport of the pottery, for which Stoke-on-Trent was so famous. The canal had drawbridges and locks and all sorts of fun. Holiday-makers would rent barges and spend two weeks traveling thirty miles up the canal. They were a breed unto themselves. Bargees were always willing to wave and even stop for a chat.

Of course, mum always warned us that, "If there's one thing worse than getting in a car with a stranger, its allowing yourself to be lured onto a barge!" Dad had a friend, Jim Shufflebotham, who had his own barge in Stone, and there was no question that Jim and his wife Clare were 'different.' They also had a bubble car, which I thought was neat but dad considered t it was cause for open mockery.

The canal was scary, yet alluring- especially, since Baby Butcher, who was the same age as Eric, had gone walk-about one day and ended up being fished out by Biffo, the lower sider, as she going down for the third time. It was ironic to me that these hooligans from the lower end were considered a constant threat to our lives but their rough exteriors were often countered by acts of great gallantry. Of course, who would not fish a drowning child out of the water? Maybe Doug Pitt, I reasoned. But most humans, right?

As mentioned, we also had our own railway track to play upon. In fact, very few trains came along our track. Time had long passed since it had been a passenger line. Our track only handled freight, usually coal, which slow-chugging steam trains would transport about ten times a day.

We would play dare devil games of chicken by racing across the track a few seconds before the train came. Sometimes, this would scare the engineer, who would pull frantically on his whistle. We also found that a strategically placed penny could be flattened to a two-inch radius by the sheer power of the train. Andrew also showed me that a small limestone rock could be completely rendered to powder as the engine and its carriages passed over it. Without trivializing my snowball faux-pas, this led me to the biggest mistake of my life!

I loved the powder trick and on a Sunday Afternoon, I decided to line up a few two-inch rocks on the track, then a few more, and more still. Soon, I had a 50 foot stretch of track completely covered with small rocks. When I heard the train coming, I instinctively hid in the bushes, at the top of the escarpment. The adrenaline rush was amazing, as I was carrying out my own experiment, completely independent of my brother and friends. The train became louder, as it thundered toward its unexpected rock-crushing task. However, excitement began to turn to trepidation and then terror, as I finally began to consider the possible consequences of my actions. The engineer must have spotted the obstructions on the track about the same time that I was realized my terrible mistake. Suddenly, there was a dreadful clanking noise. The train driver tried to abort his journey and buffers between individual carriages crashed together, with the activation of the emergency brake. However, his response was too late and a horrific grinding noise set in, as the first wheels met the limestone rocks. From my hiding place, I could see the train engineer's ashen face, as his unstoppable train rocked from side to side. Derailment was inevitable. Wheel after wheel lost contact with the track. I was a juvenile delinquent, undoubtedly heading for Borstal. Why had I not learned from the snowball/bus incident? Now the whole train disappeared in a cloud of limestone dust, as it screeched, clunked and crunched before the inevitable crash. I closed my eyes tightly as my tear-sodden face grimaced with anticipation. I suddenly realized that the engineer might die. Then it was silent. I kept my eyes closed tightly, petrified that I had vandalized the track and murdered the train driver. I would be the last one to have seen him alive. The silence was eerie until it was finally broken.

"Bloody Hell Fire!" exclaimed the welcome voice of the engineer.

"Sodding Hell!" added the voice of Reg Johnson, who was the first on the scene. "It'll be those sodding kids!"

"My sodding kid is in the house eating his dinner!" defended Bill Pratt, determined to disclaim any blame on his son's behalf. Almost instantly, there were about thirty people who had dropped everything raced across the field to be first on the scene of anticipated carnage.

"What's happened?" asked my dad's familiar voice. I could not have picked a worse time than a Sunday afternoon, when all the adults were at home.

"Some kids have just tried to derail the train," said Reg Johnson. However, the whole scene was surprisingly devoid of kids. Finally, the white dust began to settle and, to my astonishment, the train was still intact and on the track. I just lay still as my heart tried to pound its way out of my chest. I watched as the community of adults united to help the train driver clear the track of debris.

"I bet it's that Drinkwater kid, he's stupid enough to not even know what he's doing!" insisted Bill Pratt.

"No Bill," replied Reg Johnson, "this was a deliberate act of vandalism. This is attempted murder!" I shuddered at this suggestion. I was either stupider than

127

Jimmy Drinkwater or a cool, calculating, terrorist with a propensity to murder.

It might have been that dad's sons had not yet been eliminated from the inquiry but dad felt compelled to inject some perspective. "It looks to me like some idiot kids have just been experimenting. We've all done stupid things, as kids. No harm done." This seemed to calm the whole crowd.

"Suppose you're right, Pete, there's nothing to see here," announced Bill Pratt. This declaration dispersed the crowd as quickly as they had gathered and the train driver continued his journey. I personally lay low for another twenty minutes before rolling, commando style, from my hiding place and returning home.

"Where have you been?" asked dad, as soon as I walked in.

"The park," I responded nonchalantly.

"You missed some fun down by the track." said dad.

"Greyhounds?" I asked.

"No, the railway track, you fool," he retorted. "See Beryl, he hasn't a clue what I'm talking about." It was hard to tell whether an innocent person would say less or more at this point. I opted for less and my parents seemed more-than-content to probe no further. Even when a mystery white crust lined the bath, after Sunday evening ablutions, the mysterious case of the railway saboteur was never again raised in our house. On this Sunday night, I was looking forward to next day's school, purely to put a little distance between me and the crime scene.

Chapter 13: The Unfriendly Friendly

The following morning, even the pungency of the outdoor urinals at Marston Road School was a welcome comfort. At least, I was safely away from the world of the Sutton Green witch-hunt for the railway vandals; it was pretty much assumed that this was too complex a crime for a single individual. In fact, witnesses were already swearing that they had seen four kids running away from the track, toward to canal.

I had only shared my secret with Whiskey. The burden was intense and I would love to have confided in Andrew because he always had sound advice. However, I instinctively knew that the knowledge was only safe whilst it belonged to me alone (and my hamster).

Marston Road boys' toilets were no more than an L-shaped seven-foot wall with a concrete trough, at the top of the schoolyard. Regularly, the drain would get blocked with litter. Pupils would find themselves trying to manipulate their flies, while balancing, on tiptoe, in an inch of pee. As I squared up to the wall next to Alan Rollins and Pete Knight, they were literally having a pissing contest. Both had very different styles; Peter got as close to the wall as possible and leaned back. On the other hand, Alan employed a squeezing, pressure-hose technique. Both boys managed an impressive five feet up the wall and they were in the process of asking me to adjudicate, when an uninvited Paul Moore stepped up to the competition. Paul was the only kid in the school that was not white. Dad referred to him as a pickaninny because he was of mixed race.

"Peter, don't teach your son to be prejudiced!" mum scolded. She then turned to me and said, "Martin, you should never judge a person by the colour of his skin." Mum was a true advocate of all human rights, unless they were mine!

"Mrs Forsythe's already told us," I assured her. My teacher was equally passionate about equality for all, except the children in her class!

"Your mum's right, son," said dad soberly, "the kid can't help being a half-cast." Mum and Andrew glared at him.

"What have I said now?" asked my genuinely bemused dad.

Mum felt obliged to spell it out for all of us. "Well when you say he 'can't help it,' you make it sound like his skin colour is a handicap. I don't want my boys growing up thinking there is something wrong with coloured people." Andrew nodded in agreement but dad just looked exasperated.

"Can't do right for wrong," dad told himself. He was so immune to her nagging that he could not recognize a genuine point when she made one.

Once mum had pointed it out, I tried much harder to like Paul Moore. I started to notice the way some pupils were mean to Paul and even the teachers seemed to pick on him. Mr. Rice caned him once, for running down the corridor, and we had all done that on occasion. Unfortunately, however hard I looked for things to like about the boy, I could not find any redeeming features, on which to focus. He could not read, and had to go off with Kevin Dagworth to a special reading lady each day. He had the smell of a bed-wetter and his clothes were always filthy. Furthermore, he had no sense of humour and he used to bully the younger kids. Paul Moore had no discernible skills.

However, once he unbuttoned and entered the wall wetting game, he unleashed a latent talent. His pee instantly surpassed the record, reducing his fellow competitors to the 'also rans.' Soon it was touching at six feet, then seven and rising. The concentration on his face was intense.

"If only he could focus on his Janet and John book with similar purpose, he would be reading in no time," I thought to myself, superciliously.

"Then again, he didn't nearly knock a train off the tracks." I quickly rebuked myself.

Finally, Paul Moore made it! A shower of concentrated, early- morning urine disappeared over the top of the wall. Alan Rollins, Pete Knight and I broke into spontaneous applause, as Paul Moore finally realized a moment of glory. Unfortunately, this was curtailed by an unwelcome sound.

131

"Streuth, which Pommie bastard's pissing on me!" said the unmistakable voice of Parsnips the Aussie. He was back!

Paul Moore still had the offending weapon in his hand as Graham appeared around the corner - both fists flailing. Paul dropped to the ground, instantly followed by Pete. I was trying to help them up when I felt an agonizing thump to my solar plexus. Every one of his knuckles twisted in my gut, bent on inflicting maximum pain. I would have screamed but the air had already vacated my lungs. As his fist withdrew, it felt like he was ripping my innards out of my midriff. Any doubts about his fighting credentials were quashed in that instant. Luckily, I fell on top of his two other victims. Unlike them, I did not suffer the added indignity of lying in my own urine - this was obviously not a new sensation for Paul Moore. Alan Rollins' short-sightedness turned out to be his salvation.

"You're lucky you're wearing glasses, Specky-four-eyes!" said the crazed junior boxing champion. That was probably one of the few times that Alan found solace in his myopic handicap. I was wishing that I had been wearing my glasses at this point but vanity had turned out to be my enemy. I remembered one of Andrew's most annoying taunts: "Sticks and Stones may break my bones but names will never hurt me!" Paul Moore, Peter Knight and I were witness to this statement. Alan was relatively unhurt by the names, whereas bone breakage was a definite possibility for us.

As Parsnips walked away, he chuckled to himself. Then, in the aftermath of his violent attack he burst into one of the funniest things I had ever heard: "Two little Pommie birds pissing on a wall, one named Peter, on named Paul." In a way, he reminded me of The

Riddler, from my Batman comics, except he used children's rhymes to accompany his sadistic strike.

School had seemed like a sanctuary from my incessant home troubles but this Monday was turning out to be a nightmare, before the bell had even sounded. To add further dismay, Mrs Forsythe seemed to be in a foul mood.

"Dinner money," she announced. Of course, I had, yet again, forgotten it.

"Sod it!" I said, accidentally a little too loud. By the time the pump was pounding my bottom I was immune to the world. My happy place was becoming more and more frequented. I spent the rest of the day avoiding Parsnips, who seemed to feel that he still owed me a beating.

That night, I took an unprecedented step. My pensive look prompted dad to ask me if I had a problem. Perhaps, he was still trying to substantiate my innocence in the railway incident because he did not usually show such interest in my well-being. However, I took the opportunity to inform him that I was being bullied by Perth Junior Boxing Champion. Of course, the credentials sounded like the empty claims of a braggart and I knew that dad did not believe them.

He showed some relief as he said, "There's only one answer to bullies, son. You have to stand up to them!"

"But dad, you don't understand. He can beat up anybody in the school," I protested.

"Not my sons, he can't!" dad insisted, totally unaware of the sheer might of this kid. Andrew looked over, a little shocked by dad's 'sons' (plural) comment. My elder brother had heard of Parsnips' growing reputation and he could gain nothing by getting involved in such a conflict.

"I can teach you to box," dad announced. This came as news to Andrew and me because we had never once heard about dad being a fighter. On the other hand, we regularly heard about his wimpy teenage years in the Sanatorium. Of course, there was no way that Andrew was going to let me learn fighting techniques alone. It would unhinge the whole family dynamic for me to be able to outmanoeuvre my big brother at fisticuffs. So, we both listened intently to dad's coaching tips and, to our amazement, he seemed to know what he was talking about.

First, he taught us to keep our faces covered with both fists, which made perfect sense. He showed us how to 'jab,' putting the whole-body momentum behind the blow by stamping, as the arm straightened. He made us wrap scarves on our hands so that we could spar without causing too much harm. Dad insisted that everything was done in twos. Soon Andrew and I were one/two-ing in and out, picking off jabs and pokes.

"That's good, it's Sonny Liston and Cassius Clay," he encouraged, "power against agility." Occasionally, I would feel the momentum, of which dad spoke so highly, and Andrew would go reeling back. Then he would do the same to me. Next, dad showed how to duck and weave by anticipating and rolling with the punches. I had always had lightning reactions and I was particularly good at this. Andrew and I felt our telepathic link, as we skipped, thrust and countered.

"One, two, one, two," the three of us counted together. It reminded me of a Mrs Clark music class.

"One, jab, one poke, one punch, one poke," dad encouraged, "weave, two, duck two." It was almost like dancing, with us rocking and swaying to the rhythmic commands of our father. I had never pegged dad as a fighter and wondered what other talents he carried over from his misspent youth. By the end of the evening, Andrew and I were both exhausted. Dad had turned us into boxers, which seemed like the greatest gift a father could give to a child. Of course, mum did not officially approve, yet I could see that she was a little proud. She cast a rare admiring glance toward dad, which probably translated into an early night for all of us. She gave us a lecture, about power bringing responsibility. This was a speech straight from my Spiderman comic, which led me to surmise that mum must have had a sneak peek. Her speech was going a little over my head until dad decided to clarify.

"Never be the one to start a fight but always be prepared to finish one!" were dad's 'pearls of wisdom.'

It was with an air of confidence that I entered school on Tuesday. I was aching and bruised from the ordeals of the previous day but I felt mentally sharp. In fact, I even remembered my dinner money and my football boots. My Under 9s team had a 'friendly' game against the Under 11's and we fancied our chances. Admittedly, their team was taller and stronger but we had Barry Cooper, whose dribbling skills had been likened to those of the great Stanley Matthews. Gary Smith was also the most agile of goal-keepers and he was certain to frustrate the strike force of the bigger boys' team. My lightning speed was always a threat on the wing and we had four or five competent players. I hoped that the combination of the older boys' complacency and our underdog-driven motivation would produce a competitive game.

When Mr. Barton posted the team sheets at lunch time, there were a couple of surprise inclusions. Firstly, he had moved me from the right wing to Centre Forward, which put me in direct conflict with Andrew, their Centre Half. Secondly, Mr. Barton had included Paul Moore and Graham Parsons in our team.

"Unbelievable!" I uttered with disgust. Not only could neither of these outcasts play soccer, they had never even shown any interest in the game. I was not sure that Parsons even knew the rules. To me this was an insult to the game, not to mention the deserving players who had been side-lined to accommodate them.

Barry Cooper and I marched indignantly into Mr. Barton's room and demanded answers. Barry was the captain so he spoke first.

"Please sir, I think there's been a mistake," said Cooper, as respectfully as his temper would allow.

"Moore and Parsons don't like football, sir," I added, in my capacity of vice-captain, struggling to hide my emotions. Football was everything to me and Mr. Barton knew it.

"Thank you for sharing your views, boys," he said using his deliberately calming tones. "Now, I don't expect you to understand what I am about to say to you but please do me the honour of listening to my answer." We were used to Mrs Forsythe's indifference to the concerns of her flock and had half-expected him to yell at us for questioning his decision. I felt flattered that he afforded us the dignity of explaining his mystifying decision.

Barry and I both nodded silently.

He continued, "Paul and Graham are different from most children here. They don't have friends." I had no argument with this statement but failed to see what this had to do with football. "They have had a different kind of upbringings to you. Graham's dad is a terrible, terrible bully and Paul does not have a dad at all. You boys cannot imagine what it's like to be bullied or neglected by a parent." I desperately resisted rolling my eyes and just about managed to hold my tongue. "Tell me Martin, do you feel proud when you are playing for the school team?" He sprung the question upon me.

"Yes Sir," I was compelled to respond.

"Barry, will you be thinking about problems at home, when you are dribbling past everybody on the field?" he asked.

The answer was not necessary but Cooper gave it anyway, "No, sir."

His final question was posed to both of us, "Do you hate your teammates, as they play alongside you?"

"No sir," we agreed.

"I want these boys to be part of a winning team. I am relying on you to make sure that they are!" he said. His tone changed from man-to-man to formal, as he reopened the professional distance that had been temporarily bridged. He re-donned the metaphorical teacher's hat indicating that our part in the conversation was over.

"Yes sir," we answered in unison. So, the stakes were suddenly raised. Not only were we playing against boys two years older than us, we were carrying two dead weights - a moron and a psychopath. Furthermore, we were expected to defy the odds and win the game so that these two losers could fool themselves into thinking that they were part of a victory. The more I thought about it, the more unfair it seemed. I was impressed by Mr. Barton's commitment to integrating the two pariahs but why did he have to contaminate the game of football?

All afternoon I was restless, and conflicted. I had adults depending on me to pull off miracles. I still half-expecting the police to come and arrest me and cart me off to Borstal for my reckless behaviour on the railroad. Added to that, there was a mentally deranged bully thinking that he still owed me a thrashing. Where all my instincts told me to avoid Parsnips at all costs, dad expected me actively seek out and confront him. Dad was convinced that his couple of hours of coaching had turned me into Henry Cooper -the latest great British hope. Dad was relying on me to 'put the bully in his place.' Now, Mr. Barton was turning the game I loved into some sort of psychological social experiment, designed purely to boost the morale of a half-wit and crazy kid. Indeed, the very nutcase that I was vehemently trying to avoid!

It was interesting to line up in a directly complimentary position to my brother because we both knew one another's game so well. The older team kicked off and passed the ball straight back to Andrew. Of course, I anticipated the move and with my speed I reached him at almost the same instant as the ball. My brother read my intentions and merely side-stepped my tackle, stroking the ball out to Pete Knight, on the wing. Knight was fast and he cut inside, leaving Zeleski and Dagworth in his dust. Suddenly, he was in the penalty area with only Gary Smith to beat. Gary raced out to narrow the angle and dived at the attacker's feet but Pete was too quick and he skipped around our 'keeper. He was about to side-foot the ball into the empty net when, out-of-the-blue, Graham Parson's slid across the damp muddy field, with his bare studs showing. Mr. Barton blew his referee's whistle to award the penalty whilst Pete Knight hobbled off with blood gushing from both lower legs. It was only his shin-pads that had prevented a broken leg.

Alan Shaw stepped up and scored the penalty, which seemed to particularly provoke Graham Parsons. The rest of the first half we were totally out-played and we were lucky not to concede any more goals. A couple more ruthless tackles by Parsnips made the opposition nervous but it was the heroics of Gary Smith that kept the teams separated by the single goal, at half time.

Mr. Barton was, of course, the coach of both sides. First, he huddled the Under 11 team, and probably told them to just keep on doing what they were doing. Then he called us into a group to give us advice.

"Listen boys, they're probably going to keep on doing what they have been doing," he said, like he was purely guessing their plan. "Wells, I want you to make diagonal runs," he said.

"Yes sir," I agreed, not daring to admit that I did not know what diagonal meant.

"Graham, I want you to stop giving away fouls," said the teacher.

"They keep cheating, sir," Graham protested, "I hardly touch them and they dive to the ground. They're a load of cheating sissies, sir."

"Well if you don't touch them they won't be able to cheat, Graham," Mr. Barton tried to reason. You could see from the boy's bewildered expression that he did not follow the logic. Straight from the kick-off he 'shoulder charged' Ian Cook when the boy did not even have the ball. Whilst were reorganizing for the free-kick, I managed to have a word with Andrew.

"What's a diagonal run?" I asked.

"Corner to corner," he explained, "is that what Barton told you?"

"I can't say," I responded.

"I think you just have!" Andrew retorted smugly.

However, just because he knew what I was planning to do, it did not particularly mean that he could stop me. A couple of my high-speed diagonal runs almost resulted in me scoring and our team was starting to play our way back into the game. However, the biggest advantage to my catty-corner runs was that it drew the opposition defence out of shape, so that Barry Cooper could move unhindered down the middle. He virtually dribbled the equalizer into the net. Then a minute later, it was only a heroic sliding tackle by my brother that prevented us taking the lead. Against all odds, my underdog team was beginning to get the upper hand. With just a minute to go, I even heard the indelicate tones of encouragement of my Aussie nemesis, as I plundered the older boys' goalmouth.

"Come on Ink Boy, put it in the net," yelled my enemy. Perhaps, Mr. Barton's plan was working, whilst Ink Boy was not exactly my ideal Superhero name, at least it was being offered as a term of endearment. I felt a surge of confidence and coasted past their defence, like a knife through butter.

"Ink-boy, Ink-boy, Ink-boy," barked the harsh patronizing chant from behind me. Peter Sylvester, their goal-keeper raced from his goal-line, misjudging my pace, leaving me on the corner of the box with an empty net only twenty yards away. Whilst my first instinct was to score the winning goal by blasting the ball between the goal posts, an even more glorious scenario presented itself. Parallel to me in a central position was Paul Moore. Without hesitation, I tickled the ball to a mid-goal spot, about six feet from the goal posts, so that Moore could tap it in and be the hero. The pass was perfectly weighted and the defence stood motionless, accepting their inevitable loss.

"Good man, Wells," yelled the supposedly unbiased referee. I felt proud that I had won over, Graham Parsons, Paul Moore and Mr. Barton in one selfless moment. If God was watching, and what else would he rather be doing, I had just booked myself a place in heaven. Something truly magical was in the air because, although the shot was impossible to miss, Paul Moore managed to scoop the ball over the crossbar, just like his stream of pee had cleared the toilet wall.

"Bloody moron, Moore!" screamed Graham Parsons. I had to agree with this sentiment. "Bloody idiot, Wells!" he added. Again, I could not disagree. Instead, of creating a hero I had: vilified poor Paul Moore; Parsons was mad at me, again; I was an embarrassment to Andrew; Mr. Barton was mortified by the cruel backfiring of his social integration plan. You could hear the sadness in his whistle, as he brought the game to an end. I had let everyone down, including God, if he was watching. I wondered if God had exerted any control over Paul Moore's boot. If so, he must have had a rather sick sense of humour.

"Bloody Idiot, Wells!" said God.

The walk home was going to be tough because I was already exhausted from the day's events. On the brighter side, I had somehow managed to gain some standing with some of the older boys from the other team, simply being Andrew's brother bought me some favour and my lightning speed always impressed. So, as we were leaving school, taking a short-cut through a cobbled back alley, we were at the point of complimenting reciprocal virtues.

"Great penalty," I told Alan Shaw, "you sent Smithy the wrong way."

"I gave him the old hip shimmy," Alan bragged, reliving the moment with a pelvic dance.

"Bloody cheat, Shaw!" goaded an Australian voice behind us. Personally, I would have ignored it but Alan had more pride.

"You're the cheat Parsnips!" Shaw responded. "You just run around the field trying to kick everybody. If you weren't so bloody slow you'd be dangerous!"

Now the gloves were off. Graham Parson's charged in, with fists flailing. Alan was quick and leapt aside, making the Aussie look decidedly clumsy. We all cheered. I carefully studied Parsons' technique. He certainly did not use the style that dad had drilled into me and Andrew. He made no use of momentum and his approach could best described as be rapid and random. Shaw had his own haphazard responses but he was the first to draw blood. A split lip proved that Parsons was not indestructible. However, it seemed to spur the bully on. He suddenly head-butted Shaw, which was not exactly the Queensbury rules but was highly effective, all the same.

"Cheat!" cried Shaw as his face hit a cobblestone.

"Cheat, cheat, cheat!" the crowd chanted. I think that the Australian took this as an instruction, rather than an insult because he cheated more than ever. He began kicking Shaw in the abdomen rhythmically, in time to the chanting, which seemed particularly perverse. Once the audience realized that they were inadvertently orchestrating the assault they stopped. Unluckily, I stopped after everyone else.

"Cheat!" my sudden solo echoed. This distracted Parsons long enough for Alan Shaw to roll away and pick himself up. I hoped that Shaw might launch an unexpected resurgence but his groans told me that he had lost the urge to fight. Unfortunately, victory over one boy was not enough to satiate the bully and he started to move toward me.

"You lost the game for us, you bloody idiot, Wells!" Parsnips decided. I recognized the tone. Just like when mum was on the rampage, there was nothing that could be said or done that could prevent a barrage of either mental or physical abuse. Adrenaline surged oxygenated blood to my brain and I began think clearly. I was instantly in superhero mode. My fists sprang up to protect my face and I launched into the one, two, one, two, duck and weave, duck and weave, rhythm that dad had taught me.

"It's just like sparring with Drew," I said to myself, *"concentrate."* Sure enough, his swinging fists were powerful but slow. I was Cassius Clay, dodging each punch and making a monkey of my opponent. The crowd got behind me and I even managed to launch a momentum-backed blow, which made my opponent recoil. Then, I saw him draw back his head ready to nut me but my bull-fighter instincts left him butting at thin air. He was humiliated and I almost felt like taking a bow to the on-lookers. Ironically, his next move caused me to do just that. Whilst I was growing in confidence that my face was well-protected, I neglected to defend my torso. Suddenly, his fist drilled into my abdomen instantly doubling me up in agony. I had not felt such excruciating pain since, well, since the previous morning in the boys' toilets. Once I was down, all I could do is protect my head, as kicks and thumps were coming in from all angles.

"Jump down, turn around, kick him in the bollocks!" Parsnips sang, to the tune of 'pick a bale of cotton.' True to his bastardized lyrics, he tried to stomp on my goolies. I lifted my thigh just in time to prevent myself joining the 're-ascended testicles' world of Martin Butcher.

"Ouch!" I screamed, driven more by imagination than actual pain.

"Jump down, turn around kick him in the head!" he continued, as his boot met my temple.

"Ouch!" I cried again, this time motivated by real pain. He seemed ready to kick me to death, whilst he sang this sick song, such was his rage, when a voice of reason seemed to penetrate his blood-lust trance.

"Leave him alone, you bully!" came the voice of Sally Doyle. Graham Parsons instantly stopped and without further comment, walked away from the scene. The fight was over.

When I discussed the stressful events of the day with Whiskey later that evening, it was hard for us to decide whether I was a loser of winner.

Chapter 14: Doggy in the Kennel.

Two days later, the scent of ether, was presenting another tier of stressors to my endless woes. Every May and November, mum had to take me for an eye test at the hospital out-patients department. Ether was used to numb injection sites at the adjacent juvenile vaccination ward and the fumes would permeate the air, creating an anesthetizing ambiance.

Ether was mum's Red Kryptonite and she often became 'giggly tipsy' during these visits. On the other hand, the ensuing 'hangover' would invariably invoke mum's darkest moods. Anticipation of the upcoming wrath gave me bad associations with the hospital smells. Moreover, the eye tests were traumatic in their own rights.

"He has a lazy eye," mum announced to the optician's technical nurse, as she sat me down in front of the complex eye-testing machinery.

"So, you have a 'lazy' eye, Martin?" asked the technician, in such a way as to chastise mum's oversimplification of my problem.

"The rest of him is bone idle, too!" joked mum, chuckling to herself. This was the same joke she always used - the ether was kicking in. The hospital staff usually laughed politely at this point but this nurse chose to see nothing funny in the comment. Her own eyes were red and her mascara was smudgy, like she might have been crying.

"Oh, I'm sure he's not lazy, Mrs Wells," responded the technician, trying to afford me some dignity. I liked her because she was one of those rare adults that could talk to children without belittling them. However, it was obvious that her reluctance to acknowledge mum's sense of humour was not courting any popularity with my mother.

"I'm a nurse, myself," declared mum, hoping to impress. The nurse did not respond to the claim, instead she focused on me.

"Have you been wearing your glasses?" asked the technician, filling in notes on a clipboard.

"Yes," I lied, glancing furtively at mum.

"Religiously," confirmed mum in complicity, adding a reassuring wink. I breathed a sigh of relief that she had not 'snitched me out' but then the ether added, "Every time he goes to church he wears them, religiously."

"Your child's eyesight is a serious business, Mrs Wells," said the nurse, who obviously had her own issues. In truth, I 'forgot' to wear my spectacles most of the time, except when Mrs Forsythe remembered to remind me. Standard issue brown wire clinic glasses were like a red rag to a bull, not to mention a bully! I would rather risk blindness than invoke such social ridicule.

"You can see his squint, especially when he's tired," mum informed the nurse, finally dropping the banter.

"Well, we don't like to call it a squint, or a lazy eye, Mrs Wells, because some patients are offended by such terminology," she said. Whilst she treated me with the respect of an adult, she was definitely not afraid to talk down to other adults. Mum was annoyed.

"Offended? Offended?" mum mocked, "You have noticed that he's just a child?" As if a child was incapable of taking offense.

"Now I'm offended," I thought to myself.

It was during mum's sarcastic moment that the optician walked in. His face was sporting a bad mood, even before he heard my mum using disrespectful tones to his technician. Added to this, there already appeared to be an uncomfortable tension between the doctor and his nurse.

"Who do we have here?" he asked the technician curtly, ignoring mum completely, whilst snatching up my notes. It was a tone with which I was familiar - like when mum and dad were having a *neigh-silent row* in public. Such altercations were often more venomous than regular verbal sparring. Whilst the nurse was able to wear a mask of professionalism, the doctor's arrogant air afforded no such courtesy to his patients. His professional obligation to defend his staff and his apparent personal annoyance at her was obviously conflicting. It gave him the charm of a cranky American pit-bull terrier.

"This is Martin Wells," snapped the nurse, matching his tone.

"Really, that's why his notes say, 'Martin Wells,' under Patient's Name," said the doctor sardonically.

"I'm sorry, I thought when you asked, 'Who do we have here?' that you wanted to know the answer," the technician blurted.

"It was a rhetorical question, nurse," he said superciliously, emphasizing her inferior rank.

"Oh, you and your sarcastic ways," the nurse tried to play off the comment as playful banter but the forced smile was betrayed by her ever-moistening eyes.

"Great, I'm in an episode of Dr. Kildaire," I thought to myself.

"Look into the binocular eye-pieces. What do you see with your right eye?" demanded the eye-doctor.

"A dog," I responded. It was the same dog that I had had so much trouble with six months earlier.

"He can't do the dog," mum interjected. The optician glared at her contemptuously.

"Good," he responded, deliberately directing his response toward me and ignoring mum.

He manipulated the machine and asked, "Now the left eye."

"A kennel," I told him.

"Good," he replied. "Now let's put the doggy in his kennel." He was now being deliberately condescending

I wanted to say, *"I'm eight years old for God's sake,"* but I opted for silence. He turned knobs and interchanged lenses methodically.

"Tell me when the doggy goes into the kennel," he repeated, as though I was ignoring the instruction.

However, just like every previous occasion, that 'doggy' was not going anywhere near the kennel.

"Not yet," I felt obliged to let him know.

"Are you looking at the dog?" he snapped. It seemed a silly question since my eye was tight against the eyepiece.

"Yes," I replied. I thought that a single syllable answer would add less fuel to his anger.

"There it's in there now, isn't it?" he tried to bully me.

"Not really," I replied.

"The boy's lying," he told his technician.

"I'm not," I defended myself.

"I told you, he can't do the dog," mum supported me.

Perhaps the ether atmosphere was clouding his emotions because he began to lose any last semblance of civility at this point. "Look madam, I've been doing this job for twenty-three years and I've never had a patient that can't get the bloody doggy in the sodding kennel!" he sniped.

The optician's inability to control his temper seemed to empower mum, rather than put her in her place, as his comments were intended.

She took a deep breath and then in a calm, controlled voice she said, "He can get the bloody fishy in the sodding tank."

After an inordinate amount of silence, the optician regained composure and then turned to the technician and said, "Fine, try the fish one."

The nurse floundered through the box of slides with fluster and agitation. Her tears were obviously impeding her vision and she could not find the fish, "What about the kitten in the basket?" asked the technician.

"The fish one," he insisted.

"How about the parrot in the cage?" she snivelled.

"How about the choo choo in the tunnel," he suggested. This must have held some hidden meaning to the nurse because it seemed to inflame things further.

"How about the ring on the finger?" was her final whimper before ripping off her lab coat, throwing it to the floor and storming out of the room.

An even lengthier silence followed. Even mum was at a loss for words, as the optician began rooting through the slide box himself.

He started to mumble to himself, as he scrutinized then discarded each slide, "Car in garage, candle on cake, baby in the cot, bun in the oven..........bugger! Ah here's the damn fish in the tank!" he proclaimed. "Now, let's get this done."

The problem was that I had lied about seeing the fish in the tank on my previous visit. I had merely used vocal cues of the examiner to help me fake it. Unfortunately, my only potential ally had just had an emotional meltdown, for no imaginable reason. The irate optician grabbed my head and forced my eyes tight against the lenses of the machine and stated turning the knobs; and so the fish game began.

"Closer of further away?" he asked.

"Closer," I guessed.

"I told you he can do the fish," insisted mum, where common intuition advocated quiet.

"And now?" he asked.

"Mmmm," was all I could muster, hoping that my deliberate ambiguity would be heard whichever way he wanted to hear it.

"Right," he replied, no longer interested in the game. Then he turned to mum and said, "Your son has not been wearing his glasses, Mrs Wells, and his lazy eye is getting lazier."

"Oh dear," said mum, suddenly feeling guilty. She was an accomplice to her son's negligence. We all knew what came next. It was something that they had threatened for the last two years. Only the cruellest thing you could ever do to a child. Ruth Parsons, no relation to Graham, had become school-phobic as a victim of this inhuman treatment. It was a death sentence and I could not bear to hear the optician's next words.

"So, we're going to cover the right lens, his good eye, with plaster so that his lazy eye will be forced to work harder.

"How long?" mum asked, somewhat feeling my pain.

"Oh, three to six months," the optician replied, seemingly arbitrarily. The man was completely indifferent to the life-changing decision he had just made, on a whim.

"I'm not wearing them," I blurted, feeling the urge to make the same exit as his highly-strung technician.

Throughout the bus journey home, I felt like a total outcast. Mum reassured me that the pink patch over my 'good eye' was hardly noticeable. However, as my tears started to draw attention - even more attention than my freak glasses, mum became embarrassed.

"If you had worn them like you're supposed to, it wouldn't have come to this," she insisted. The ether effect was moving to its new phase.

"I can see better than anybody, I don't need glasses," I sobbed.

"I'll give you something to cry about if you don't stop," was mum's familiar war-cry.

Now, this was what she meant by me being 'awkward.' The most obvious move would be to try, with all my worth, to stop crying, at this juncture. However, the full degradation of my grotesque eye-wear left me feeling that life could get no lower. I was truly helpless. So as she began to publicly humiliate me with a series of slaps, my cries remained unrelentingly defiant. Tears trickled out from under my latest 'cross to bear.'

"You're not supposed to hit a person with glasses," I shouted. This caused the bus conductor to approach.

"Can't you keep him quiet, love? He asked. "He's upsetting the other passengers." There was sympathy in his voice but it was hard to tell whether he felt sorry for me having to wear these gimp glasses or mum, for having a retarded child. Either way, his intervention seemed to work.

"Sorry," she apologized, "he's had a traumatic day."

"That's okay love, my brother has a spastic kid, I know how hard it can be," he commiserated.

The conductor made my point for me and later, when dad came home his face betrayed his inner thoughts.

"They look fine, son," he lied, under heavy prompting from the rest of the family, then ducked under his newspaper where I am sure that he was feeling the same shame as me.

I later overheard mum and dad, in the next bedroom, talking about my predicament.

"Six sodding months, they'll crucify him!" exclaimed dad's raised voice from their bedroom.

Mum shushed him, and I could only hear mumbled snippets after that. The argument seemed to resolve quite quickly and then I heard her telling dad about the strange behaviour of the optical nurse. I heard the word 'affair' and pregnant which was not the vibe that I was getting. It caused me to re-evaluate my perceptions because I was under the distinct impression that the two detested one-another.

The next morning, I conveniently forgot to pick up my glasses case off the kitchen table, fully expecting to encounter more wrath that evening. However, when I got home after school, mum had moved my spectacles into the top drawer- the messy one, where things got lost for weeks at a time. Furthermore, it soon became obvious that everyone was as happy to forget about the glasses, as I was. They could stay there until November, as far as I was concerned. Sally Doyle would, hopefully, never witness me wearing my Ruth Parsons specials. Another, insoluble solution had resolved itself, at least for the time being. Of course, that was assuming mum did not enter a vengeful phase. I made an unspoken pact, to stifle my *awkward streak* for a while.

Chapter 15: Bukowski

The smell of burning dust, on the old valves of our television, stirs mixed emotions. Admittedly, it was the place that I first met Bill and Ben, the Beatles and Blue Peter but the best event of the year was always FA Cup Final day. This was the only televised football match of the year. It brought this extended season, riddled with frozen-pitch postponements, to a close.

The television went on at eleven o'clock in the morning, so that Kenneth Wolstanholme could treat us to four hours of pre-match ramblings. By the kick-off, all members of the Manchester United and Leicester City teams, and their wives, would be permanently etched into our memory-banks. We would know how each team had navigated the road to Wembley, their idiosyncrasies and superstitions. Apparently, United striker, Ian Herd, had a father who had played in two FA cup finals in the 1930's.

"Quite a coincidence," I thought.

Dad, for all his normal traits, had a few obsessions. For instance, he had heard that televisions only 'acted out' when they had been subjected to some form of kinesis. On reflection, somebody must have been secretly moving it, because our BBC-only, black-and-white television broke down with great regularity. Of course, mum was the prime suspect. She was more than capable of deliberately shaking it when she was alone, just to dislodge the valves. Bringing disharmony to dad's life was a powerful motivator for mum. The TV had an annoying habit of 'flicking,' as we called it. The vertical hold would stray, so the picture would hover with people's legs at the top of the screen and their bodies at the bottom. Sometimes a strategically placed screwdriver, held in a hole on the side, would alleviate the problem. On this day, the valves must have overheated from the pre-match because, just as Bobby Charlton drew back his foot for one of his signature 30-yarders, the flicking began. We were only ten minutes into the game. Dad summoned the screwdriver, like a surgeon demands the scalpel, but the patient did not respond. I felt nauseous to think that I would miss a goal by Charlton or a famous bicycle kick by Scottish International, Dennis Law. It seemed that life could turn no sourer, but then it did!

"Go and fetch Ivan Bukowski," dad commanded, in his resistance-is-useless voice. Now, my childhood was haunted by a series of unpleasant experiences with the local TV repair man, Mr. Bukowski. How I dreaded being sent to get this scary man. He was the only foreigner I had ever met and I think that I interpreted the cultural differences as hostility. His thick, eastern European accent seemed so phony and his apparent psychotic gaze and abrupt manner were truly intimidating.

"But dad, he won't want to come, he'll be watching the cup!" I protested.

"Don't be stupid, kid, he's Polish. They don't watch football," he explained.

A frenzied bike-ride later, my faint tapping on the backdoor of the Bukowski household was finally acknowledged.

"Jesus Christ Almighty! Who the hell's knocking in the middle of the FA Cup?" yelled Mr. Bukowski. His tones were a little more decipherable than his usual mutterings.

"My dad wants you to come and fix the television," I managed to convey.

"Who the Hell's your dad?" he screamed.

I am not sure whether my protective genes kicked in at this point or if I was simply distracted by the background sound of the football match on Mr. Bukowski's perfectly good TV. However, I was suddenly dumbstruck. He tried a few bullying tactics but to no avail. I had involuntarily retracted to my 'safe place' where nothing could harm me. I was spending more and more time there, of late. Yes, I could see his contorted facial expressions spouting venom. True, I was aware of the blend of Polish spirit and Polish spittle saturating my face. Admittedly, I was aware that extremely unpleasant sounds were being unleashed upon me. But basically, I was solid gone. Outside my safe place, I might have caved under this pressure. Somehow, during this phenomenal onslaught of my senses, I remained focused on one thing. Dennis Law had beaten the offside trap, side-stepped Gordon Banks, the England goalkeeper, and slipped the ball into the net. United had taken the lead!

This seemed to jolt my consciousness back to reality and I began to understand the words that Mr.

Bukowski was yelling. He was listing the "arse-holes," that he thought might have the audacity to think that he should abandon his own pleasures to accommodate theirs. He obviously stored up resentments.

"Are you Pickerton's son?" was his first guess. I was hurt that he was confusing me for Arthur Pickerton; a genuine retard. Still I could not speak.

"Are you one of the Drinkwater kids?" he interrogated. It was getting worse and I just managed to give my head the slightest shake of denial. How could anyone mistake me for Jimmy, or worse still, one of his brothers?

Eventually, my dad's name came up, on his extensive 'hate list,' to which I must have given a discernible nod. Instantly, he was cranking up his motorbike, with sidecar, and screeching off toward my house. I mounted my bike and scrambled back home, fully expecting to witness a bloodbath on my return. Hopefully, mum would not be sending me, to ask the only neighbour with a phone, to call for an ambulance.

"United have scored," I informed Andrew, as I re-entered the room. Then I looked around to see whether dad had survived Mr. Bukowski's wrath. To my amazement, all was calm. Mr. Bukowski had managed to insert his own screwdriver in the vertical hold hole and completely stopped the 'flicking.'

"Thanks for coming at such short notice, Ivan," my dad said, slipping a ten shilling note into his hand.

"Anytime, Pete," Mr. Bukowski retorted, as he headed off to catch the second half. He even afforded me a little tweak of the cheek. For on-lookers this looked like a gesture of affection but I suspected that it was some sort of Polish death threat.

157

United went on to win comfortably in the end, with two goals from Ian Herd.

"His dad must be proud," I thought to myself.

According to the Monday playground chatter, the underdogs put up a brave fight, apparently having their best spell whilst I was on my emergency Bukowski errand. According to Kevin Simkins, the Leicester goal came from a diving header only a foot from the ground. I had learned to take what Simkins said, with a pinch of salt.

Chapter 16: Rosy Apples

Nature has a way of balancing itself out and, just as January had been the worst on record, June was exceptionally pleasant and mild and the smell of freshly cut hay filled the air. As soon as we got home from school we would throw on our tracksuit tops and play until sunset, stopping only for a chip-butty, or a round of beans on toast, for tea.

Games of cricket in the field, or balancing acts on the iron-bridge across the canal, were regular pleasures. Then there was the rope swing located in the valley, down at the bottom of the field. Death defying acrobatics went on for weeks. Our parents were oblivious to our risk-taking, until Bill Pratt 'caught us in the act' and felt a moral obligation to cut down the rope. He was probably right because our buckers and doffers were becoming braver each day and eventually someone would have suffered an unpleasant fate.

Bill's rope removal ceremony had to be seen to be believed and it confirmed dad's numerous statements that "Bill Pratt is an idiot!" The thirty-foot rope, originally used to tie boats to their moorings, hung from a thick lateral branch of an old Oak tree. I was intrigued as to how he was even going to get to the point where the rope was tied, and then how he would undo the knot. Anyone could see that it was tightly fused, a result of a thousand centrifugal tugs. Bill had already considered these challenges and he had a plan.

Firstly, despite his well-earned beer-gut, he climbed the rope with surprising agility. His tattoos danced as his biceps moved his grip, arm over arm. First, the anchor on his left arm distorted, then the naked lady on his right arm fattened up. I could see that Barry was proud but, of course, he did not know about the Gypsy Queen. Bill sat on the branch, straddled the rope, and took out a Bowie knife from a holster on his belt. After a couple of cuts the rope dropped to the floor. Then everybody cheered Bill, especially Barry, who rarely had a reason to applaud his wastrel father. Unfortunately, the admiration was short-lived. A wave of realization spread through the gathering audience, that Bill had just discarded his only feasible mode of descent. It was too far to jump and the branch, upon which he was balanced, was impossible to manoeuvre. He sat bemused on his branch for an embarrassingly long hour, before somebody finally fetched Fred the Window Cleaner. Fred, who had apparently seen Bill in more humiliating predicaments, carried his double ladder across the entire field to rescue 'Bill the Idiot.' I could see that Barry was ready to renounce his birth right.

Once the rope swing was gone we needed a new game.

As usual, Andrew had fresh inspiration, he declared, "Let's play Rosy Apples."

At first, we just rang people's doorbells and ran off. I was always the one selected to ring the bell, while the others hid behind privet hedges. The fancier people had illuminated doorbells and they were made to suffer most for their vanity. We never tired of watching their infuriation as they answered their doors to 'The Invisible Man.' No doubt, some dived under tables to avoid collectors, as our family had often done, in response to the unexpected ring. However, most came out and, almost to the man, they would curse in the same way:

"Bloody kids!" was the standard retort. The first run was easy. What was more challenging was to throw in a repeat performance straight after the first. Most adults will chalk up one occurrence as 'kids being kids.' They would even rationalize that they played the same games when they were young. However, after two or three repetitions their definition quickly deteriorated from 'kids' to 'hooligans' to 'delinquents.' That was when the adrenaline truly started to flow.

Now, at a 999er's meeting in the shed one Thursday evening, Andrew recounted a story that dad had once confessed to him. Apparently, dad and his rascal younger brother, Uncle Bennie, had tied together the doorknobs of two attached houses, with just a little slack, and then knocked on both doors simultaneously. According to the legend, an old lady opened the first door and just as she was about to peak out to see who was calling, the other door opened, slamming the old lady's door closed. The man in the other house was just about to ask, "Who's there?" when the old lady, thinking that wind had played a part in the sudden slamming, tugged firmly, causing the man's door to slam violently. If the story was to be believed, the tug-of-war went on for ages before the two home-owners twigged as to what was going on.

"Brilliant in its simplicity," we all agreed, using what was becoming our gang motto.

Unfortunately, Bill Pratt had disposed of all available rope and all we could find was about two feet of string. This was clearly not enough to repeat the original wheeze. So, Andrew suggested that we attach a rock to the string and tie it to the door-knocker of our unsuspecting victim. In theory, we thought that the rock would continue to knock as the door was opened and then when it was closed again. In hindsight, even if the rock had a mind of its own, it would not have been a good plan. However, it deserved exploration.

We selected a house next to an area of rough land. We could easily hide behind some conveniently placed brambles. As usual, Andrew thought that the job called for my level of bravery, so I tiptoed up to the door and fastened the hanging rock. I retreated to the place where Andrew, Barry, Jimmy and Tony were crouched. We watched for several minutes and, of course, nothing happened.

"You'll have to knock," said Tony.

"Once they open the door, the bugger will keep knocking on its own," said Jimmy optimistically. He seemed to have a different image in his head to the rest of us.

So, I crept silently back to the door and reached for the doorknocker, all the time being coaxed by the other gang members. I was going to hammer like crazy and run like the wind. However, the knocker was not quite where I was anticipating. In fact, as I leaned more forward, the knocker began to back away. I was not the only one with a plan. The house holder suddenly sprang from the house.

162

"Come here you bugger!" yelled a big thickset man. He pounced in an instant and I felt his arm around my neck. I felt my heart start pounding in my chest. This was more adrenaline than I had ever wanted to feel. I struggled to avoid throwing up. Instinctively, I raised my arms above my head and slid free of his grip. I rolled and ran for the bushes, where my friends had been hiding. They were already starting to take flight. Chaos broke out, as my friends scattered and the man's children and wife were screaming, "Get him, dad!" and "Don't hurt him, Ken!"

"Don't hurt him? I'll bloody kill him!" replied Ken. I took off down the path on the spare ground with Kenneth matching my pace, stride for stride. I overtook Jimmy and Barry, and half-expected Ken to grab one of them instead. But this man was on a mission; it was like a cheetah at the heels of a gazelle.

"Come here you little bastard," he screamed.

"Sorry mister, it was just a joke," I gasped as I sprinted at full pelt. I hoped my apology would weaken his resolve.

"You can tell that to the police!" he panted, seemingly madder than ever.

I suddenly darted into a back yard, down the side of the house and came out on Kennilworth Road. I assumed that Ken would not follow me across somebody else's property but he did! I felt him grab a handful of tracksuit, causing me to arch my back; I could not believe that this giant man could keep up with me. I sprinted down Ripperton Road, toward Chilton Lane High School and still the Cheetah locked on. I was hyper-ventilating and knew that I could not run much further, when he finally gave up the chase. I darted into a section of rough ground at the side of the school, where there was some long grass.

I lay panting for about thirty minutes, terrified that the man would find me.

Eventually, I came out of my hiding place and doubled back to meet the rest of the gang in the shed, checking regularly that I was not being followed. The gang was relieved to see me. Jimmy was insisting that he had seen the man had got me in a headlock. Barry had supposedly heard Ken's wife say that she was calling the police.

Once again, I spent the night, worried sick that the police would turn up ready to handcuff me and whisk me off to Borstal. On the other hand, I was a hero amongst my peers.

SUMMER

Chapter 17: To the Zoo.

The Marston Road summer trip to Chester Zoo always flashes to mind, whenever I detect the odour of exotic animal dung and sawdust. The excursion to the zoo commenced, as any good school trip does, with a vying for position on the bus. Of course, the person you sat by was important, but more pressing was the people you managed to avoid. Graham Parsons, Ruth Parsons and Paul Moore were universally shunned. Then on an individual level, I did not want to be near Yvonne Clamp, Ivy Morrison, Sandra Adams or Tina Carolla. Of course, the worst-case scenario was to have to sit with Mrs Forsythe - Ruth Parsons earned that privilege. I ended up with Michael Johnson, the witty one, not his pain-in-the-arse namesake.

'Funny Michael' kept me entertained with knock-knock teasers. For instance: *Knock, knock. Who's there? Doctor: Dr Who?* This was a reference to a new science fiction program that was sweeping the nation. It was typical of the quality of his jokes. Although, I had heard much funnier things, the atmosphere on the bus was such that anything Michael said seemed to make us laugh.

When we arrived, we were each assigned to a different group. Again, I lucked out because I ended up in the group with Mrs Forsythe's best friend, Miss Devonport, who had volunteered to help for the day. I think that they deliberately gave her the 'easy kids' because she was not experienced at bossing children around; we were the group judged least likely to steal a penguin and smuggle it home. My group included Michael Johnson, Ian McKay, Penelope Evans and Sally Doyle. Miss Devonport had a rather irritating high-pitched voice but she was actually quite nice and she treated us all to a bottle of pop. Furthermore, she did not feel the same obligation to 'educate' us, as the other teachers - although, she made the occasional obvious statement.

"Look at the elephants, children. Who knows the difference between Indian and African elephants?" she asked.

"Who doesn't?" I uttered to myself, much to the amusement of Sally Doyle and Penelope Evans.

"What was that, Martin?" she asked, seemingly oblivious to my mockery.

"I think It's something to do with their ears, Miss," I replied, still showing off to the others. This caused Michael Johnson to blow out his mouthful of Vimto.

"That's right, Martin, the Africans have bigger ones," she explained.

"I've heard that, Miss," said Michael Johnson, quick as a flash, chuckling at the double entendre. You should not laugh when you are drinking pop. Now I had a stream of Hubbly Bubbly gushing down my nose. Luckily, Miss. Devonport failed to recognize Michael's dirty hidden meaning. We moved to primate section and that is when the shit really started to fly- quite literally.

"Look at the chimpanzee, children," she asserted in her increasingly shrill tone, "they look so human." At this, the chimp picked up a lump of excrement and launched it in our direction.

"It's throwing poo!" Michael Johnson stated. We started snickering and the chimpanzee joined in the laughter.

"Naughty monkey," said Penelope Evans, and the chimp did a backward somersault, as if to emphasize how 'naughty' he could be.

"It's Mitch the Monkey," I named him, after a puppet character from my favourite TV show, Supercar. "Ooo, ooo, ooo." The chimpanzee seemed to like the impression and tried to talk back to me.

"Ooo, ooo, ooo," he replied. We repeated this conversation several times, although I think that the animal knew more about what we were saying than I did.

"Technically, chimps are not monkeys," shrieked Mrs Forsythe's friend. Instantly, the chimpanzee picked up some more faeces and flung it toward us.

"Bad Mitch," Sally giggled. The ape responded by covering his mouth and snickering, too.

"You see they have opposable thumbs," the teacher's friend added, in an even more grating voice than before. Again, the chimp became irate and threw more crap. It dawned on all of us, except for Miss Devonport, that her annoying frequency was triggering Mitch's anti-social habit. Michael could not resist prolonging the game.

"Does he live in the jungle, Miss?" he asked. This caused her to check her zoo guide, for fear of giving us any wrong information.

"Yes, they are found in all parts of the African forests," she replied. The ape looked around for some more waste to throw but there was nothing available. So he decided to demonstrate the true versatility of his opposable thumbs. His long arm disappeared behind his back and he deliberately shat on his own hand.

"Urgh!" we all exclaimed in unison. The ape gave a wicked grin then hurled the poo directly at the source of irritation.

"Oh, my God!" screamed our chaperon, as the sloppy, fresh, ape-shit whizzer hit her smack in the face. She finally got the message. It was pretty funny, except that she made us wait outside the ladies' toilets for half an hour, while she was trying to wash the stuff out of her hair, face and clothes.

In fact, this made us miss feeding time in the Lion's den, which had been heavily billed, by Mrs Forsythe, as the event of the day. Indeed, Mrs Forsythe seemed a little miffed at her friend, when our group finally did arrive.

"Where've you been Eunice?" she snapped. I was not surprised that Mrs Forsythe was short-tempered because she had the six biggest trouble-makers in her group and they had undoubtedly been testing her patience.

"Sorry, I've been washing monkey-doo-doo out of my hair," she apologized.

"What?" snapped a disbelieving Mrs Forsythe.

"I think she means ape-doo-doo, Miss Forsythe," corrected Michael Johnson.

"It's Mrs Forsythe, Michael," corrected the teacher, in her usual fashion. However, I noticed that this seemed to trigger a weird response from Miss Devonport.

"Oh, its Mrs Forsythe, is it?" Eunice sniped, no longer in an apologetic mood.

168

"Yes, Miss Devonport, as the children all know, a married woman is referred to as a Missus not a Miss," she announced. It was altogether odd and there was obviously some undisclosed tension between these two best friends.

"What a shame that your husband could not join you for the zoo trip, today," jibed Eunice. It was the first time that I ever observed Mrs Forsythe blushing. It was hard to read between the lines but I came to two possible conclusions: either Miss Devonport did not know that Mrs Forsythe was married, or she detested Mrs Forsythe's husband. I watched for further clues but both ladies seemed to suddenly become aware that this was not a topic for public consumption. Miss Devonport quickly changed the subject.

"Michael, why don't you tell Miss, whoops, I mean Mrs Forsythe what you have learned about African elephants?" she asked. I was hoping that he would not repeat his earlier innuendo because I knew that Mrs Forsythe was less naïve than her friend. Instead, he came out with a brilliant joke.

"They're just like little Noddy, Miss," said Michael with a totally straight face.

Confused, Miss Devonport said again, "I'm talking about African elephants, Michael."

"That's right Miss, they're just like Noddy," he insisted.

Mrs Forsythe intervened, "Michael, what are you talking about? How are African elephants like Noddy?"

"They both have Big Ears!" Michael announced. It was hysterical and the whole class laughed. Any tension seemed to dissipate thanks to 'Funny Michael Johnson,'

Watching the feeding lions seemed to prompt the teachers to call an early lunchtime and we all took out our packed lunches. Mine was a little embarrassing compared to most kids. I had a mangled cream cheese and Branston Pickle sandwich wrapped in a bread wrapper that dad had botched together, on the Sunday night, whilst mum was at work. Everybody else seemed to have fancy baps and bags of crisps and cake. Paul Moore and Ruth Parsons were entitled to free dinners, so the school canteen had prepared them a particularly fine array of foods. Dad had given me a shilling to spend which would have handsomely supplemented my lunch. Unfortunately, I had already spent it on a souvenir present for mum. It was a two-inch plastic African elephant. I knew that she would love it, especially if I delivered the Noddy joke as I gave it to her. I showed Miss Devonport and she told me that she would be 'truly thrilled' if her son bought her such a gift. Then, she seemed to get all choked up and offered me her cupcake. It was home-made and could only be described as blissful. Then I noticed that Mrs Forsythe had a matching cupcake, which seemed an amazing coincidence.

After lunch, we went to see the bears. I had always had a phobia about these creatures. The first nightmare I had ever remembered involved three bears.

I was in my bed and mum initiated the normal, "Goodnight, God bless, See you tomorrow, I love you" but then she accidentally broke with tradition and switched off the landing light. This was the opportunity for which the bears had been patiently waiting. They lived in a secret panel, in the wall and I heard them come into the bedroom as soon as mum left. I was terrified! I thought that they were after Andrew, at first, but they walked straight past his bed and came to mine. "This one's just right!" said the smallest of the bears. I wanted to shout to mum but I instinctively knew that they would kill me if I

170

spoke. I remained silent, as they dragged me through the space in the dislodged wall and then replaced it behind us. The bears seemed to want me as a 'toy' for their son. He started to maul me and hurt me whilst his parents laughed. Then I heard mum and Andrew talking from the other side of the wall.

"The bears took Martin," Andrew's muffled voice insisted.

Mum started to shout hysterically, "Martin!" I knew that I only had one chance to let them know where I was before the bears killed me.

"The bears have got me in the wall," I tried to yell.

"It's okay, son, I'm here!" mum replied.

"There are bears in the bedroom," I tried to warn her.

"It's okay, son there are no bears," mum's voice was now clear. "The bears have gone." The bears had gone. I was back in my bed, sweating profusely, awakening from a dream.

This nightmare recurred several times. I could not stop it coming but I eventually learned to recognize that I was dreaming, and wake myself up, before the bears did any damage.

Seeing real-life bears provoked a post-traumatic stress episode. I simply froze as three black bears paced menacingly up and down in their shared cage. I felt petrified and Miss Devonport must have noticed that all the blood had drained from my face.

She grabbed my hand and calmly stated, "You're perfectly safe, Martin." Funnily enough, her voice was no longer screechy; it was beautifully modulated and reassuring. I felt the fear lift.

Then Michael Johnson broke the tension with a question that the bears had probably heard a thousand times before, "Where's Goldilocks?"

"They're just like Teddy Bears," Sally Doyle quipped. Then one of the bears did the goofiest thing. He went over to a metal bath, full of drinking water, and plopped himself down in it; he hung his arms and legs over the side. It looked ridiculous and any remaining fear dissipated in that instant. We all found ourselves drawn to empathetic giggles with Sally Doyle - even Miss Devonport could not stop laughing. Her temporary pleasant tone had completely disappeared again, as her laugh turned out to be more irritating than her normal voice. It occurred to me that it was a good job that the bears did not have opposable thumbs because they would surely have been lobbing bear shit in no time!

The rest of the day went without a hitch, until five minutes before we were supposed to meet the coach. Miss Devonport left our group on the car park where we were about to meet the others, whilst she went off to the toilets to check on the status of her monkey-poo. Unfortunately, for no imaginable reason, I suddenly walked through a ten-foot turnstile and found myself outside the zoo. There was an equally high fence, topped with barbed wire, designed to keep intruders out. So, there I was, five minutes away from my class' departure time, stuck the wrong side of the fence. Michael Johnson could find no humorous words to lighten my predicament. Sally Doyle started crying and Ian McKay tried to comfort her, provoking a new emotion in me – jealousy. This must have triggered the superhero in me because, without further thought, I scaled the huge turnstile and found myself balancing on top of the barbed wire. Then, with the grace of a gazelle, I launched myself into the air. My landing was far from graceful, as my legs buckled and I took several rolls. However, the manoeuvre solved both my problems. Not only was I returned to the confines of the zoo but I also found Sally Doyle helping me to my feet. Ian McKay's unexpected advances had been foiled.

The trip back started with lots of singing. Michael led a few choruses of old army songs that his dad had taught him.

"There were beans, beans as big as submarines, in the stores, in the stores." he sang, and then we all joined in the chorus:

"My eyes are dim I cannot see, I have not brought my specks with me, I have not brought my specs with me!"

"Miss Forsythe," complained 'pain-in-the-arse' Michael Johnson, they're singing about my glasses.

"It's not Miss it's……….." Mrs Forsythe cast a glance over at her friend and the stopped herself, "Michael, it's not your specs they're singing about, silly boy!"

"Mrs Forsythe's right. Michael, it's an old army song," added Miss Devonport. The two friends smiled at each other.

We started to make up some verses of our own. My favourite was:

There were eggs, eggs with little hairy legs in the stores, in the stores.

Then there was a lull in the singing and suddenly everyone was asleep. It was five o'clock when we arrived back at school and nearer to six by the time I had completed the long walk home.

Chapter 18: Funny Men.

Tea leaves have a unique odour that always reminds me of collectible cards, that Brook Bond's 'PG Tips' used to include in their quarter pound packs. It took me two months to persuade mum to change from her favoured Typhoo tea, which also happened to be a halfpenny cheaper.

The card series of the day celebrated fifty different native birds of the British Isles. In addition to a picture of the bird, each card had a load of information about habitat and nesting habits. Certain cards were ubiquitous and my peers would gladly give away spare Reed Warblers, Blackbirds and Mistell Thrushes. Others, like the Kestrel and Curlew were so rare that many doubted whether they existed at all. I became absorbed, if not obsessed, with bird facts and quoted them daily, hoping that my parents would see the educational value of the more expensive tea.

"Oh look, there's a Turdis turdis negra," I announced, when I noticed the singing blackbird in the back garden. Unfortunately, the only one paying any attention to my comment was Doodle.

Andrew joined the conversation, "I wonder why PG Tips doesn't have any blue tits?" It was an endless source of amusement that we could say 'tits,' when referring to the bird but not at any other time.

"I don't know. Card forty-seven has Great Tits," I told him, unable to resist the opportunity to play the 'tit' card.

"Stop it, boys," snapped mum.

"It's a kind of bird, mum," Andrew and I responded, as one voice.

She reiterated, "I said, 'Stop!'"

However, dad was obviously enjoying her embarrassment because he chipped in, "I'd like to see card forty-seven." I pulled out the card for him and he made a point of reading it out loud.

"Great Tits have olive upper parts and yellowish under parts," he read, adding, "You can't argue with that!"

Andrew laughed.

"What are you tittering about boy?" dad added with his overly-blatant reference.

"Peter, stop encouraging them," mum insisted, desperately trying to quell his inappropriateness.

However, dad was on a roll. "Hey listen to this Beryl, *'They have two prominent white cheeks!'* Great tits, big white cheeks; sounds like Diana Dawes."

"Daa...aaa...ad!" we all said, knowing he had overstepped the line of decency.

Then I had a lightning brainwave. "Diana Jackdaws," I added, keeping the bird reference alive. According to card eighteen, the words Jackdaw and Magpie were synonymous.

Everyone laughed at my pun, inspiring Andrew to come up with another play on words.

"Marilyn Mun-crow," he quipped

"What's the other name for the blackbird, son?" he asked me.

"Turdis negra," I told him, handing him the blackbird card.

"Hey look, Beryl, there's a little turdis flying through the air," he joked.

Then she gave him, one of her 'That's enough!' looks, which curtailed any further comments. However, this very moment, Doodle chose to jump in through the open window, with the aforementioned Blackbird, half-dead but still flapping, in his mouth. Talk about coincidence.

"Thanks Doodle," I thought to myself, *"I'll never get any tea cards now!"*

However, when mum returned from the Co-op the following day, there were two packets of Brooke Bond PG Tips, which she gave me the privilege of emptying into the tea caddie. There was something thrilling about getting my own cards, even though there was only a Kingfisher and Reed Warbler, both of which I already possessed. Still, they could always be used as swaps. Indeed, on the way home the next day, I managed to exchange them with Kevin Simkins, for a Sparrow Hawk and a Common House Sparrow. Funnily enough, the latter was often preyed upon by the former - hence its name.

Simkins lived down Bognor Drive, so we went our separate ways when we reached the top of his road. When I turned into the northern loop of Bladon Circle, I had noticed that an older man was following me close behind. Since I was on my own, I felt slightly perturbed when I realized that he was tracking me. Mum had drilled me and Andrew repeatedly about not talking to strangers, and Mrs Forsythe had also stressed the point. The golden rule was to never get in a car with a stranger, or accept sweets off them. I would certainly never have done that. I startled when he spoke to me from behind.

"You collect those tea cards, do you?" came his voice. I turned around and was surprised to discover that he was actually older than I had first perceived. He had a pink face, probably from playing catch up, and his teeth were yellowish and crooked.

"Yes," I reluctantly answered, in response to his question about cards. My heart was pounding but I reasoned that my house was only around the corner and, if I could out-run 'doorknob Ken,' I could certainly leave this old guy in my dust.

"I've got a whole biscuit tin full of those cards, if you're interested," he told me. His stained teeth certainly gave testimony to years of tea-drinking. Now I had a dilemma because there was nothing I wanted more in life than a biscuit tin full of tea cards. On the other hand, this could definitely be one of those 'funny men' that everybody warned us children about.

"Mmm," I responded, thinking an ambiguous answer would be the least offensive. I resisted the 'Scream loudly and run-like-the-wind' pledge, that I had made to my parents.

"Good," he said, "I live just down here."

I followed timidly behind him, as he literally led me down his garden path, to the backdoor, which was on the side of his house. His home had an identical layout to that of the Butchers; I half-expected a waft of poo and cabbage to hit me when he opened his backdoor.

Being mid-July, there were still hours of light remaining. All the same, the old man's house seemed really secluded. It was up a blind corner of Bladon Circle and his high privet hedge added an extra level of vulnerability. Ironically, it was the only door in the block that I had never knocked upon when playing rosy apples. I had always assessed the getaway to be too unpredictable. So, I was now here, calculating my escape for the first time, when the front gate creaked and then clunked shut in a sinister fashion.

"Bugger," I whispered to myself, trembling on his backdoor step.

"Don't just stand there, come in," he shouted, as old people do.

"I'm okay," I replied.

"Do you like cake?" he yelled. It sounded like a trick question. I mean a full-fledged, Hansel and Gretel, put-your-head-in-this-oven-to-see-if-its-hot-enough trap! He was undoubtedly going to kidnap me and do to me whatever it was that 'funny men' did to little boys. He came out of his kitchen and crossed the outhouse, arms out-stretched and a biscuit tin leading the way. For a second, I thought that it might be the tea cards but there was a vanilla slice and a chocolate éclair; my two favourite types of cake. Part of me knew that I should be sprinting down the street; cakes were practically sweets – the legendary lure of all 'funny men.' Instinct told me to run but greed held the stronger hand over fear, keeping me rooted to his backdoor step. I reached into the tin for the éclair but I had procrastinated too long. He was already pulling it out of reach and backing toward his kitchen.

"You'll need a plate, come in and eat your cake whilst I find you those tea cards" he insisted. As well as his face and tooth colour, I noticed that his lips were blood red.

"I'm supposed to go straight home," I told him, as I crossed his outhouse and stood in his kitchen doorway. I was determined to not let him block my exit. He dragged a stool over to his pantry.

"I say, hold this steady for me while I stand on it," he insisted, "I think the cards are on the top shelf." As he climbed, he supported himself by placing his bony right hand on my shoulder. It felt a bit creepy but I stood perfectly still, too petrified to move. I was almost in that place in my head where I no longer cared what happened to me. He squeezed a little harder and lowered himself back down to the ground. Amazingly, he was clutching a biscuit tin, choc-a-block full of tea cards.

"Here, you can have them all but I'd like the tin back, if you don't mind," he told me, thrusting it into my hand.

"Th-th-thanks mister," I stammered, pushing past him in his kitchen doorway. A split second later, I was fumbling with the latch of his creaky gate. I was almost safe, when at the last second I felt his skeletal hand on my shoulder again. Andrew had always said, "Kick 'em in the bollocks and run!'

I turned around with the intention of firing a Clark's Double E into his goolies, only to have him say, "Don't forget your cake!" I grabbed the éclair from the plate and took off post haste, clutching my freshly acquired treasure trove.

"Wow, where'd you get them from?" asked Andrew.

"Simkins' grandad has been saving them for me," I lied.

"Lucky bugger!" he added. He had no idea just how lucky I had been. Nor did he know how irresponsible I had been, taking such a foolish chance for some tea cards. This was yet another secret, for Whiskey's ears only. On the other hand, this was a serious haul. There were Curlews and Kestrels galore. There were also complete sets of other tea cards that I had never even heard about: Flags of the World; Prime Ministers of England; Famous Stately Homes; Trees of Great Britain; Vintage Cars and my new favourite - Unusual Animals around the Globe. In hindsight, he might have simply been a nice old man, who innocently wanted to do a random act of kindness. All the same, one thing of which I was certain was that I would not be returning his biscuit tin in a hurry. In fact, I vowed that I would not be going back there ever again!

Chapter 19: The Weetabix Tale

Weetabix used to have a saliva-eliciting bouquet, until Andrew told me about an unfortunate incident. The first day of the six week's holidays had finally arrived and we were up at the crack of dawn, determined to savor every minute of the summer school break. As every Monday morning, mum was already pegging out her first batch of washing. She did not have the same enthusiasm for our holidays as we did. I had just poured milk on my Weetabix and was reaching for the sugar, when Andrew chose to relate the story.

"A boy was putting milk on his Weetabix, just like you are right now," he explained, "when the milk started to curdle and turn red." I looked down at my own bowl of food for a similar reaction. The green custard incident, back in March, flashed through my mind and I thought that the solution to this unfolding riddle might be similar.

"What was it?" I asked. He was obviously at not at the stage of the story where he could reveal the answer. Sometimes Andrew had a real flare for the melodramatic. I sprinkled my usual conservative covering of sugar over the two cereal bricks.

"He had a sweet tooth, rather like you," Andrew added. It was a trait I could hardly deny. I was building a definite empathy with this boy.

"What made the milk curdle? I bet he used bicarbonate of soda rather than sugar," I guessed.

"You think?" Andrew tantalized. "As I said, the boy had a sweet tooth, so he covered the Weetabix with a thick coating of mystery crystalline powder."

"I knew it!" I replied, excited that I might have solved the mystery. "It's bicarbonate of soda. Did he taste it?"

"Oh yes, the boy took a mouthful of Weetabix but it didn't taste like bicarbonate of soda," he announced, obviously ready for the punch line.

"What was it?" I had to know.

"Well," Andrew dragged out the answer, "when the boy realized that it tasted nasty, I mean really nasty, he scraped the sugar off his Weetabix and what do you think he found?"

"What?" I begged with wide open eyes.

"Compressed into the Weetabix was the body of a dead rat!"

"Urg...rhh!" I groaned, slamming down my spoon.

"Urg...rhh!" mimicked Eric; he loved to copy me.

"Okay boys, finish your breakfast and off you go, out to play," she insisted. There was no way that she wanted us adding to the annoyance of her Monday routine.

Andrew polished off his Cornflakes, and Eric enjoyed his Farley's Rusk. However, the rat story had totally destroyed my appetite. I tried to leave the table and, nine times out of ten, mum would not have turned a hair at me abandoning my breakfast. However, she was already in a bad mood; mum seemed to get a dark malaise every few weeks and I sensed that another one was about to start. The skies were darkening and rain would destroy her drying regime and make it so we could not play outside.

"Eat your Weetabix, Martin," commanded mum.

"I don't want it" I foolishly replied.

"Well, you'll eat it anyway. I'm not going to put up with your awkward ways - not this holiday," she insisted. There was something about the word 'awkward' that triggered an uncontrollable antagonistic response in me.

"I don't want it!" I asserted.

"Eat it!" said the demon voice of her past. I looked down at the food and all I could see in my mind was crushed rat. I almost threw up and I could not even pick up the spoon.

"It's too soggy!" I insisted.

"It'll soon be soggy inside your stomach! Now eat it, you, awkward little boy!" mum's psycho voice insisted.

"No," I refused, welling up in anticipation of the inevitable slap. I knew that some form of violence had to occur before mum's temper would be satiated. I had seen the pattern so many times.

"I'll pour it on your bloody head if you don't eat it!" she yelled. I shrugged, at a loss for words, mentally striving for my 'fortress of solitude,' and the next thing I knew, the contents of the dish had been turned over on my head.

Now, this was when my *awkward streak* kicked in because, just as with the nosebleed session back in February, I did not rush to clean up the damage. Instead,

I sat crying with two dripping Weetabix balanced on my head, as milk and sugar dribbled down my neck. The drama was over and now I held the power. Mum went about her washing chores for a while but I sensed that some remorse was setting in.

After what seemed like half-an-hour she eventually said, "Come here silly," and wiped the Weetabix off my head. Andrew, who had scampered out of the kitchen at the start of the episode, returned sheepishly. He knew that his rat story had inadvertently triggered the whole incident. He was also aware that the actual cause of the flash-point was irrelevant; if it was not uneaten Weetabix, it would have been something else. We also sensed that, having 'blown out,' mum was probably in a post-crisis lull. However, because it was morning, there was no great race to' patch things up before sleep time, so mum did not make the normal apology.

By the time that she was retelling the epic Weetabix-on-the-head story to Ted and Bertha it was a very different scenario.

"Martin's always been finicky about his food," she told everyone.

"He won't eat meat, at all!" added dad.

"Isn't that dangerous, Beryl?" asked Bertha.

"Well he still eats cheese and eggs and Weetabix," she added, segueing back to her story.

"Weetabix?" queried Bertha, anticipating an epic story. Ted's ears picked up, too. Mum had the stage.

"Yes, the other day, his majesty here decided he was too good for Weetabix," she misrepresented.

"Too good for Weetabix?" echoed Ted, as though he was agreeing with mum but then he turned and winked at me as though he was mocking her.

"Oh yes, he gets in those awkward moods," commented mum.

"Don't they all?" agreed Bertha, rolling her eyes toward her own son, Robert.

"Anyway, his Royal Highness decided that his Weetabix was too soggy," she told them. I was beginning to feel highly uncomfortable with this conversation because, not only was it misrepresenting the true facts, it was painting me in an even worse light than I had originally been.

"Not, too soggy?" added Ted again winking empathetically. "So, what did you say, Bet?"

"Tell him what I said I'd do, Martin," she said, adding, "Its okay, we laughed about it afterwards."

"She said she'd 'put it on my bloody head if I didn't eat it!'" I quoted.

"I didn't swear," she lied. "Tell him what I did next."

"She put it on my bloody head," I explained.

"Ha. You put soggy Weetabix on his head?" clarified Ted.

"What happened then?" asked Bertha, thinking there must be a punch line, because what she had heard was not really that funny.

"We had a good laugh about it!" mum told them. I had no memory of any laughter. I looked over at Andrew, to check if this was his recollection of events. He shrugged, to confirm that reality was truly being distorted. This was more distressing than the initial event. To mum's disappointment, the story did not receive the raucous response that she expected. All the same, I felt slighted. It was unforgivable that she had tried to exploit an experience that was so painful, just to get a cheap laugh. That was the moment when my *awkward streak* kicked in.

"There was a crushed dead rat in the Weetabix," I mumbled, just loud enough to be heard. Now it was silent. "I put milk on it and red blood started oozing into the milk."

"Blood?" asked Ted, looking shocked at mum.

"Yes, and the rat's bones were sticking out through the fur and mum said I had to eat it!" I embroidered. I was entirely deadpan in my delivery and I was convincing. Obviously, it was not a story that anyone would just make up.

"Damn, I'm never eating Weetabix again!" laughed Ted nervously. "Kids today have strange imaginations."

"He's making it all up," blushed mum, no longer seeing the hilarity of the situation. I could see her reliving the whole event in her mind. Perhaps she had been so caught up in her own 'power trip' that she had failed to notice a mangled rodent in the Weetabix?

"That's quite a story, Beryl," Bertha commented, implying that it sounded too authentic to have been imagined.

"Oh, he's in a world of his own sometimes," explained mum, now sounding extremely defensive. "You should see him and his friend Barry, playing with the Teddy bear and Panda. They go into a complete fantasy world. Peter will tell you that, won't you, Pete?" Each extra word made her sound guiltier and, if ever she needed dad's support, it was now. Unfortunately, dad was showing a few doubts, himself. My acting had been very convincing.

"Maybe, the rat was crushed by the threshing machine," said dad, missing the opportunity to show some unity with his wife.

"There was no rat, Peter. What the hell do you think I am?" mum reiterated. Now, it really did go quiet.

"Yeah, I'm having trouble swallowing that one," added Ted.

"So was I!" I smiled, finally revealing that it was a fabrication - much to the relief of everyone. Everybody laughed hysterically, except mum.

"Brilliant!" said Ted. The kid had me going for a minute.

"Me, too!" admitted dad, who was particularly relieved, secretly knowing the true perversity of mum's dark side. Mum was, of course, deeply offended that her friends could consider that she would be capable of such a despicable act. It seems that, on this occasion, I really was 'awkward,' after all!

Chapter 20: Stevensons

I was not sure whether it was the dog food or their old dog, Loxley which gave such an unfortunate tang to the Stevenson's house. The Stevenson family lived just up the road, on the bend, and mum and dad treated them with a certain reverence. Whilst we had a shed, they had a garage! What was more, they had a car to put in it! Dad seemed oblivious to the dank dog smell that attacked your throat, as soon as you entered their backdoor.

"That Jack Stevenson is a real gentleman," mum would often observe. The man's name was actually John, but he allowed my parents to call him Jack. It was the same with President Kennedy, in America.

"They're a classy family," confirmed dad. He would often draw parallels between our families, suggesting that we and the Stevenson family were only temporary residents of the council estate. We really did not belong there and were destined to own our own houses one day.

Both their children were eccentric. Christopher, who was Andrew's age, was a 'mad scientist' - always making explosives from everyday items, such as weed-killer and sugar. On the other hand, his younger sister, Judith was an actress. All through the summer she would put on street theatre and we were drafted in, as last minute audiences, to watch their improvised pantomimes. They had a box of dress up clothes, including authentic Chinese garb. Therefore, Aladdin usually entered the *avant garde* shows, somewhere along the line.

The garage door opened to reveal a backdrop of Japanese temples and Jane Dawson appeared, dressed in a Kimono, which dragged along the floor behind her.

"Oh, where is my lost love, Aladdin?" Jane's character over-projected.

"I'm here, Nancy Poo," announced Christopher, wearing a lampshade, as he entered from the side. We all laughed at her name.

"Nancy Poo," Eric mimicked, and everybody laughed again.

"Oh, my darling," Jane Dawson declared, already straying 'off script.' She proceeded to place her hands on both of Christopher's cheeks and kiss him full on the lips. I was familiar with this manoeuvre and I began to salivate involuntarily. Tony Boswell wolf-whistled, Christopher desperately tried to wrestle free. I could have warned him that resistance was hopeless and soon her tongue was exploring his mouth.

"At least it's not riddled with German Measles," I thought to myself.

"Bloody Hell," exclaimed Jimmy Drinkwater.

Eventually, Aladdin broke free but not before losing his lampshade hat. He pulled out a papier-mâché magic lamp, which had obviously taken an inordinate

189

amount of time to make, and placed it on the ground. Then he struck a match and dropped it into the top of the lamp.

"Poof!" a flame and cloud of smoke leaped three feet in the air. The audience marvelled and gasped. Judith emerged from behind the backdrop, as the Genie of the lamp.

"Master, your wish is my command," announced Judith's character, who was wearing a heavy coating of make-up and lipstick, a magnificent turquoise silk dress and red high heeled shoes.

"What can I wish for, oh Genie?" Aladdin asked.

"Alas, I cannot advise you but to say choose your wishes wisely, for they cannot be undone," replied the Genie.

Aladdin turned to the audience. It was participation time and we were being prompted to heckle.

"What shall I wish for?" Aladdin asked.

"Another kiss from Nancy Poo!" yelled Jimmy. Christopher visibly shivered as Jane licked her lips.

"Nancy Poo," shouted Eric, still tickled by the name.

"I know, I wish that Presidents Kennedy and Khrushchev will join for world peace," declared Aladdin. I think that their dad must have helped with the script because it sounded like an awfully grown up wish.

"It is done, master!" granted the genie, much to the disappointment to the puckering Nancy Poo.

"Hurray," we cheered, like a good audience, but we really hoped that the next two wishes were more tangible.

"Liquorices for everyone," was Aladdin's second wish.

"That's more like it!" I thought, as the genie produced a plate of liquorice sticks and proceeded to distribute it throughout the audience.

"You have one wish left," announced Judith Stevenson to her brother.

"What do you think people?" asked Aladdin.

"Kiss Nancy Poo!" yelled Jimmy, strangely obsessed.

"Who's your favourite group?" asked the genie.

"The Beatles!" we all screamed. This was the cue for the record player to kick in:

"Last Night I said these words to my girl. You know you never even tried girl," sang John and Paul.

The cast started dancing and then they moved into the audience, grabbing our hands and encouraging us to join in. Andrew, Tom and I were too shy but Barry jumped up straight away. Then Jimmy started his unique style of rhythmic pacing, making a beeline for Jane Dawson. He had heard about the tongue and witnessing it with his own eyes had stirred something within Jimmy.

"Come on, come on," sang John Lennon,

"Come on, come on," sang Jimmy to Jane.

"Please, please me, oh yea, like I please you" harmonized John, Paul and Jimmy, as the latter moved in for a kiss.

"Urgh!" said Jane, obviously repulsed by Jimmy's advances. Apparently, even Jane 'the tongue' Dawson had some standards and poor Jimmy Drinkwater was below them.

All the same, it was a fine show and, just like my parents, I was now a Stevenson fan. So, the next week, when they asked if we could look after Loxley, whilst they went on holiday to Great Yarmouth, we were more than willing. They gave Andrew the key and asked if he would take Loxley for morning and evening walks, I simply tagged along; they also wanted my brother to feed the dog each night. Loxley seemed content to just sit around in his kitchen basket, in his own fumes. Andrew said that the smell was from Loxley trumping and I was amazed to think that animals could do that. Doodle and Whiskey certainly never farted!

The first three days went well. However, on our way back from the Stevenson house on the forth evening, there was an unfortunate accident. I was swinging their key on its string, around my finger, when it slipped off. This was not the first time that this had happened and mum had even warned me that I would 'lose it.' I fully expected the key to tinkle on the ground, as usual. However, in a fate-riddled moment, time seemed to slow down as the key took an elliptical arc, straight down a grid.

"Oh, my God, you stupid, stupid bugger!" shouted Andrew. It was not just the key that had entered the sewers, it was his reputation. He had been entrusted to take care of the Stevensons' dog, and now he had betrayed that trust, by letting his idiot brother throw the key down the grid. All we would be able to do is watch their farting old dog through their kitchen window, peeing and pooing, whilst it simultaneously starved.

"Martin's dropped the key down the grid!" Andrew told mum. Then he started crying, which was quite a rare sight, as the full impact of the lost key dawned on him. The Stevensons would not be happy when they returned home to find their dead dog lying in a pile of shit and piss!

"Martin's done what?" asked mum. "Which key?"

"Stevensons' key!" he blurted.

192

"Oh, my God," mum said, "your dad's going to be so embarrassed!" She had added another layer of guilt. Dad could hardly claim parity with Jack Stevenson, if we weren't even fit to feed his dog!

"Which grid?" she asked which seemed somewhat superfluous.

"The one by Sparky Ears'" I explained. The next thing mum was shining a torch into the deep dark drainage grid. The grid was slightly bigger than a foot square and it seemed a fruitless exercise. However, just as mum was about to declare the key "gone forever" and undoubtedly exact unyielding wrath upon me, Andrew spotted something shiny on an inch-wide ledge, about two feet down the drain. The odds of the key falling down the grid were remote, in the first place, but to land and stick to this tiny ledge had to be considered a miracle.

"Don't touch anything!" mum insisted. She went into the house and returned a few minutes later with thin metal scraper which we usually used for scooping ashes from the hearth. I was put in charge of the torch.

"Shine the light on the key," mum must have repeated seven times. It was harder than getting the 'doggy in the kennel,' because, however I held it a shadow was always cast upon the area where the key was situated. "Give the flashlight to your brother," mum eventually told me. It was a duty I was glad to pass on. After several attempts, mum finally managed to hook the string onto the hearth cleaner and she carefully maneuvered the device back out through the spaces in the grid. Things were going well until the tension in the string caused the key to slide off the ledge, which in turn slid the string off the scraper. I gasped, as it seemed that all was lost but Andrew, driven by his reputation, lunged toward the string and emerged with it hooked on the very tip of his index finger. In one movement, he discarded the torch and grabbed the string with his other hand. Andrew had the key. It was a miracle to match anything Jesus had done.

"Somebody's looking down on you today," mum told me. We were so engrossed in the whole incident that we had not really noticed that some on-lookers had appeared.

"Seen enough, Mrs Johnson?" mum confronted our neighbour.

"What have you got there?" Sparky Ears asked, overcome by curiosity.

"It's the key to your chastity belt, Reg threw it down there!" mum told her, adding, "Mind your own business, bloody busy body!" This seemed to effectively disperse the gathering, as well as absorb the anger, that I was fully anticipating.

"It truly is a miracle," I told myself.

Chapter 21: The 50 Kilometre Walk.

Nana Lena only wore the latest, most expensive, Estee Lauder perfumes. The overpriced fragrance triggered mixed emotions. People as poor as us should not move in circles where we encountered such rich aromatic delights. On the other hand, the smell became intrinsically linked with all the trepidations that we associated with a visit from Nana Lena. Mum would have to interrupt her full schedule to scrub and clean every inch of the house, only to have her mother-in-law demonstratively stroke a white-gloved finger across a surface and examine it for dirt. Whether she saw dirt or not was hardly the point, it was the gesture that did the damage.

All my friends had nice Grandmas, who used to buy them Easter eggs and baby-sit. Our Grandma made us call her Aunty Lena until little Eric was born. Her second husband, Grandpa Eric, who my little brother was named after, owned a Pottery firm and he was rich - filthy sinking rich! According to information, that I had eavesdropped from mum's Babycham-enhanced talk with Kate Dawson, Nana Lena had to convert to Catholic before Grandpa Eric's mum would allow her to even marry him. From what I overheard, there was talk of disinheriting Eric if he married a Protestant but love had forced him to call his parent's bluff. It seemed that he really loved her but it was hard to see what she had to offer. He had a thin moustache and was the spitting image of a film star called Clark Gable.

Occasionally, on a Sunday afternoon, when they were returning from church, Grandpa Eric and Nana Lena would pull up outside our house in their Rolls Royce Silver Cloud. There were only a few vehicles that ever came up our road; Jack Stevenson's Ford Anglia; David Foot's three-wheeler Reliant; Paul Freedman's dad's petrol tanker; Mr. Walker's motorbike with side-car; a couple of traveling shops; three ice-cream vans; the milkman; the postman; the coalman and the odd rag-and-bone man would be the sum-total of a typical summer's day. So, when a car, fit for the Queen of England, arrived, the streets were suddenly lined with Nosey Parkers. I enjoyed the attention, personally, but I could see how mum detested it and dad seemed more embarrassed than proud. One time, they decided to take Andrew, me and toddler Eric on a ride around the block in the Rolls Royce and we called at Nadin's shop for some lemon sherbet dips and brand new American comics.

"Here we are, riding in a stranger's car and accepting sweets off them," my awkward streak observed. Unfortunately, little Eric sneezed some powdered sherbet

across the back of Lena's seat and some went in her hair. Mum and dad got us back sooner than anticipated and the next time the 'royalty' turned up in their Sunbeam Rapier, which caused far less of a stir.

There was nothing that illustrated the bridge between poverty and affluence, more than the day mum entered a women's 50-kilometre walking race. Apparently, President Kennedy, in America, had started a fitness fad, challenging people to walk 50 miles in a day. Kennedy's own brother had taken up the challenge and completed the task and the whole country was following suit. Mum's race organizers had diluted the distance to kilometres but it was still a hefty thirty-four miles. The first prize was to be two hundred pounds, just for walking from Trentham Gardens to Leek and back, taking a detour around the six towns of Stoke-on-Trent and Rudyard Lake. Many women were semi-professional and had been training for months for the event. Mum, on the other hand, entered on a whim. It was a big event and the Evening Sentinel published the walkers in the same format as the Grand National. It also explained the difference between walking and running. Apparently, there were strict rules about having to put the heel down first and always keeping one foot on the ground, all the time.

Grandpa Eric, who was quite nice if you ignored the cigar stench, saw mum's name in the paper and persuaded Nana Lena to lend some backing to mum's brave cause. Lena agreed, so long as they could have a splendid picnic. The conversations that I heard left no doubt that mum did not care for their support. However, she was in no position to decline.

At six o'clock, on a Saturday morning in August, Grandpa Eric dropped mum at the starting point in

Trentham. The plan was to meet up with mum at various points around the course, plying her with sustenance.

It was ten o'clock by the time Lena was ready and the Rolls turned up in Bladon Circle. We had already missed the first two planned rendezvous sites but at least Lena had her fancy picnic set and Champagne-on-ice. Mum was still with the leading packing when we caught up with her on Bentilee stretch. Dad leaped out of the car and walked alongside her for a few minutes, feeding her tea from a thermos flask, and French pastries, which had apparently been 'highly sought-after' at Nana Lena's last 'soirée.'

"*What a snob!*" I thought to myself. The cakes were okay but were certainly no chocolate éclairs or vanilla slices. We were supposed to track mum down again at lunchtime, on the Leek Road but Lena was peckish by that time, so she decided that we would lay down a blanket in a field and start our picnic.

Grandpa Eric, Nana Lena and dad poured themselves some Moet-Chandon champagne, which she repeatedly assured us, was the 'best you can get!' Then, to apparently make it even better, she topped it up with copious amounts of a drink called Cognac. Soon all three adults were acting goofy and more pompous than ever.

"You're a good boy, Peter," Nana Lena gushed, "and a fine father to these three boys."

"It's not easy sometimes, mum," dad confessed, holding out his glass for a refill.

"To Peter and his magnificent sons," toasted Grandpa Eric, raising his champagne flume.

"Here's to Peter!" Lena reciprocated, already beginning to slur her words. A champagne rush forced a visible cogitation. "Beryl doesn't know how lucky she was, the way you stood by her, son." I thought that she

198

was talking about the fact that he walked beside her for a few minutes during the race. It occurred to me that dad's part was trivial, albeit Bentilee, compared to the sacrifice mum was making.

"I'm not one to run away from my mistakes, mum," dad announced proudly.

"I'm going to have to say it, son," insisted Lena. Causing a grimace on dad's and Grandpa's faces, imploring her to not 'say it.'

"Mum, let it drop, its water under the bridge," said dad.

"That trollop trapped you!" insisted Lena, completing her thought. "I'm sorry but there, I've said it!"

"Yes, we're all sorry, dear," said Grandpa Eric, in a tone identical to the one dad frequently employed, to demonstrate contempt. Grandpa Eric was the only one to notice that we children were listening to every word. He quickly changed the subject. "Have you boys ever tasted Black Forest Gateau?"

"No!" we said together, as keen as Grandpa Eric, to avoid Nana Lena from saying anything else. Whilst we had no clue what she was talking about, it was obvious that the conversation was embarrassing dad. It was obviously the Champagne/Cognac cocktail that was inspiring Nana Lena to speak her true conscience. Grandpa Eric pulled out a massive chocolate, fresh cream and black cherry cake and a special silver device for cutting and serving it. I had never known such decadence. It truly was the most splendid of cakes and we all had two massive slices. Little Eric got more on his face than in his mouth and then he had to suffer the old handkerchief-and-spit face wash. Andrew and I quickly went to climb a nearby tree before the saliva-moistened hankie became our fate.

"What's a trollop?" I immediately asked him.

"I think she was talking about mum," Andrew explained. I could see that the conversation had troubled him even more than it bothered me. Andrew had a special bond with mum, being her first-born, and he did not like hearing her being insulted.

"Well how did mum trap dad?" I asked.

"Don't know, don't care!" he blurted at me, obviously caring a great deal. Apparently, question-time had just ended. It was a huge tree and we climbed really high up before we stopped. It was neat because we could spy, Jimmy Drinkwater-style, on the unsuspecting scene below. They got louder for a while and then silent. All three adults, and my little brother, were sound asleep on the blanket.

It was another hour before dad finally stirred. He looked disorientated and panicked.

"Mum, Eric....err...sir," dad floundered, struggling to find the appropriate way to address his stepfather, "we are supposed to have met Beryl!"

"Bloody Hell!" exclaimed Eric senior.

"Bloody Hell!" echoed Eric junior. It took us a few minutes to rush all the picnic gear into the enormous boot of the Rolls Royce and then we headed off toward the Rudyard Lake meeting point. Amazingly, four women in front of mum had dropped out and she was in third position. What is more, the lady in second place was flagging. You could see that mum was pleased to see the plate of red salmon sandwiches and Black Forest gateaux. On the other hand, it was apparent that she disapproved of our fun day.

"I'm flogging myself to death whilst you're 'Hooray Henrying' around the countryside," we heard her saying to dad, when Nana Lena rolled down the window.

Dad seemed to be trying to appease her about something when she became all sarcastic and said, "I don't know, Peter! Why would I be upset?" Dad got back in the car, looking a little huffy. Nana Lena consoled him with a shrug and tut, as if to say, *"There's no pleasing some people."*

"She does know its red salmon, does she?" Lena asked.

"I doubt it," dad replied, milking his mother's sympathy.

"It's red salmon, Beryl!" Lena yelled through the car window, for all to hear. Mum was obviously ravenous because she had been attacking the sandwich with relish. However, when her mother-in-law shouted this, from the comfort of our luxury ride, mum turned almost as red as the salmon and the sandwich came flying in through the open window. My first thought was that it had been a freak accident. *"Perhaps her hands were sweaty and she had lost her grip."* However, when a big slab of Black Forest Gateaux splattered onto the windshield there was no more denial of intent. The resultant surge of adrenaline saw mum accelerate and the crowd lining the roadside began to cheer. Whether their approval was for her food rejection, mother-in-law admonishment, or her actual spurt, was hard to determine.

"Take me home, now!" ordered Lena. Surely, an hour earlier she would have giggled hopelessly but the next phase of the alcohol had kicked in. Grandpa Eric pulled the car off into a country lane.

"You embarrassed her dear," reasoned Grandpa Eric, as he activated his windshield wiper.

"Nonsense, she just doesn't appreciate class," insisted Nana Lena. Now, even I was becoming offended at the negative talk about my mother.

Grandpa Eric looked over at our confused faces and brought the argument to an instantaneously impressive end by saying, "Beryl is one of the classiest people I know and she has entered this race purely to help her family. You need to respect that!" Nana Lena was silenced. The quiet triggered little Eric to start crying but his namesake calmly said, "There, there," and he stopped.

Meanwhile, mum's heightened pace was closing the gap on the second-placed walker. She was ex-WRAF and expected by many to win. The sensation of mum in her rear radar caused her to quicken which, in turn started to dramatically close the gap on the lady in poll position. This would have made a thrilling climax to any race. Unfortunately, there was still thirteen miles to go.

Although we were parked in a side country lane during this stretch of the race, a BBC new team happened to have set up camera, at this stage and the full drama was later broadcast on the television. I am sure that mum was cursing Mr. Bukowski, because our television clearly showed the end of mum's race on Monday evening's six o'clock news:

Firstly, the WRAF woman tried to block mum's way, as she made a move to overtake. Whilst this was within the rules, it did not appear to be sporting. It went entirely against the grain of camaraderie that President Kennedy was trying to harness in his own country.

"Get out of the way, stupid cow!" is what mum mouthed, if my lip-reading skills were accurate. Her 'angry face' filled the whole screen which I found rather disconcerting. Luckily, the commentator's voice was the only sound track.

"Now, now, ladies it's only a race," the announcer patronized. I could see how it might have been funny if it was not your mum being mocked, and she did not happen to be sitting on the settee next to you during the report. The WRAF lady, who walked more like a middle-aged man, zigzagged repeatedly blocking mum off. However, mum was tenacious and a double-bluffing manoeuvre suddenly saw her level. The commentator was becoming excited at this point, especially as the pair was encroaching on the lead position. The stubborn nature of both women made for excellent TV footage.

"And the younger filly's coming up on the rails," the commentator reported.

"Well, at least he said you're the younger one, dear," said dad, trying to soften the blow but failing miserably.

Unfortunately, they became over-competitive and the WRAF lady broke into a trot. Mum followed suit. Next, they were sprinting and then it seemed to dawn on them simultaneously that they had just disqualified themselves. Blaming each other they began to wrestle, which weirdly turned into an empathetic hug. Finally, they both sat down on the ground panting and sobbing.

"Oh, they've both gone lame," the insensitive voice quipped, determined to perpetuate his horse race analogy, "let's hope we don't have to have them put down." Mum forced a smile for our benefit but it was certainly a humiliation that she could have done without.

At the actual time of the event, mum ended up sitting by the roadside for another half-an-hour before we found her and picked her up. She was red from sunburn and her twisted feet were swollen and blistered. I expected her to be mad but she was totally emotionless.

Eventually, Grandpa Eric broke the silence and said, "You were spectacular, Beryl. You should be proud." Mum smiled and opened her mouth to speak but the words turned into a snore. Mum was fast asleep. Her ordeal was over as far as she knew. Of course, she was not yet aware that, through the wonders of modern technology, she would have to relive it two days later, along with the rest of the country.

Chapter 22: The love letter.

The reek of lavender perfume etched itself onto my long-term memory banks the day a letter landed on our hallway doormat. It was addressed to me. Discounting the annual birthday cards from Nana Lena and Auntie Evelyn, in my whole life I had received three pieces of correspondence: Firstly, my Butlin's Beaver Club card, earned from our summer vacation of 1961. Secondly, my Supercar Club Secret Agent badge, along with cryptic number. And now, a strongly scented letter loaded with amorous tell-tale signs.

"Looks like somebody's got an admirer," smiled mum, sniffing the lilac envelope before handing it to me. I was already blushing.

I examined the letter for clues. My first thought was that it was probably the work of Ivy Morrison or Sandra Adams, determined to give me no respite from the embarrassment, even on my summer furlough. It had to be a joke because the emanating fragrance seemed like deliberate overkill. The writing looked like that of a child but it was all spelled correctly. As with any love letter, there were abbreviations over the seal.

It read: "S.W.A.L.K.," which was a common love letter seal. I knew this to mean, 'Sealed with a Loving Kiss.'

I took the letter off to the shed, away from the prying eyes. I opened it carefully and read it to myself; and then again to Whiskey. I often practiced my reading skills on the hamster because he had patience with my semi-dyslexic verbal clumsiness. The letter read:

My darling Martin,

My heart misses a beat every time I see you. I want you to hold me in your arms, forever. I want to shower you with kisses. I love you, darling. Be mine forever.

Yours sincerely,
Guess who?

I felt a surge of butterflies in the stomach. It was almost certainly a joke but it was still exciting to even pretend that a girl was harbouring such feelings toward me. I had always told mum that I hated girls, just like all eight-year-old boys and she had regularly reassured me that these feelings would change when I got older.

"One day you will meet the girl of your dreams and fall in love and get married," she told me, "and you'll be as happy as your dad and me." The last part somewhat shattered the fantasy. It was hard to envisage that mum and dad saw themselves as a romantic couple because they seemed to dislike one another much of the time. However, mum's perception was that they had an enviable relationship, to which others would want to aspire.

I scrutinized the letter for clues. Firstly, the postmark on the envelope was from the Main Post Office, Hanley. Someone had gone to a great deal of trouble to disguise its origin. The hand-writing was neat and carefully crafted, as though the author had taken her time to print every syllable. I could not imagine Ivy Morrison going to such subtle lengths. Also, the spelling and grammar seemed too good for my initial suspects. Furthermore, I had experienced previous shenanigans from these two: Back in February, on St. Valentine's Day, Ivy and Sandra put an anonymous homemade card in my school desk. It read:

Roses are red,
Violets are blue,
I think you're gorgeous,
Ooo!.....Ooo!...Ooo!

On that occasion, the culprits had revealed themselves almost instantly - taking pains to point out to the rest of the class how much I was blushing. However, this time the pranksters were prepared to deny themselves the pleasure of watching me squirm. Also, although the latest love letter was riddled with clichés, it was completely devoid of humour. The only flippant part was the invitation to 'Guess who?' at the end. Perhaps the Rubella-laced kiss in the spring had altered Ivy's attitude toward me; we certainly shared a moment, as the German measles germs goose-stepped from my lips to hers.

Of course, it could have been my friends playing a trick. I instantly eliminated Jimmy Drinkwater. He could not possibly produce such a sophisticated hoax. Barry Pratt was too good a friend to play a practical joke of this nature. Andrew certainly had the skills and the cunning. In fact, it occurred that he might be running some kind of 999 club test. If so, was I expected to show him the letter or keep it secret? Surely, he would be dropping hints before long if he was involved. I decided that the only course of action was to sit tight until someone else brought it up. Meanwhile, I could fantasize that it was the genuine article and I hid it inside my mum's gardening gloves in the shed.

Later that day, we had a cricket match in the field. It was going well until a couple of lower-siders ventured into our territory, walking a vicious looking pit bull mutt. Andrew invited the two yobs to join our game, much to my dismay. However, we had Tony Boswell, so there was little to fear. The elder boy was Biffo, the teenager, who I remembered from the day of the great slide last winter. He was the kid who had been straddled by the girl outside Butcher's house. The other was his younger brother, Corky. It dawned on me that both their nicknames came from comic characters: Biffo the Bear and Corky the Cat. Any doubts about this being mere coincidences were dispelled when I heard their dog's name: Gnasher – Dennis the Menace's pet.

The game was fiercely competitive. Corky hit a six off an experimental off-spin bowl that I was trying.

Gnasher retrieved the ball and dropped it at my feet. My full toss was similarly driven for a four. Once again, the dog returned the ball. My third bowl pitched in front of Corky and he opened his shoulders and drilled the ball like a rocket back in my direction. Driven purely by instinct I leaped into the air and launched my right arm above my head.

"Slap!" I heard as the ball miraculously hit my outstretched hand, triggering my fingers to clench. To everyone's astonishment the ball stuck. It was the catch of the century! Andrew raced over and patted me on the back.

"Great catch!" he acknowledged, in a rare moment of praise. Tony and Jimmy agreed. Then I looked over at Biffo and Corky. They were struggling to demonstrate the sportsmanship usually associated with the national game. Cricket was almost a synonym for integrity, which led people to talk of sneaky behavior as 'just not cricket.'

Eventually, Corky came over and shook my hand and said, "Nice catch." His big brother followed suit and this was something of an olive branch between the rival camps. Next Biffo was bowling fast balls at Andrew, who blocked them expertly. Mutual respect was beginning to emerge and consolidate, when Gnasher suddenly ruined the day.

"What you got there, Gnash?" asked Corky, in response to the dog's sudden snarling.

"Gnasher's got a rabbit!" exclaimed Biffo. "Kill, boy, kill!" We were all excited and ran toward the commotion to get a better view. However, the thrill turned to horror as the truth began to dawn.

"It's a cat!" yelled Corky.

"It's Doodle!" I screamed. It was true, the dog had his jaws firmly locked on the scruff of Doodle's neck. My cat screeched a haunting noise, as death undoubtedly loomed. Without consideration for danger, I flew like Superman, fists first, straight at the dog. With my full momentum, I caught Gnasher hard on the side of his head. Doodle broke free and shot through the hole in the fence to our back garden. The dog bit my shoulder and arm and then charged after the cat. I had to throw my whole body after the beast, rugby-tackling him around his waist, receiving another bite on my stomach. Gnasher was a fighting dog, driven by a desire to kill. Frustrated from losing his initial prey, his need to end a life suddenly focused his attention on me. The snarling and gnashing of teeth was terrifying, as his jaws snapped together close to my face. A shower of frothy dog spittle sprayed my cheek and slopped into my ear. I was in danger. Then, our backdoor flew open and Doodle shot in the house. With the same lightning speed, mum emerged clutching a toasting fork.

"Call the dog off or I'll kill it!" demanded mum, as she stomped fearlessly toward us.

"Leave, Gnasher, leave!" commanded Biffo. This, amazingly, snapped the dog out of its trance. He instantly ran to his master, saving its own life, as well as mine. There was no question that mum would have impaled the dog on the three prongs of the toasting fork without hesitation.

"Now bugger off back to your own end and don't come back!" Mum's manic voice commanded. The same voice that usually induced terror was now a source of great comfort. The enemy retreated without need for repetition. Mum grabbed me and tossed me over her shoulder in a fireman's lift, carried me into the house and dropped me onto the settee. I fully expected her to finish the job that she had just denied Gnasher. Mum's wrath was at full tilt. It was difficult to know how she was going to attribute the situation to my *awkward streak* but I assumed that I had done something wrong and I was about to find out what. However, her face slowly metamorphosed, before my eyes, as she clicked into nurse mode; she began checking my wounds. They were all pretty superficial, although the one on my stomach was bleeding. My abdomen had certainly seen quite a year, including gunshots, rashes, punches and now dog bites.

"How's Doodle?" I asked.

"He's in a state of shock," mum responded. I did not know what that meant, probably because I was in a similar state myself.

"Will I get rabies?" I asked, remembering the dog's foaming mouth. Until this point, mum had held her professional discipline well, but this question seemed to upset her. Tears welled up in her eyes.

"No, you won't get rabies," she wept. "You're such a brave little boy. I could have lost you."

"I'm okay," I reassured her.

"Let's have a nice cup of tea," mum insisted, "hot, sweet tea!" She was back in control. Within two minutes all was right again, especially when she produced some emergency Cadbury's chocolate fingers. Doodle finally entered the room and climbed cautiously onto my stomach. He licked his wounds and I mentally licked mine. It was a good day: a secret love letter; my best cricket ball catch ever; and I was a hero by saving my cat's life.

Chapter 23: The Mystery of Horace's Trousers

The Thursday night vapours of hairspray and Babycham told me that Kate Dawson was doing mum's hair. More to the point, there was a small pile of magazines on the arm of the settee waiting to be scrutinized.

"Woman's Realm is boring!" I said. It was a kind of unwritten ritual that we had developed

"Keep going," Kate prompted.

I read another title, "Tit Bits," Mum and Kate giggled, suggesting that the Champagne Perry was already taking effect.

"Tit Bits," repeated Eric, whose face was already covered with his penny chocolate bar. Kate laughed but mum was obviously less comfortable about Eric saying the t-word.

"Reader's Digest, double boring," I added. Kate would always make us work for the American comics. Then I discovered it. "The Flash: my third favourite superhero!" I assumed my usual position on the floor and allowed my mind to fluctuate between the world of 'The flash' and the gossip of Sutton Green.

"I found out why Mrs Baggot is not speaking to you," Kate revealed.

"Really?" mum responded. "I don't even care. I have been so nice to that family and now they're all shunning me. I mean, just because Nancy is blind it doesn't give her an excuse to be rude."

"I know Beryl, she's a moody bugger," agreed Kate feeling obliged to add, "still it can't be easy being blind."

"But Kate, I've done so much for her out of the kindness of my heart. I took down her filthy curtain nets and washed them. I mean, she wouldn't know the difference, of course but I'm sure the neighbours appreciated it."

"They were disgusting weren't they," admitted Kate.

"Years of grime," mum said. "I hemmed young Horace's new trousers back in spring and now its August, and not so much as a 'Thank You.'"

"Actually Beryl, I think that's what it's about," said Kate. "Mrs Baggot wasn't happy about Horace's trousers."

"What because I took too long? I know I had them a couple of weeks but I was dead busy. I mean, all the boys had German measles, thanks to your Jane. And I had just started working nights at Bucknall Hospital. She's a cheeky bugger if you ask me."

"I'm just telling you what Nancy is saying, Beryl," Kate reminded her.

"Go on," insisted mum, eager to defend whatever lies were being spread by her neighbour.

"She says that Horace's trousers had big holes in them," Kate explained.

"Nonsense," said mum, as she tried to recall the return of Horace's trousers. "I hemmed them, ironed them and rolled them up in a plastic bag to keep them immaculate. They were still in the bag when I gave them back." Mum seemed bewildered. "I remember it well, because it was just before Martin started with German Measles. Whiskey had been missing for days and we eventually found her in a nest under the washer. Remember when Whiskey went missing, Martin?"

"Yes mum," I answered, not wanting to relive the worst day of the year, except for getting shot, or getting beaten up.

"Well Beryl it seems like a funny thing for Nancy to make up," reasoned Kate. "Maybe Horace ripped his trousers and blamed you for it?"

"That'll be it." agreed mum, clutching at straws. "Unless..........." Then it dawned on her, "......that bloody hamster! He ate Horace's bloody trousers!"

"Oh, I doubt it, Beryl," said Kate trying to console her. The full embarrassment of the situation was hard to digest but mum was not one to shirk her responsibilities. Within ten seconds she was hammering on the Baggots' backdoor whilst simultaneously ringing the illuminated doorbell and yelling "Nancy!"

214

Reluctantly old Horace and a blast of cigar smoke answered the door. "I don't think we're speaking to you, Beryl," was Horace's paradoxical statement.

"Horace, go and get Nancy, now," mum insisted. Horace was a hen-pecked husband and was used to being ordered about.

Ten seconds later the blind lady had felt her way to the door. "You're useless, Horace," she stated. "What is it, Beryl?"

"Nancy, there's been a big misunderstanding. Kate told me that Horace's trousers had big holes in them. Remember, I hemmed them for you?"

"Oh, I remember, the poor boy was distraught," she confirmed.

"Well, it was Martin's hamster that did it. He escaped for three days and he must have used Horace's trousers for nesting material," mum revealed.

"Well why didn't you tell me, instead of just giving them back with the bloody crotch missing?" was Nancy's pertinent question.

"I've only just found out about the holes," mum revealed. "I'll buy Horace a new pair of trousers."

Once Nancy Baggot understood the situation she became magnanimous and said, "Don't worry about it Beryl, those trousers made little Horace look fat, anyway."

Kate and mum returned to the house and cracked open their third Babychams. "I always wondered what made Horace Baggot's arse look so fat." Kate snickered, "it was those trousers all the time."

"And I thought it was all those steak and kidney puddings," laughed mum.

"Oh, Beryl you are wicked," Kate chuckled.

"You're a real friend Kate Dawson," spoke mum's alcohol. "You're the only one brave enough to tell me to my face, what others were saying behind my back."

"Well Beryl, you're such a kind person. You're like a mother to me," reciprocated Kate's drink.

"She's not like a mother to you, Kate Dawson," I reflected, *"otherwise she'd be slapping you silly and calling you 'awkward' all bloody day long."* Of course, it was tempting fate just thinking these irreverent thoughts about mum's mothering skills. Indeed, she went on to make me feel guilty, by saying something nice about me.

"Martin's brave, too," mum added. She then forced me to tell the story of my heroic rescue of Doodle. Whilst I was recounting and embroidering the story, mum chipped in with comments about her own role, which made us both seem like we should get medals. I could not wait to hear how it would sound by the time it was unveiled, at the next Ted-and-Bertha gathering.

"You should be very proud, Martin," smiled Kate.

"You should write a letter, apologizing to Horace Baggot," mum's Babycham decided, out of the blue.

"Why?" I asked.

"Because your hamster ate his trousers, silly," mum replied.

"Good idea, Beryl," agreed Kate, consolidating mum's idea and making resistance useless.

So, I took out my personal writing pad, which had been a Christmas present nine months earlier, and wrote:

Dear Horace Baggot,
I would like to apologize, on behalf of my hamster. He accidentally chewed a big hole in your best

trousers so he could build a nest in the washing machine.
We are both very sorry.

Yours sincerely,

Martin Wells.

I showed mum, who's first thought was that it sounded sarcastic, so she handed it to Kate for a second opinion.

"Oh Beryl, its sweet," Kate told her.

"You don't think it sounds a bit awkward?" mum checked.

"Not, at all. It'll be perfect," said Kate, turning to me and adding, "This is very nicely written, Martin."

"Okay, seal it up," insisted mum. I've got a stamp somewhere. She had me write his name and address on the envelope and, before the glue was even dry, I was sent to post it in the mailbox on Ripperton Road. It seemed ludicrous to waste the stamp money, when I could easily stick it directly through their letterbox. However, mum insisted that it was better social etiquette to send my apology this way. I personally felt that the apology letter was not necessary but mum was adamant that it was a good move. The intent was to rebuild a bridge with our neighbours and it might have worked if it was not for one detail.

The next morning, I was putting my special writing pad away in my drawer and, to my horror, the letter to Horace Baggot was tucked under the second sheet. I blushed and cringed at what I must have sent instead. You see, after receiving my mystery love letter, I had experimented with a reply. It was only meant as a practice exercise and I thoroughly intended to destroy my writings. However, my arch enemies - distraction and procrastination, had conspired to keep my mock love letter very much alive. The letter that Horace Baggot would be opening the next morning would contain no talk of holey trousers, hamsters or washing machines. Instead it actually read:

> *My darling,*
> *I want your kisses so badly. I can't wait until you are in my arms. I will always love you. Meet me in the usual place.*
>
> *Yours sincerely,*
>
> *You know who.*

My scalp tightened with embarrassment. It was a pure fantasy, intended for nobody's eyes but mine. Young Horace Baggot should never be privy to such innermost thoughts and he would surely take every opportunity to humiliate me. What if it got back to Ivy Morrison? I would be mortified! She would make my life a living Hell and I would have to change schools.

Then it occurred to me, that my letter was totally anonymous. As far as Horace was concerned, it could be a genuine love letter, written by a love-struck admirer. He would be in an identical predicament to me, ambiguous, if not paranoid, about the sincerity.

Then another thought entered my head. Supposing old Horace Baggot opened the letter and thought it was for him. It was funny to think that either of the Horace Baggots might consider that they had a secret

218

admirer. On the other hand, someone, somewhere, was undeniably laughing about the love letter that I had received.

Chapter 23: Holiday at the McDermotts'

The smell of duck poo is far more rancid than cow dung. It almost eats into the gums below your bottom teeth and this was a daily experience, during the last two weeks of August.

It turned out that it had been mum's entire motivation, on the 50km walk, to earn some money for a family vacation at Butlin's Holiday Camp. We had been there two years prior and that was when they 'decided' to have my little brother Eric, from what I overheard mum tell Bertha.

"The only rubbers you'll find in Wales are wellies," added dad, much to Ted's amusement and mum's horror.

"Peter," mum scolded, as if he'd betrayed a family secret.

Anyway, even though someone had spray-painted "Velcome to Butlitz!" on the entrance, the camp held fond memories for all of us. Mum's dreams of recreating her Butlin's moment in the sun, and maybe a baby daughter, disappeared on that faithful day when she had turned the walking race into a run. A daytrip to Auntie Val's in Prestatyn was looking like our only hope for 1963, when dad came home with the news.

"The boss is going to Greece for a fortnight and he's asked us to take care of Inglewood Hall whilst he's gone. It's a million times better than any chalet or caravan. All we have to do is feed the dogs, collect the chicken eggs and look after the ducks and horse."

Mum looked dubious at first, "It sounds like you'll still be working for Dr McDermott, only without getting paid for it."

"Nonsense," dad added, "the kids can groom the horse and put the ducks away each night. I can teach them how to collect eggs and I can take them hunting and fishing."

"Can we mum?" Andrew cajoled. He had always been a little jealous of my winter hunting day with dad, unaware that it was plagued with chilblains and the minor matter of 'getting shot.'

"Sounds great," mum finally conceded, somewhat won over by the fact that dad was intending doing all sorts of father/son bonding activities. Perhaps, that baby sister was still on the cards. Next thing we knew, Carl Wagstaff was dropping us off at the McDermott mansion.

Inglewood Hall was like a stately home, and it certainly had that old, damp musty smell. Two sets of banisters led to an upstairs with seven bedrooms and three bathrooms. The boss' master suite was strictly 'out-of-

221

bounds,' on threat of death, along with the cellars and the gun cupboard.

Dr M., as dad had affectionately started referring to him, had several fields, including a wood and a fish pond. He also had a huge croquet lawn, a massive vegetable garden and an orchard. An old Welshman, named Mr. Jennings lived in a caravan at the bottom of the orchard. His job was to maintain the fruit and vegetables and then do odd jobs around the mansion. He was very polite but all I ever heard him say was, 'Yes' or 'Don't mind if I do,' or 'If it's not too much trouble.' Apparently, he used to be taller but he was getting smaller, like the Incredible Shrinking Man. It seemed that, during previous vacations, Dr McDermott had left the daily chores to Jennings. Unfortunately, he was getting too old. There was a strong suspicion that he had completely forgotten to feed the dogs for the last four days of the last trip!

It was hard to see how Mr. Jennings could have ever put the ducks away each evening because it was an hour-long task when Andrew, Eric and I tried it. The first day was not so bad - we formed a half-moon shape around the lower end of the water-filled hollow and slowly manipulated all five ducks up the field and into the duck shed. However, this task became harder each day, as if they were learning from their previous mistakes. By the fifth night, after an inordinate amount of wasted time, Andrew decided that we should give up.

Unfortunately, Eric ratted us out by saying, "Ducks," one too many times. Then mum gave us a lecture, explaining vividly how the fox would come along and bite the duck's heads off.

Dad felt obliged to clarify, as if mum's imagery was not clear enough. "You see, foxes get something called blood lust," he told us. "Once they get a taste for killing, they won't stop until everything is dead!" Foxes joined the rats and bears as my latest nightmare adversaries.

Unfortunately, darkness had descended and we had to round up the ducks by torchlight, desperately trying to avoid horse poop. After a frustrating ninety minutes, we were all thinking that it would be the ducks' own stupid faults if a fox got them. Even dad was about to throw in the towel, when a minor miracle happened. The ducks suddenly began to capitulate. They appeared to sense that they had teased us enough, and waddled, inexplicably, single-file into the shed. A quack and a laugh seem remarkably similar at times - this was one of them.

Egg collecting was a fun chore. Chickens had a way of hiding their eggs and so every day was like an Easter-egg hunt. Andrew and I were each given a silver bucket and we would be locked in with the chickens until we emerged with about forty to fifty eggs each. Sometimes they were still warm and occasionally we could watch them being laid, which seemed an anatomically impossible task.

I do not know how Andrew learned this, but he discovered how to hypnotize the hens. All you had to do was hold them down and repeatedly draw a line in front of their beaks. They would sit staring blankly for half-an-hour, after doing this. On one occasion, we had seventeen chickens, in the outside pen, in a deep trance. Then dad spoiled it.

"What the bloody hell have you done to the chickens?" he demanded. This seemed to stir them all from their spell. In fact, they burst into a state of pandemonium, as they tried to recover all of their lost clucks. Mr. Jennings came running - well walking as fast as his ninety-year-old legs could shuffle.

"It's okay Mr. J! I bet you thought there was a fox in the chicken pen?" dad said.

"Yes," admitted the old man.

Andrew and I were masters of the chickens and would gather their eggs with increasing confidence each day. The art was to distract them with a strategically scattered handful of grain. Food made the birds far less defensive over their eggs. However, one day I had just fastidiously latched myself into the pen, when I was confronted by an altogether different kind of beast, which I later discovered had been borrowed by Mr. Jennings from Podmores' farm. This was not a hen at all, it was a rooster. Furthermore, he viewed me as a direct competitor for the affections of his harem of hens. He leaped over the top of the food bucket and began flapping and pecking furiously. I panicked and threw the whole bucketful of grain directly at the irate cockerel. This distraction failed; in fact, it seemed to make him more crazed than ever. He started jumping up trying to attack my face. I swear to this day, that he was going for my eyes. It was truly terrifying! This was even scarier than my fight with Parsnips. Without further hesitation, I swung the metal bucket at the rooster smacking him hard on the side of the head. I was worried that it may have been a fatal blow; the bird reared for a split second. However, it recovered quickly and the next thing I knew it was on my shoulder pecking mercilessly at my face.

"Bloody Hell," yelled Andrew, finally coming to my rescue. He bravely knocked the rooster off me then, in the same motion, leaped on it from behind, pinning it to the ground.

"It's bloody crazy!" I screamed.

"Hypnotize it!" he insisted. The beast was trying hard to struggle free but I followed my big brother's advice. I began to stroke the ground in front of his face. At first, he tried to peck my finger but after a few strokes we witnessed him fall under the familiar spell, which had previously entranced his female counterparts. After about fifty repetitions, Andrew told me to back slowly toward the door. I willingly obeyed. There was a gathering of chickens around the pile of jettisoned grain. They were blocking my escape and I had to carefully usher them out of the way, without creating further disturbance. After fumbling with the latch a few times, I got it open. Andrew let go of the memorized cockerel with the intention of backing discreetly away. However, it seems that crafty bird had been faking the trance, all along. On release, he was instantly pecking at Andrew, with renewed tenacity. We raced for the exit, kicking hens out of the way, in fear of our lives.

"Bloody hell!" we screamed in unison, as we slammed the cage door shut, not a second too soon.

At this moment, Mr. Jennings appeared, presumably checking for another potential fox attack, and we cajoled him into going in and finishing the egg-collecting job.

"Yes," was his only choice. We watched sheepishly through the cage, as the frail old fellow stepped into impending doom. His first action was to thrust his hand under a broody hen, who was trying to hatch an egg. The hen's annoyance was only surpassed by the cockerel's rage.

"Manslaughter," Andrew uttered to himself, rehearsing the defence for our Juvenile Court hearing. We should, by rights, have fetched an adult but we were rooted to the spot. It was not that we wanted to see this kindly old man pecked to death - but we didn't want to miss it either! The rooster was up for the challenge. Cockerel's had a reputation of fighting to-the-death and it set upon Mr. Jennings with a vengeance. The pecking and flapping were intense and the noise was dreadful but then it turned beautiful. Mr. Jennings began to sing:

"There'll be a welcome on the hillside,

There'll be a welcome in the vale," sang his melodious Welsh tones. This seemed to have a similar hypnotic effect to the line-drawing; within seconds, the rooster walked away. Mr. Jennings turned and winked at the two of us. The cockerel flipped into a completely different mode and began visiting one hen after another giving each a few seconds of attention, much to their annoyance. Andrew said that Mr. Jennings' singing had seduced the rooster.

Dad wanted to let us have the experience of firing a shotgun but mum was adamant that this was not allowed. By way of compromise, when he took us hunting, he let Andrew and I take turns in carrying an empty air rifle. This was to teach us gun etiquette. You always had to keep the gun broken open during the hunt, so that an accidental stumble would not result in someone getting shot.

"Like that could ever happen!" I told myself sarcastically.

An added precaution is to never point the gun at anyone, even in jest, and never fire when anybody is in front of you. *"Perhaps, Gordon Podmore, my would-be assassin, should be taught these rules."* I mused, continuing my uncharacteristically sardonic inner dialogue.

Dad underestimated Andrew's resilience when he thought that denying us air gun pellets rendered the weapon harmless. On the contrary, it became more lethal. Another room in the mansion was the workshop, where we weren't exactly encouraged, but not officially banished. Soon, thanks to a hacksaw, vice and a bag of nails, Andrew had made some home-made pellets. The initial targets were points on walls and a derelict tractor. Then we progressed to bottles and cans, set on a wall. Of course, these inanimate objects did not satiate our hunting instincts for long, so before we knew it, we had escalated to birds. The short range of about forty feet made the chance of a kill neigh-impossible but it was enough for us to experience the true 'joy of the hunt.' In hindsight, we were naive to think that the high-pitched discharge of our air guns would remain unobserved and Farmer Podmore soon arrived to talk to dad about the dangers young kids firing guns.

"Them bane just baerns, Pete. Town folk kids should'na bay shooting guns. They dunna know country rules." he grunted. I felt like he should have been reminded of his own son's serious lapse of etiquette. However, since nobody could admit that a crime was ever committed, it seemed fruitless. Luckily, dad never caught the man's drift, that we had been firing 'live ammunition.' Instead, he thought the farmer was just being awkward but he decided to lock our 'toys' in the gun cupboard to avoid further provocation his boss' neighbours.

Having exhausted outdoor fun, we diverted our attentions indoors. Andrew discovered that the eighteen little bells along the top of the kitchen wall, were each controlled by a lever or rope in a different room. Obviously, these were originally to attract the attention of servants. But the McDermott's did not use hired help, except Mr. Jennings, who dad thought was more a hindrance than help. Of course, he had not observed him charm the rooster with his dulcet tones. Many bell-pulls were hidden behind wardrobes or reduced to insignificant, painted-over stumps. Also, some of the bells had lost their clappers. This all added to the intrigue and, before we knew it, we had discovered fifteen of the bell sources. It added an extra level of excitement to playing hide-and-seek, ringing bells, then racing up and down the two stairwells trying to catch one another in the act. I used Eric as a red herring on a couple of occasions.

"Sing Baa Baa black sheep, all the way through, and then pull this string." I told him in the downstairs study. The plan worked perfectly. I was already upstairs ringing the one in Alexander's room, by the time Andrew discovered that my little brother was an accomplice. Unfortunately, Eric spent most of the rest of the week returning to the study and ringing the same bell, over and over. It takes far longer for the novelty to wear off with younger kids, I discovered.

Fifteen out of eighteen was good enough for me. However, Andrew's curiosity could not let the mystery of the other three lie. The master bedroom was an obvious candidate and Andrew reasoned that he should keep lookout in the kitchen whilst I entered the forbidden zone. The master suite was at the opposite end of the house. While mum was busy cooking the dogs' dinner and dad was sorting eggs in the outhouse Andrew gave me the nod and, off I set.

The master suite was not as luxurious as I expected. The paintwork was flaky and the pink flowery wallpaper was torn and hanging off the walls in a few places. There was an attached bathroom with an ugly turquoise bath, with a thick rim of scum about a foot up the tub, and a toilet that matched in every way. The ancient double bed had a massive dip in the middle - the

228

indelible imprint of generations of McDermotts. It shattered my illusions because I had anticipated an ultramodern bedroom, with a James Bond level of sophistication. However, old technology was present, in the form of a two-foot dangling bell chord right above the centre of the bed. Even with the high ceiling, I calculated that I would be able to jump and give the remaining string enough of a tug. I took off my shoes and carefully circumvented the dent in the mattress and leaped, grabbing the cord as planned. Of course, there was no way of knowing whether the people in the kitchen were hearing a clear ring, or simply the clumsy rattle of the unclappered bell.

I intended a rapid exit. Unfortunately, when I turned around there was little Eric, playing his regular game of wearing my shoes and he was making motions to combine this with his other favourite pastime - bouncing on the bed! To make matters worse, Judy the fourteen-year-old golden retriever had managed to drag her arthritic legs up the stairs and was also showing an interest in settling in the dip in the mattress.

"Bounce on bed," Eric announced.

"No!" I said in a whispered panic.

Like any toddler that realizes that someone really wants them to remain quiet, Eric became uncontrollably loud. The next thing I knew, I was tugging at Eric's legs, trying desperately to keep my grubby shoes from doing damage, as he clung fiercely to the bed-cover and screamed out his protest. Meanwhile, Judy was practically salivating at the prospect of testing the comfort of the forbidden mattress and I found myself pushing at her face at the same time. It was upon this farce that mum entered the room.

"What the hell are you doing, Martin?" she yelled. I felt the blood drain from my face and an all-too-familiar nauseous feeling in my stomach. Mum's rage had been activated and we had the whole cycle ahead of us. In some sort of displacement action, I tugged extra hard at Eric and we were suddenly on the floor with the bed-covers and the semi-paralyzed dog on top of us.

Knowing what was to come, I slipped into my mental "fortress of solitude." The eider down offered little physical protection and, let me say, slaps are even more frightening when you cannot anticipate them coming. Dad had explained to us about the effectiveness of 'riding the punch,' during his boxing lessons but it was impossible, under these circumstances. I thought that I counted five smacks but I only felt four of them. That was because she accidentally caught Eric with the fifth smack, which silenced everyone. I lay perfectly still, wondering whether the 'threat of death' was metaphorical or literal. Either way, instinct told me that feigning unconsciousness was my best option. Per my tea cards, the opossum used a similar ploy to stave off the attack of predators. I was torn between an open-eye and closed-eye pose. I ended up with a hybrid of the two, as the cover was pulled back to reveal my limp body. Eric scampered out of the door but my eyes did not respond to his movement. Instead, they stared blankly through the small slits in my eyelids. Dad came in to see what was causing the commotion. He still had an egg in each hand.

"Is he okay, Beryl?" dad's concerned voice asked.

"Have you seen what he's done to Dr McDermott's room?" snapped mum.

"But is the bugger okay?" asked dad, showing a more appropriate set of priorities. Mum gave no response,

230

which told me that I had at least injected some doubt, if not guilt into her mind. I could feel an accumulation of slobber in the corner of my mouth and there was a great temptation to reclaim it with my tongue. However, I knew that this would expose me as a faker, so I just let it dribble down the side of my face and I felt it flow right down to my neck. I did not think that I could hold this any longer when dad picked me up in his arms.

"It's okay son," he said. I was not sure whether dad was trying to lure me from unconsciousness or simply assure me that he was not going to allow any further assault. He kissed me on my forehead, just like the time he saved me from the dolly tub and I again felt the tears welling. I had no choice but to jerk myself out of my fake coma and act confused.

"What happened?" I mumbled.

"It's okay, son," dad repeated. "He's going to be okay, Beryl."

"Mmmm…mmm," said mum, sounding a little suspicious but somewhat shamed into suspending her attack. The opossum tactic had worked but I instinctively knew that it was a stunt that I could never repeat. Firstly, it would be unbelievable that I would blackout more than once. Secondly, a further such incident would retrospectively nullify their belief that I had passed out this time. Dad was a little wary because he put me to bed and made regular tests for concussion, over the evening.

The next day, mum allowed us to choose any cereal we liked from a Kellogg's variety pack and her only mention of the intrusion into forbidden territory was reduced to a one line.

"I hope you learned your lesson yesterday?" mum stated.

I nodded, trying to avoid any addendum to the conversation. It worked because mum also wanted to put the whole episode behind us. I suspected that, with no Evening Sentinel to hide beneath, dad had been forced to engage in a conversation with mum. Perhaps, he had discussed alternative methods of tempering my 'awkwardness,' other than beating it out of me. After all, we were supposed to be 'on vacation.'

When I was finally got alone with Andrew he told me that the third bell along had rung from the Master Suite but it had a decidedly different tone to all the others and that was what alerted mum to investigate in the first place.

"Sixteen down, two to go!" insisted Andrew. I could not believe that, after all that had happened, he still wanted to continue the search. The fact that he never asked whether I had truly been knocked out, led me to believe that he knew that I was faking. On the other hand, Andrew never seemed to acknowledge any of these things. It was as if it was a special thing between me and mum of which he wanted no part. I did not blame him for this.

"We've tried everywhere that we are allowed to go," I reminded him.

Andrew raised an eyebrow, leaving me in no doubt that our quest was still a priority. "We only need bells four and eighteen."

The cellar door was truly locked and the key was nowhere to be found. However, Andrew discovered two hinged doors on the ground outside the house. We found a couple of flashlights and checked that parents, Eric and the dogs were all well occupied. Then, we lifted the heavy doors and were soon skulking around a dank dungeon, lined with hundreds of bottles of wine on racks. This was a creepy place; even when Andrew found the light switch and provided real illumination, it felt no less scary.

"I don't like it down here," I told him, and I was just about to insist that we leave, when Andrew discovered a bell pull. It was a handle type, like the one in the study that had so attracted Eric.

"Okay, you stay here and pull it when I'm back in the kitchen," my big brother decided.

"No bloody way!" I told him.

"Okay, you go to the kitchen and I'll ring it," he decided. This seemed the better option. So, I went back out through the delivery doors and raced off to the kitchen. Sure enough, the end bell could be checked off – it peeled in response to the handle in the cellar. I raced back to tell Andrew of the success but when I got back to the outside entrance, dad and Mr. Jennings were standing on the cellar doors, deeply engaged in conversation. I was worried that Andrew would start banging from the inside when he could not lift the doors. I knew that I would have panicked. After twenty minutes of talk they seemed to reach some sort of agreement and Mr. Jennings handed over some keys.

"Where's your brother?" dad shouted to me.

I shrugged with fake nonchalance.

"Pity, I was going to teach you boys how to drive a tractor," dad explained. Excitement instantly purged my mind of my brother's current plight.

"I want to learn!" I exclaimed.

"Let's do it!" said dad with equal enthusiasm.

He had Jennings turning a crank handle, on the front of the tractor, whilst he tried to 'catch the revs' with the accelerator. This went on for ten minutes and the little Welshman looked just about beat when the tractor motor finally 'kicked in.' Soon dad was driving around the to field, with me sitting on his knee; he let me steer. Next, he was letting me work the accelerator, as well as steering. I was truly driving a tractor. It was sensational and I was feeling more confident by the minute. I gave the ducks something to think about, as I accidentally ploughed straight through their pond, scattering them in all directions. The fox was no longer their greatest threat, I was! The lesson was probably about thirty minutes long before the tractor finally ran out of petrol and spluttered to a halt.

I jumped out of the seat and raced up the field to tell mum what I had done. Apparently, mum had given pre-approval, if dad promised to take all precautions. Mum was standing at the top of the field holding Eric up to see his brother in action. Andrew was also there but he was not smiling like the others - he was scowling. It was bad enough that I had left him trapped in a cellar, worse still, I had stolen his birth right. Apparently, as the eldest son, he felt that he should be the first, if not only, child to drive a tractor. Now I had used up all the fuel and robbed him of true position in the family pecking order. Andrew did not speak to me for the next two days, even when I told him that it was bell eighteen that he had rung from the cellar.

The final deadlock came when he was forced to be sociable. Dad had persuaded Old Farmer Podmore to let us come and watch a milking session. By design, Andrew was the first to be allowed to have a go at milking a cow. The cow was patient, as the farmers laughed at the 'town kid' tugging with all his might at the teats. Andrew was blushing, which was usually my trick.

Then Old Podmore said, "Show him how it's done, Gordon." His trigger-happy son jumped in and obliged. Gordon grabbed the same giant nipple that

234

Andrew had virtually been swinging from, and with the gentlest of twists a river of milk began to flow.

"Pull like it's your own," advised Gordon Podmore, offering the udder back to Andrew. It seemed like a meaningless statement but, somehow it made sense to my brother, as he began to coax out surges of milk into the silver urn held below. The farmers cheered and clapped as my brother mastered the art. As well as the cow, Andrew milked the applause and it took ages before he was willing to hand over the udder to me. Much to his delight, I could not squeeze a drop out of any of the cow's four teats.

"I think you must have emptied it, Andrew," I claimed, much to the amusement of the farmers.

"Let me show, you," insisted Andrew, and sure enough, with the lightest of touches, the milk began to gush again. It seemed prudent to give up because it was embarrassing to have a bunch of country bumpkins having fun at my expense. Moreover, Andrew's superior milking skills had redressed the imbalance that the tractor had brought about. The family dynamic was restored.

It had been such an exceptional holiday, where dad had really tried to educate us in the ways of the country and we had so many moments of growth. Even the day that we went fishing, sitting silent for seven hours without the slightest hint of a bite, was character-building. It did not seem like two weeks had passed when Wagstaff's Land Rover was pulling up in the driveway, to taxi us away from Inglewood Hall.

Andrew and I had only a single regret, as we said our farewells to Snowy the horse, the ducks, Captain Billibones, the cat, Judy the dog and old Mr. Jennings. We would be leaving tantalizingly unfulfilled. An unresolved puzzle would plague us and taint our memories. Then a miracle happened, that was too far-fetched to invent - my little brother sang a whole nursery rhyme with the eloquence of a mature five-year-old:

> *"Baa baa black sheep,*
> *Have you any wool?*
> *Yes sir, yes sir, three bags full.*
> *One for the master and one for the dame,*
> *And one for the little boy who lived down the*
> lane."

He had previously tended to get stuck in a tape loop around the 'three bags full' mark. Whilst we were all engrossed in our own adventures, he too had been growing from the vacation experience. We were not greatly shocked when his song was followed by the vibrant ringing of a bell. After all, I had initially taught him to do it, as part of my diversionary tactics, in the study.

It did not seem a big deal, until Andrew looked up and exclaimed, "Its bell four!"

"Bell four?" I repeated in disbelief. I looked up at the bell pelmet and, sure enough, number four was still reverberating with the sweetest of all sounds. First we looked at each other, then back at the bell, and then over at Eric who was sitting under the oak table in the kitchen. We ducked down together to see Eric pulling on a bell handle. The one place that we had assumed that there would be no need for a bell pull was the kitchen where all the bells hung. It defied logic but it was completely satisfying. My precious little brother had made it the perfect end to a perfect holiday.

Chapter 25: Back to School.

Summer ended quickly after our vacation in Endon and it was no time before the stench of freshly painted classrooms was infesting my nostrils. School paint evoked more nausea than the ordinary house variety. Mr. Locket, my new Class Four teacher, said that unique odour of school paint was due to addition of extra lashings of a substance called Lead. Apparently, the paint took weeks to completely dry, hanging solvents in the atmosphere for longer than normal. Eventually, it would harden tougher than normal gloss, making it the perfect paint to be used around clumsy, boisterous children.

It was the first time that I had ever had a male teacher. He was not as moody as Mrs Forsythe. Furthermore, Mr. Locket treated us like we were more grown up, which we were. Paul Moore seemed to have grown four inches in his six weeks off and you could see some of his ex-persecutors becoming rather nervous. He had also stopped smelling of pee, suggesting that he had finally acquired some bladder control at night. I pondered whether this would enhance or diminish his uncanny vertical piddling skills. It was a riddle that was likely to remain unanswered. As well as the paint job, the school had splashed out on state-of-the-art indoor toilets. They were fancy, with a modern hand-drying system, where you just tugged gently and a fresh region of towel magically appeared from a machine. Also, some thought had gone into modesty. Instead of a continuous urinal and there were individual porcelain bowls to providing a modicum of privacy. This put pay to any future pissing contests, so Paul Moore would have to work on a different talent.

Mr. Locket was the first teacher that I had known who had not claimed some first-day-back planning time, with the traditional, "What I did on my holidays" essay. It was a shame because I was looking forward to bragging about staying in a mansion, feeding chickens, hunting, driving tractors and milking cows. I know I did not actually draw milk, but Andrew had explained to me, *ad nauseam*, what I had been doing wrong. I figured that I could describe the task in enough detail to claim the skill as my own.

Instead, Mr. Locket was the sort of teacher that wanted us to feel challenged from Day One.

He stressed, "We are not infants anymore; we are juniors!" He often referred to his pupils as 'we,' rather than 'you' as though he shared responsibility for our behaviour. "We will have just a week to learn our times tables; up to the sevens."

"You'd think he'd already know them," was my whispered jest. This drew a convulsive snort from

Penelope Evans, which gave Mr. Locket the opportunity to assert his authority with a 'we-don't-suffer-fools' glare.

Rote learning of so many multiples in a week seemed an impossible task - Whiskey must have been so sick of hearing me chant "Six sixes are thirty-six. Seven sixes are forty-two." Funnily enough, I was the only student in the room that managed to get full marks. Sally Doyle, who had also blossomed during the break, was doing fine until she got to eight sevens, and then she caved. Ian McKay would normally have won a contest of this nature but he became overconfident on his fives, of all numbers, and he spewed out some nonsensical answers - like six fives are eighteen. Ian had been Mrs Forsythe's undisputed favourite but he was suddenly being made to work, to impress his new teacher. The position was up-for-grabs and Mr. Locket was already making some affirming comments toward me. Of course, he was not yet aware of my annoying procrastinations, my scatterbrain ways or my *awkward streak*.

No longer was I expected to read, "See Jane and John fly their kite in the park." Mr. Locket insisted that we read a real book called *Wind in the Willows*. It was about a world where animals were having real adventures. He allowed me to take it home each night and this was the perfect book to practice my reading on my hamster. Whiskey seemed fascinated by the exploits of Mole and Ratty and Mr. Toad, who lived in Toad Hall. I was lucky because I had recently lived in such a mansion and so I could really visualize it. The book was not a 'page-turner,' like the Secret Seven books, but Mr. Locket pointed out that the descriptions painted a picture in your head.

Ivy Morrison and Sandra Adams arrived on their first day, wearing 'mod' backcombed haircuts, trouser suits, and cakes of make-up. At break-time, I overheard

Mrs Forsythe making an inappropriate comment about them, to Miss Heath.

"They look like little tarts," whispered my ex-teacher.

"They wouldn't dare to turn up to my class looking like that!" announced Miss Heath, feeling no need to keep her opinion under wraps. Mr. Locket must have overheard the comment. Until this point, he had seemed indifferent to their appearance but his colleague's comment embarrassed him into action. He marched Ivy and Sandra into the girls' new restroom to 'de-tartify' them. I was shocked to see a man go into the girl's toilets.

"Make sure we wash all that muck off our faces!" he yelled demonstratively slamming the door. "We are young ladies!" This comment tickled me, especially since he was emerging from the Ladies Room as he said it. Unfortunately, he saw me grinning.

"Wipe that smirk off your face, Wells!" he barked. It was startling to hear my surname used in the classroom. One minute I was enjoying watching my arch-nemeses fall out of favour, the next minute, I had blotted my own copybook.

As well as the real subjects, fourth years could also go swimming every Monday, and, even though we did not have trunks with us, the bus had been booked and Mr. Locket decided to take us, just to get used to the trip. This was another way by which he differed from my previous teacher. Mrs Forsythe would never have done a spontaneous field trip. Mr. Locket justified this by saying that it would make things go smoother the next week.

"Think of it as a 'dry run' boys and girls," he announced.

"Unless somebody falls in the water," I added, without thinking. The class laughed then silenced themselves, awaiting a response from Mr. Locket.

"So, Wells, we're the class clown, are we?" he asked. "Are we as clever as our brother?"

"No Sir," I responded. Unsure to which part of the question I was responding.

"No, you're not a clown or 'No,' you're not clever?" he asked.

"Don't know, sir," was all I could think to respond.

"Well I guess that rules out the latter," he said to himself. I think that he was being sarcastic but it was hard to tell whether he was genuinely annoyed or simply 'putting me in my place.' My *awkward streak* was already sabotaging my new image.

The steamy chlorine atmosphere, along with the unique reverberations of the swimming baths, was quite a hostile environment. First, Mr. Locket introduced the Swimming instructor, who explained that he was going to take all the fun out of swimming - at least this was my interpretation of his rules. I just knew that it was going to be a series of endlessly tedious lectures, while we all dripped and shivered at the side of the pool. It was only on the journey back when Michael Johnson started a chorus of 'In the stores' that the trip livened up. I was relieved to see that Mr. Locket sanctioned this and he even added a verse of his own:

"There were peas, peas, that smelled a bit like cheese, in the stores, in the stores," was his contribution. I had to admit that this was hilarious - a step up from Mrs Forsythe's sense of humour. I made a point of letting him see me laugh heartily, hoping to worm my way back into his good books.

My reward came swiftly. For, Mr. Locket chose me to be the points and Merit Badge monitor, which was a serious step up from my former ink duties. My job was to visit all the classrooms, collecting their point totals and nominations for the highly-sought Merit Badge. Each week, a member of each class was awarded this shield-shaped broach of recognition. The job was a privilege because I already knew the night before, who was going to win. It was entrusted information and it was so exciting to look at unsuspecting receivers and think to myself, *"His life is about to change forever!"*

To me there was often an irony to the whole Merit Badge system, in that the hard–working, talented pupils, like Ian McKay were always overlooked. On the other hand, Graham Parsons might get it for simply going a couple of days without beating somebody up. Paul Moore once received it for his reading skills, even though he could hardly read. Ruth Parsons got to wear the Merit Badge for "attendance," the one and only time that she managed to turn up for five consecutive days. She celebrated by missing the entire next week.

My first visit, in my new role, was to Mrs Forsythe's class. She welcomed me, with affection. She seemed to be struggling to train her new Class Three and was pining for her old class.

"Children, this is Martin, one of my favourite pupils," she announced.

"If only she had told me that at the time," I mused. "I've come for your house points and merit badge nomination, Mrs Forsythe," I announced, bristling with pride and importance. Her class went silent and all sat bolt upright with their arms folded, as if their behaviour at that precise moment would have any influence over the canny teacher.

"Oh, the naivety of seven-year-olds!" I thought to myself.

"Mmmmm…, let me think," she said, perusing the whole room. I empathized with their emotions. Was it best to avoid eye contact or not? Danny Dagworth, Kevin's little brother, had adopted a tactic of trying to divert her attention to the star board. He was in pole position, with seven coloureds and two silvers, and he obviously assumed that his stars reflected his claim to the merit badge. Of course, he had no grasp of the true perversity of the Merit system.

"Why don't you copy down the class points, Martin, whilst I think about who has earned the first merit badge of the term?" she told me. I dutifully followed her directions as she milked the class' attention. There were four different houses, named after the four valleys in Staffordshire: Dove, Churnet, Derwent and Manifold. I belonged to Derwent, and we traditionally came last. Class Three's Derwent points seemed to be upholding that tradition, with only three points on the board, compared to Dove's sixteen.

Eventually, Mrs Forsythe was ready to insert her nomination. She took the notebook off me and duly jotted down the name of the lucky winner. I could hardly wait to get out of the class so I could read the name. I was not disappointed, as I read, "Liam Doyle: for being quiet and polite." It was so typical that Mrs Forsythe would manipulate her pupils, by picking an attribute that would encourage better behaviour from all of them. Of course, the next week she would be picking a conflicting quality, like "Most energetic," just to keep her class on their toes.

Liam Doyle was Sally's little brother, no less! Oh, how I wanted to run back and divulge my secret to his big sister! But I knew that such a betrayal of trust would jeopardize my privileged position. The other class badges were nominated for a variety of reasons; I almost got the impression that the teachers were all trying to upstage one another. Miss Heath's prize went to a boy for "The Cleanest Shoes." I took this to be a subtle pro-establishment dig at Mr. Locket's initial acceptance the high-fashion appearances of tarts Morrison and Adams. For Miss Heath, polished shoes epitomized an adherence to standards that progressives, like Mr. Locket, would never comprehend. Miss Elliot's Class One winner was for a girl who had mastered "Colouring within the lines." Even my little two-year-old brother could do this, to some extent. Whereas Mr. Barton, who was Andrew's teacher for the second year running, picked Alan Rollins for "Wearing his glasses all the time."

"*A braver man than I, Gunga Din*" I told myself, using one of Andrew's favourite quotes. Hopefully, my brother would resist telling mum about Alan's merit badge, because it might resurrect my greatest nightmare. Mr. Locket had no knowledge of my lazy eye and I wanted it to stay that way!

Mr. Locket would not divulge his merit badge selection to me, for fear of me 'spilling the beans.' It was certainly a heavy load to carry but nothing compared to some of the secrets I was sitting on. Instead, he established a routine where he would personally hand the notebook to Mr. Rice for the Friday assembly. I toyed with the idea that he was working a double bluff on me, and that he was going to give me the award but I had not actually done anything to earn it.

For the Friday assembly, we marched in to a tune by Sebelius and sat cross-legged on the floor. Mr. Rice always tried to introduce a piece of classical music into assemblies. My favorite composer was Mozart but

Beethoven's Moonlight Sonata was also quite pleasant. One week, Mr. Rice made the mistake of playing the William Tell overture, which was also used as the theme music to a television show called "The Lone Ranger." Instead of the expected single-file march, we practically galloped into the room. Barry Cooper was unable to resist the masked cowboy's famous battle cry:

"Hail Silver, ahoy!" he yelled. Mr. Rice sent everyone back to their classrooms, that day and when we returned it was to the dirge from "Bambi." This was far less rousing.

I awaited the Class Four Merit badge announcement with trepidation. In my cynicism, I thought he may give it to Ivy Morrison for "Cleaning the muck off her face!" or Paul Moore for "Ridding himself of the smell of urine!" However, this was not to happen.

Mr. Rice declared, "For bringing a good sense of fun into the classroom, Mr. Locket has chosen: Martin Wells." Suddenly, the award was meaningful and important. I walked out and took up my position next to Liam Doyle. I savoured every moment of applause in my moment of victory. My eyes made brief contact with my brother. He showed no sign of jealousy, only pride. I caught a glimpse of Sally Doyle, who was applauding heartily, especially when I turned and shook her brother's hand. Fourth Year was going to be so much better than Third Year.

AUTUMN

Chapter 26: Saturday Morning Pictures

Years of penetrating cigarette smoke and grime lurked in the seats of all three of the Hanley cinemas: the Odeon; the Gaumont; and the Capital. The smell was so unique that you could have been blindfolded and taken there and you would instantly know where you were.

With our move up to the next school year had come more freedoms. We were finally allowed to take ourselves off to Hanley, to Saturday Morning Pictures. The Capital provided exceptional value for money and entertainment. It was sixpence to sit in the downstairs stalls, but Andrew discovered that the old lady usher, collecting tickets to the nine-penny balcony, was so dozy that you could turn your ticket upside down and fool her into seating you in the upper Escalon. I personally suspected that she was not dozy at all but just very kind.

The formula was always the same: First a cartoon, like Mighty Mouse or Donald Duck, would open events. Then there was an episode of Captain Marvel, which was always left as a cliff-hanger. Captain Marvel was pathetic as superheroes go. When he was needed, he would say "Shazzam!" and a poof of smoke would instantly kit him out in a Superman-type outfit. He could fly but his body remained vertical throughout the flight, which was not too convincing. He only fought with his fists and his costume offered him little protection. Most annoying, was the fact that the facts changed from week to week. In one week's finale, Captain Marvel was trapped in an out-of-control car. A close up showed the terror on his face, as the car plummeted off the cliff – the archetypal cliff-hanger. The next week, the Captain managed to open the door handle and leap out ten feet from the edge.

A Disney animal movie, about pesky skunks or ornery grizzly bears, always brought the performance to the interval. The lights brought time for a stretch, a choc ice and a chance for the ushers to do some entertaining. Ushers were like budding Butlin's Red Coats, professionally trained to pep up the audience. One week, four of them dressed up in Beatles suits and mimed to "Twist and Shout." A little hysteria broke out as girls screamed uncontrollably, as if they were the real thing. The next week they called for volunteers from the audience to take part in a yo-yo contest. Jimmy Drinkwater and Barry Pratt and Andrew pointed at me and the ushers were instantly dragging me to the stage. Six of us competed to see who could keep the yo-yo going the longest.

"Martin, Martin," the chant came, but it was not from my group. It dawned on me that it was the voices of Ivy Morrison and her cronies, urging me on. Now I had to do well, or I would be the laughing stock at school, on Monday. Soon there were just two of us left and it became apparent that we could both go on for hours. Therefore, the ushers had a bright idea of making us run a yo-yo from each hand. This was impossible and it was judged that my effort failed a micro-second before my competitor. However, we both got the same prizes –a highly collectible glow-in-the-dark Capital Theatre badge, and a Majestic yo-yo. This was the Rolls Royce of all yo-yos. The packaging said that it was electronically balanced with superior waxed string. All tricks, such as 'walking the dog' and 'around the world' were suddenly accessible with my Majestic yo-yo. There was to be no ridicule at school on Monday, when I sported these spoils!

The end of the intermission was heralded by another cartoon, like Speedy Gonzales or Daffy Duck and then there was my favourite series: Famous Five on Kirren Island. The characters from my book were brought to life, exactly like I had imagined them: Dick, Ann, Julian, Georgina (George, for short, because she was a tomboy) and Timmy the Dog. They only showed about fifteen minutes a week but I felt like I was watching my own friends upon that screen. The final feature was usually a comedy like a Jerry Lewis, Bob Hope or Abbot and Costello film.

After the movies, we would pop into the Goldfish Bowl, opposite the theatre, to buy fish, chips and mushy peas. We had to smuggle these onto the bus because many conductors banned them. September of 1963, saw the start of this Saturday morning ritual, which continued week after week for several years.

After the first week of school, an added duty of the Merit Monitor was to collect the Merit Badges back in, every Thursday. This way, they would be ready for redistribution, during the following Friday assembly. Therefore, you can only imagine my horror, when I set off to the bus stop with my own merit badge left sitting on the kitchen table. Andrew told me I should leave it but that was not an option for me. Not only would that be a dereliction of duty but it would also destroy my chances of ever earning the coveted prize again. By the time that I had raced back to collect it, my bus had gone without me. It seemed inevitable that my new image would not last. Up to this point, I had managed to fool Mr. Locket that I was reliable but the 'old awkward Martin' had returned with a vengeance. I was disgusted with myself, which is my only excuse for doing what I did next.

"Need a ride, kid?" asked a voice from a white Reliant three-wheeler car. David Foot, the local pervert was trying to lure me into the very car my friends had warned me about.

"*No thanks!*" is what I should have said. However, I needed to get to school on time. So, "Yes please," were the words that left my mouth. Barry and Tony had both survived lifts from him, in the past.

"Your name's Martin, isn't it?" he asked as we took off with surprising acceleration. I nodded timidly. He was a neighbour but, in a way, it was worse than getting in a car with a stranger because he was a known sex maniac. He was a stereotypical pervert, in that he was morbidly obese and his off-white shirt was a little too tight, straining the buttons and accentuating the roles of fat. Under the armpits were permanent sweat stains that no amount of Daz would ever eliminate. Perspiration was a major issue and his stale body odour was not even masked after he took out a cigarette and lit it.

'Fag?" he said, offering me a Woodbine.

"No thanks," I declined.

"Too young," he pondered out loud. Then he afforded himself an ambiguous chuckle which sent a shiver down my spine. I felt dizzy and sick, as adrenaline diverted blood away from my stomach and skin. My cold sweat suddenly matched his clamminess. My heart was thumping so loud that I thought that he would be able to hear it. I put my hand to my chest and felt the shield-shaped Merit badge pinned to my jumper. Strangely, it offered a modicum of comfort, as though it was a source of protection - like Green Lantern's ring. It helped me focus enough to resist my urge to vomit. He was obviously trying to impress me by speeding, yet the journey seemed to be taking an eternity. Eventually, we reached the half-way mark and no further conversation had taken place. My pulse settled, a little blood returned to my face, and I began to rationalize. Perhaps he was not a pervert after all and people were judging him by his appearance. I was beginning to wonder whether his whole reputation was based on myth. Of course, the gypsy prostitute incident was an unnerving memory, but he was acting extremely normally to me. I kept my right hand on the door handle, as a precaution but we were nearly there. That was when it happened!

"The windows steaming up," he announced, "there's a rag in the glove compartment, can you reach it for me?" He was right; the condensation on the windshield was certainly affecting visibility. However, I opened his glove compartment and two dirty magazines dropped to the floor of the car. Inside the magazines were colour pictures of naked women, like I had never seen in my life.

"Sorry," I said, trying to pretend that I had not noticed the contents of the magazines, I picked them up and attempted to cram them back into the glove compartment but it was like trying to force a butterfly back into its chrysalis. They simply would not fit. My heart shot back to emergency throb mode, I could feel blood gushing through my brain. I threw open the car door as we were approaching a junction and the two magazines shot out of the car.

"Hey, what are you doing, kid?" he screamed, slamming on his brakes. The car stopped dead.

"I can walk from here, thanks!" I yelled, leaping out. In a second, I was sprinting down back alleys and side streets, all the time expecting the pervert's three-wheeler to screech around the corner, so that he could complete his abduction. By the time that I got to school I was panting so hard that I thought I was going to pass out. I sat on the school step with my head between my knees. I might have briefly passed out because I never heard my friends approaching.

"How'd you get here before us?" demanded Andrew, rousing me from my semi-conscious state.

"I caught the Berwick bus," I lied. Once again, I was sitting on a secret too big to entrust to my brother. He would have, quite rightly, been obliged to inform mum and dad.

"You got the badge then?" he noticed.

I placed my hand on the shield over my heart. Again, I sensed its power. The mystical Merit badge had protected me and it was going to be a difficult thing to give up.

Chapter 27: The Conkerers.

Vinegar conjures up more than just a reminiscence of fish and chips. It was also the secret ingredient for hardening up your horse chestnuts, in preparation for conker battles.

One of the finest aspects of autumn had to be the ripening of the fruits of the conker tree. Unlike their edible chestnut cousins, the horse variety only served one purpose – hand-to-hand combat, on every school playground in England!

Unfortunately, Sutton Green was a relatively new estate and no such trees existed, in the local vicinity. I checked through my collection of Brooke Bond 'Trees of Britain' cards to see exactly what we were looking for, but no nearby trees matched the multiple leaf arrangements, or spiky green nut-bearing cases, as illustrated by the tea makers. However, Jimmy Drinkwater assured us that his Red Indian instincts could lead us to a whole forest of Horse Chestnut trees, at the top of Bagnall Lane. So, early in the morning hours on the first Sunday in October, we loaded the saddlebags of our bikes with blackcurrant jam sandwiches. Then we set off on a crusade in search of the 'holy conker,' as opposed to the famous Holy Grail that King Arthur had sought.

Andrew had studied this at the reference library and made himself an expert. Jimmy did seem to have some knowledge of nature and he loved leading us on our quest.

The steepness of Bagnall Lane offered too much resistance. While my legs are packed with sprint muscle fibres, they have no capacity for stamina. So, Jimmy, Tony and Andrew's bikes zigzagged up the hill, leaving Barry and me pushing our bikes in a steady plod. When we finally caught up, they were already throwing rocks and broken branches at a tree, trying to fetch down conkers. The only problem was, the singular, serrated, lime-green leaves told me that they were wasting their time.

"They're Beech nuts," I enlightened them.

"I told you, Jimmy!" Tony added. He had secretly believed that he should have been the leader of the expedition from the start. So, we all sat down, tired and disillusioned, and shared our jam butties. We had ridden such a long way, on a wild goose chase and now the skies were beginning to darken. Drizzle dampened our spirits further and Andrew decided that we should head home before the heavens really opened. The ride down Bagnall Lane was spectacular, especially as the light rain suddenly turned to brutal hail. As we met the frozen rain bullets at speeds approaching forty miles an hour, we were forced to divert into Bagnall churchyard for shelter - that is when I had my first ever religious experience. The huge tree, underneath which we had chosen to hide from the rain, turned out to be a Horse Chestnut. Furthermore, the hailstorm was dislodging some of its fruits. Literally, conker cases were raining down and splitting open before our very eyes. Andrew christened a three-inch beauty 'the holy conker' as we packed our pockets and saddle bags with our newfound treasure. We hardly noticed the torrential conditions on our return journey, as the incentive to get our spoils home protected our spirits from the elements.

The 999ers spent the whole afternoon in the shed drilling out bore holes and 'doctoring' them, in preparation for the Monday battles. I was pretty much sold on dad's legendary stories, about overnight soaking in vinegar, but all my patience would allow was about an hour. Andrew impregnated the holy conker with Bostick glue, by pumping it into the middle drill hole. Jimmy was committed to dripping candle wax onto his specimens, whereas Barry took his home and baked them on a low oven for a couple of hours. That evening we honed our skills with some practice conkers. The rules apparently varied from one area to another, just like they did for hide-and-seek, or 'Rallio Rallio,' as my Welsh cousins called it.

The Official Rules of Conkers

1   After deciding who goes first, using scout's pick, the defender must hold their conker, hanging freely from at least 6 clear inches of string, whilst the attacker is allowed a swing with their conker. In case of a miss, two more attempts are allowed.

2   Players alternate roles until one of the conkers is completely broken off.

3   The winning conker is the one left hanging.

4   Each time a conker defeats another, it acquires a number. For instance, a three-time winner becomes a Three-er. However, if you beat a numbered conker, then you acquire

their accumulated score; plus, one for the win. For instance, if an eight-er beats a fiver, then the winner becomes a fourteen-er.

5   There are also rules about tangled strings, where you can declare 'tugs' and then wrench it from your opponent's hands. Also, a conker which ends on the ground can be crushed under foot if you shout 'stamps' before the owner yells 'no stamps.' Failure to follow these protocols can lead to forfeiture of the winning conker.

I learned that 'tugs' and 'stamps' were the most common causes of escalation from conkers to fisticuffs. Even Jimmy, who was always pliable, took a swing at Andrew after his favourite conker, Waxy, was crushed under a Clarke's Double E. I made a mental note to myself to keep clear of Parsnips the Aussie, if he entered the contests.

The next morning, we set off to school with a pocketful of conkers. Of course, I forgot my dinner money and was introduced to Mr. Locket's slipper, but he did not make a big fuss, as was Mrs Forsythe's way.

He matter-of-factly said, "Bend over," slippered me once, and added, "Don't forget tomorrow!"

"No sir," I responded, and even though I was pre-occupied for the rest of the day with conker battles, my sore bottom was enough to remind me to pick up my dinner money as soon as I got home that evening. I preferred his style.

By the end of first break, my vinegar-hardened two-er, nick-named Vinegar Horace had defeated Ronnie Pinkerton's sixer, without incurring any damage. I was already on the verge of double figures. Andrew was enjoying similar success with the Holy Conker, which had taken eight scalps by the end of the day. I was proud of my brother and his adhesive-enhanced champion. Ironically, rather like a boxing champion, as a conker gains prowess, its owner can be more selective about the bouts he is willing to accept. I deliberately allowed Drew to crank up his score by finishing off a few of my runts and he similarly let me bolster Vinegar Horace's ratings. By Friday, Marston Road had reduced the entire conker population to six legends. Peter Knight's 'Invincible Brown Slammer' failed to live up to its name when it encountered Kevin Simkins' "Nitro Nugget." Barry's "Baked Beauty" finally gave up the ghost in a contrived war-of-tugs. The winner was Pinkerton's Dingleberry but this was literally hanging by a thread by the end of a sappy encounter. Andrew's Holy conker mopped up the spoils, leaving my Vinegar Joe to succumb to the increasingly mysterious Nitro Nugget.

The game of Conkers had the perfect blend of luck, skill, skulduggery and honour to satisfy everyone. It was analogous to the FA Cup, in that there was always a Yeovil Town or Blythe Spartan's to upset the odd Liverpool or Stoke City. However, by the time you reached the semi-finals you could guarantee that the Manchester United's' and Tottenham Hotspurs' would be there and about. Once defeated, the confessions about various jiggery-pokeries came out. There were no rules about doctoring because there was never any proof that it gave any advantage. However, a rumour about Nitro Nugget was beginning to spread before the final showdown.

256

"Simkins's uncle works at the British Aluminium Works and he was alleged to have dipped Nitro Nugget into liquid Nitrogen," Andrew explained.

"What does liquid Nitrogen do?" I asked.

"It turns it to rock!" Andrew insisted

"Fiendish! Are you going to challenge or forfeit?" I asked, wondering whether Simkins's actions were any more crooked than Andrew's Bostick impregnations.

"I'll challenge!" Andrew insisted, having already established an excuse for losing. The scouts pick went in Andrew's favour, as his closed hand became rock to Simkins' two-fingered scissors. Andrew was an accomplished expert and he maximized his swing. The "crack" was unnerving, sounding more like two ball-bearings colliding than conkers. However, each conker remained untarnished. Now, Simkins swung the mighty Nitro Nugget with great intensity.

"Missed!" Andrew goaded.

"You moved it!" insisted Simkins, "I still have three goes left."

"I never moved but you can still have three lives," my brother calmly announced, psyching out his competitor. Simkins' second swing hit well, making another ear-piercing clacking sound and Andrew's conker completed a 360-degree rotation on its string. He inspected it for damage but it remained unharmed.

"Round-the-world, I get an extra go!" yelled Simkins, invoking a rare rule.

"Fire away," my brother insisted nonchalantly adding, "How many is the Nitro-dipped Nugget?"

"It's a thirty-two-er!" Simkins declared in the excitement, forgetting to deny the secret treatment.

"The Holy Conker's only a twenty-sevener," Andrew reminded him. "So, the winner will be a sixty-er." It truly was the World Heavyweight Championship - one of those bouts when different belts are combined to make a champion of champions. Simkins's next shot struck well but I noticed that Andrew raised his arm on collision to cushion any 'round-the-world' repeat. Now it was Andrew's turn. He took slide-rule aim but the strings twisted around each other.

"Tugs!" declared Simkins ripping the string from Andrew's hand. My brother grimaced but he still had the gumption to yell, "No stamps," before Simkins' clodhopper could bring about an anti-climactic end. Simkins uncharacteristically missed all three swings on his next turn. Once again, Andrew was the epitome of concentration as he measured his swing.

"Smash!" was the sound that seemed to echo around the playground as the Nitro Nugget exploded into a hundred pieces of what appeared to be pure porcelain.

"Wow!" yelled the congregation of engrossed onlookers, as the Holy Conker hung proudly from Andrew's string, sparkling with shiny residue of its victim. A sixty-er! The undefeated Holy Conker was retired for the season, knowing that a year of maturation could only harden the miracle nut. Conker week was over and everyone's plans soon diverted toward the best night of the year - bonfire night.

Chapter 28: Penny for the Guy?

Singed hair and gunpowder smells combine to epitomize the lead-up to Guy Fawkes Night. A month was hardly enough time to prepare for the event.

The first step was to make an effigy of the most famous terrorist in British history. Every teacher spent a whole autumn morning, explaining how Geido Fawkes had nearly succeeded in blowing up the Houses of Parliament. This happened on the opening day of Government, hundreds of years earlier. Funnily enough, despite the teacher's compelling argument about how naughty the famous gunpowder plot was, children always viewed Fawkes as a hero. He would have succeeded if he had not been betrayed by a couple of cowardly turncoats in his gang of co-conspirators. According to Mr. Locket, Robert Cantner, was the chief 'snitch.' This weasel was so reviled by children over the ages that his name remained synonymous with betrayal. "Canty canty, custard!" was the goading chant, aimed at tell-tales on every playground in England.

The custom was to build a 'guy' a couple of weeks prior to the big day, and then burn him on top of the bonfire, on November the fifth. However, the main function of the guy was to stand on street corners and beg for money, to buy fireworks.

"Penny for the guy," we would demand of every passing adult. Some took this literally, and threw in just a penny but others might give up to sixpence. It was an unwritten law that no adult could pass without contribution, which made it a particularly lucrative venture. A carefully nurtured tone and a puppy-dog-eyes expression could easily bolster the funds. Barry's dad was the only grown-up prepared to unabashedly ignore our cuteness.

"Can you spare a copper for the Guy, please" I asked with full charm.

"Bugger off, kid!" was his curt rejection.

Andrew whispered to me, "He probably spent all his spare money on beer and gypsy prostitutes."

I stifled a giggle and asked, "Why, how much do they cost?" still mystified as to the service they could possibly be providing.

"Two Catherine Wheels and a Roman Candle," he replied. It was one of those meaningless statements that were packed with innuendo which genuinely tickled me. Unfortunately, I was in the process of swallowing a mouthful of orange Hubbly Bubbly, and the urge to laugh sent it surging up behind my soft palate and down both nostrils, accompanied by an uncontrollably loud snort. I was blushing as Mr. Pratt turned and glared and I wondered whether he had overheard us. He looked angry at first but then suddenly reached in his pocket and dropped two three penny bits into our collection jam jar.

"Sorry kids, I didn't recognize you. You're our Barry's friends, aren't you?" he asked rhetorically.

Andrew and I nodded in unison. We were not sure whether we had just accidentally blackmailed my best friend's father. Still the excitement of the haul stifled any conscience. It was quite feasible to earn a couple shillings and buy a box of bangers in an hour. You were supposed to be fourteen-year's old to purchase fireworks and we had to send Tony Boswell in to buy the first couple of packs. However, we soon discovered that Mr. Nadin had more respect for money than the law, or firework safety. He would happily sell to kids of any age. Once we all had a supply of two dozen bangers, we spent the rest of the day lighting their fuses and throwing them indiscriminately. Mr. Nadin had no qualms about selling matches to kids, either. We quickly became impervious to the standard warning of "Light the blue touch paper and retire to a safe place!" According to all parents, teachers and news reporters, hundreds of children were maimed and killed by abuse of fireworks each year and it was always due to negligence. However, there was really no thrill in placing a banger on the ground, lighting it and stepping back until it went "bang!" It was far more exciting to light the fuse whilst it was still in your hand and throw it, preferably so that it exploded in mid-air. Of course, we were ultra-cautious at first but after a couple of dozen we became decidedly blasé.

Andrew even showed me a trick that you could do with unexploded bangers. By breaking them open, having waited a suitable amount of time, you could pour the gunpowder into a heap and light it with a match.

"Won't it explode in my face?" I asked, as he handed me the box of matches.

"Don't be stupid! He said, "It can only cause an explosion when it is in a confined space." Andrew knew everything about science.

"Poof!" went the gunpowder, confirming Andrew's word, in that it did not make a sound. Unfortunately, there was still a huge flash, which I could still see for several minutes afterwards, even with my eyes closed. I was worried at first that I had just become one of those hospital statistics my teachers would be describing to future generations of students. I was so relieved when my vision returned to normal. Natural consequences instilled in me a fresh respect for gunpowder, where all the adults, teachers and news reporters had previously failed.

In what can only be described as pure irony, the unexploded banger had yet one more explosion up its sleeve. When I got home my mum instantly asked, "Have you been playing with fireworks?" in her grandma-possessed voice. Dad looked around for his Sentinel sanctuary and Andrew grabbed Eric's hand and took him off to the shed to 'feed Whiskey.'

"She can't possibly know about the fireworks," I convinced myself. "No, we've just been collecting wood for the bonfire." I lied.

"Look me in the eye and tell me that!" mum growled, bringing her reddening face toward mine. This was a tactic she was employing more and more in recent weeks. Apparently, she was working on a hunch that a liar could not maintain eye contact, whilst perpetrating the lie.

She had underestimated me. I was no longer a naive kid that succumbed to such primitive adult trickery. Only my hamster knew the truly deceptive levels to which

I was willing to plunge. I had already dodged several banishments to Borstal, with some seriously convincing full-eye-contact lies.

Her hyperthyroid eyes penetrated my comfort zone, demanding a response. I called her bluff! I opened my eyes equally wide moved in even closer and said, "I promise I have not been playing with fireworks." My tone of sincerity was perfect - she had no choice but to believe me. I could sense that she was taken aback by my response and she was going to have to eat some humble pie. Mum backed off seemingly convinced that she had made a blunder. Undoubtedly, she was drawing breath to apologize, big time!

I allowed myself a self-congratulatory moment when, "Slap!" mum's hand stung my face. "You're an awkward liar!" she screamed, following up with a crack to the back of my head. Coincidentally, I saw fireworks in my mind, at the moment of impact. Then events became confusing. I dropped to the ground, with the intent of feigning unconsciousness, like I had in Doctor McDermott's master bedroom. Mum would think that she had killed me and be filled with remorse. It was a spontaneous decision with an ironic twist. In my commitment to authentic acting, I allowed my head to hit the ground as I went down. I felt no contact. The whoosh of dolly-tub flavoured death smells coursed into my head and sounds pulsed with an odd distortion. I held my comatose pose, as I drifted in and out of reality. One second, I was an awkward boy deliberately playing possum to prevent further attacks. The next moment, I was genuinely out of it, with electrical sparks flashing all around my brain. I fluctuated between these two conditions for what seemed like an age.

"Get up!" were the words that greeted me as I re-entered the real world, accompanied by a stinging sensation in my legs. I was The Boy Who Cried Wolf. I was oscillating in and out of consciousness and yet here she was continuing to smack me. This seemed unjust. She must have been working purely on a hunch, when she accused me of playing with fireworks. She had totally ignored my most convincing, Oscar-worthy, eye-on-eye denial. Even my apparent death was not stirring any signs of sorrow or remorse. My sense of indignation was so strong that I forgot that I had been initially lying.

"Get up!" the demonic voice and slapping hand commanded in tandem. I pretended to be roused from my suspended state and stood up. However, my legs genuinely buckled under my body and the familiar dolly-tub haze returned, along with muffled voices.

"He's acting!" I heard mum say, still not yet sated in her blood lust.

"It doesn't matter!" said a deeper voice, presumably belonging to dad.

"Leave him alone!" screamed another voice, which bounced around my head several times before my mind identified it as my brother, Andrew. I slowly opened my eyes and perused the scene. Dad was standing with his hands on his hips between mum and me. He had finally stepped in. Andrew stood at my left shoulder and Eric at my right. I stood up and we were the three musketeers.

"All for one and one for all!" rang my thoughts, over the silence. Psychic sibling harmony between all three brothers bought a mystical moment, in the face of my greatest adversity.

Eric grabbed my hand and said, "Come see Whiskey." He led me to the shed, clumsily unbolted the door and gestured that I enter. Eric instinctively knew that I needed to be alone with my hamster.

For some reason, I was not as honest with Whiskey as I would normally be. "I never touched any fireworks!" I told him, feeling compelled to convince the little rodent of the injustice of the whole situation. Whiskey cocked his head on one side and made eye-contact, as though he did not fully believe me. I looked away in shame. Lying to mum to save my skin was one thing but I had always been honest with my hamster.

"Okay, I did it!" I finally confessed. "But mum doesn't know - she's just guessing!" Whiskey seemed to nod at this point, as though he understood every word. The revelation was somewhat purging.

"Am I such a bad liar that I can't even fool a hamster? I asked myself. I did not have to wait long for the answer. I checked my eyes for evidence of tears in the bathroom mirror, on the way to bed; I had not cried at all, throughout the entire onslaught. However, my reflection presented as a weird parody of myself and I had an odd look of surprise on my face. Was I still unconscious and dreaming? Had I fallen into a surreal world, like "Alice through the Looking Glass?" There was something peculiar going on and I felt decidedly queasy. Perhaps, I had died, slaughtered by a crazed mother in an act of infanticide? I made eye-contact with my image, hoping it would reveal the truth. Then it came to me: my eyebrows were completely gone! The gunpowder had burned them off. This explained why Whiskey had been looking at me strangely. It also enlightened me, as to how mum knew that I had been playing with fireworks.

Mum did not come to tuck me in and apologize, for the first time ever. Perhaps, it was because it was the first time that I had not shed a single tear. Or maybe she had less conscience than usual, with indisputable evidence written all over my face. However, I suspected that the intervention of dad, Andrew and Eric had disrupted the usual cycle, and she was probably still too angry to forgive my awkwardness.

Dad checked in, kissed me on the forehead and said, "I love you, son." Now, the stifled tears flowed freely.

Chapter 29: Gunpowder, treason and plot!

Every time my nostrils encounter the pungency of burning rubber, my mind flashes back to the eve of my eighth bonfire night. On November 4th 1963, many Sutton Greeners were convinced that the Apocalypse had arrived.

The first week of November was half-term, so we had a whole week to collect wood and other combustibles and build a bonfire on the spare ground. We pitched in with some Chilton Lane High School kids so there were about thirty of us, scavenging the whole estate, all day and late into the evening. Once it was dark, we would raid people's back yards for old doors, planks, window frames, loose shed panels. We became obsessed and everything became fair game. One day, six of us stole a yet-to-be-situated replacement railway sleeper, from right under the nose of the signal operator. It was the heaviest thing we had ever known. Another day, an old lady took advantage of our naivety by giving us a piano to cart away. Luckily it had wheels and it was downhill all the way; on three occasions, it tipped over with the most unbelievable disharmony.

With four days to go we had constructed Sutton Green's biggest ever bonfire - guaranteed to burn for hours!

Unfortunately, with three days to go, we no longer had the largest construction. The lower-side's bonfire, only three hundred yards away, had miraculously grown in the night. By coincidence, our bonfire had shrunk by approximately the same amount. We had originally accumulated seven doors but now we were down to one. The two toughest high schoolers from our neck-of-the-woods were Barry Fowler and Gezzer Jones. They decided to go over and confront the South-siders about the missing wood. We were intrigued as to how the conflict would unfold, so the 999ers tagged on surreptitiously.

As we approached the enemy bonfire, we noticed that they had built a small shelter out of six doors, and the sounds of older boys laughing, and girls giggling, was coming from inside the shelter.

"We've come to take our wood back!" yelled the enraged Gezzer Jones. The people behind the doors were obviously preoccupied with their jokes because the sounds of high-jinx continued. Gezzer's decree had fallen on deaf ears. As well as the door construction, the panels from our piano were clearly visible, along with an unmistakable chest of drawers.

"Take the chest!" Gezzer insisted, looking directly at me and Jimmy Drinkwater. I was beginning to regret my inquisitive nature. Reluctantly, we moved toward the sideboard, hoping that we could escape with it, without attracting attention. I had a fleeting thought that we were coincidentally standing in the exact spot that we had settled, the night of the gypsy camp invasion. However, I was soon distracted from that thought when a girl spilled out of the door construction. Her turquoise blouse was unbuttoned and you could clearly see her bra underneath. I sent a message with my eyes, deploring her not to blow the whistle but, she either did not read eye language, or she chose to ignore it.

"Biffo!" she shouted. I quickly backed away from the chest of drawers.

"I was only playing, duck," came the familiar voice of Biffo, obviously mistaking the intent of her alarmed voice.

"These boys are stealing your bonfire!" she clarified. This caused Biffo to emerge from the hut.

"Bloody hell fire!" Biffo exclaimed, "Bugger off you lot!"

"This is our wood," braved Gezzer Jones, showing no signs of intimidation.

"We don't want any trouble, we just want our wood back," added a less confident Barry Fowler.

"Yeah, we stole this wood first!" Jimmy felt obliged to add, trying to diffuse the situation with humour, but failing miserably.

"This is our wood," argued Biffo.

"That chest of drawers was given to us by an old lady on Bognor Drive, these pieces are all off our piano, and those doors are all ours as well," said Barry Fowler.

"They're our doors pal!" added Jimmy Drinkwater, wanting to be part of the story.

"Shut up Jimmy!" said Biffo and Gezzer Jones in ironic unison. Jimmy was silent but not because he had been instructed. He made no further sound because he was the first to notice who had appeared in the entrance of the 'house of doors.' The red-headed highly-freckled face of Doug Pitt emerged from the bunker. Then, in an uncharacteristically gentle gesture, he helped a girl out of

269

the hut. I had learned, from previous experience, not to focus on Doug's face but now I found myself transfixed by his girlfriend. She had short bright ginger hair and a glut of freckles, as though she was a clone of Doug. As if that was not weird enough, her red Cocker Spaniel followed her out. I would have laughed if I was not so terrified.

"What the bloody hell's going on?" asked the hardest boy in Staffordshire.

"They've stolen our wood, Doug," the suddenly less self-assured Gezzer Jones retorted.

"So?" responded Doug, as if he genuinely did not see the problem. His confidence would have been completely disconcerting to anyone.

"Well, we want our wood, back," said Gezzer timidly.

"So?" Doug again replied, in a tone underlining the futility of the request. This was far more discussion than Doug would normally tolerate - he was partially pacified by the presence of his female doppelganger.

"Doug, you're not going to let them take our love den?" said his impossible-to-not-stare-at girlfriend.

"Let 'em try!" said Doug Pitt, cracking his knuckles then punching the palm of his hand. Biffo parroted the sentiment with a similar gesture.

"Ah, let's forget it, Gezz!" insisted Barry Fowler.

"Fists only!" declared Doug, taking any passive resolution off the table. "Who's first?" A fixed stare at the ground was the only wise tactic; we all fought our desires to check out the curious double spectacle in front of us. Then, would you believe it, my lazy eye chose this exact moment to shake off its laziness? Suddenly, I envisioned putting the 'doggy in the kennel,' and unbelievably, my eyes were combining images of the two ginger phenomena, to make a single 3-dimensional freckled-freak hermaphrodite. I was a rabbit in the headlights. I felt Andrew tugging at my arm but still failed to snap out of my spell.

"What are you looking at bog eyes?" asked Doug Pitt. Oh, how I was wishing that I had my glasses, at this point. Surely, even Doug Pitt would not hit a boy with glasses in front of his girlfriend. I fixed my stare on the ground hoping to reverse the damage.

"What are you looking at?" is the most common battle cry, and I was wondering if they were going to be the last words that I ever heard. However, another voice emerged from the makeshift hut.

"Aren't you the kid that looked after Titch?" said Pablo. "Leave him DP, he's my little mate!"

"Where's Titch?" I asked, welcoming the distraction.

"Flew back east," he told me, with 'that's nature' matter-of-factness.

"Well they're not taking our wood," said Doug, only partially diverted.

"Our wood!" was the unwelcome addition of Jimmy Drinkwater.

"Shut up, Jimmy," retorted just about everybody.

"Course they don't want your wood Doug," Pablo confirmed, gesturing to us as we all made exaggerated head shaking movements of confirmation. Once again, this stranger had saved me from a certain battering. I would not even entertain adopting a boxing stance against the legendary Doug Pitt because that would probably turn a beating into a murder. Mine!

Luckily, a man approached our group to bring a further distraction. "You gentlemen want some tires?"

"Sure," we all agreed and before we knew it we were 'as one,' united by a legitimate invite into Cooper's Haulage Company, at the top of Paxton Lane. Our escort pointed to pile of seventy-two bald truck tires. Soon, there were thirteen of us, bowling tire after tire between the storage yard and the sparc ground. We were two rival gangs with a camaraderie emerging from a common task. Not only did Doug Pitt not want to kill me anymore, he was jogging alongside me, racing and cracking jokes. His jokes were punctuated with swear words and not in the slightest bit funny. However, I laughed like he was the funniest thing since Ken Dodd. I also stifled my urge to hit full speed because winning the race could easily reverse any kudos.

Andrew explained to me later that a shared enemy can cause the most unlikely of alliances. Manchester United and Liverpool supporters hate one another, and are segregated at a game. However, the same fans will stand shoulder to shoulder when they are at Wembley, supporting England against foreign invaders. On this occasion, the enemy was a big pile of tires.

I suddenly felt like I was friends with a rock star! He let me light a couple of bangers off his cigarette and toss them. He even offered us a couple of doors back but we gracefully declined.

Without discussion, we built a pyramid of rubber exactly half way between the two bonfires. Our mutual 'bonfire of tires' was suddenly our focus. The consensus was that we should burn the tires the day before the real bonfire night, so that we could give it our full attention and so that it would not prove to be too much of a distraction on the actual day.

So, at 6pm, on the fourth day of November 1963, Doug Pitt poured half-a-gallon of petrol, freshly siphoned from his dad's motorcycle, onto the rubber tower. The initial flare up drew a cheer, as Pablo ceremoniously dropped a lighted match. Then, the flames waned and there was a temporary concern that the tires would not even catch fire. However, by 6:15pm five or six tires were burning freely, with black smoke bellowing above the flames. This was when we began to realize that, if a small fraction of the tires could generate this much smoke, the pollution from seventy-two tires would be unimaginable. Five minutes later, we no longer had to imagine. The thirty-foot flames should have created enough brightness to illuminate the whole sky, yet there was so much thick black smog, which gushed from the source, that it blocked off visibility in all directions. Added to this, the stench of so much burning rubber permeated every molecule of air. Shortly, the whole of Sutton Green was engulfed in a cloud of rubber fumes.

By 6:40pm the fire brigade arrived. They were working with a skeletal crew, resting their top men so that they would have all-hands-on-deck the following evening. They decided that the location of the inferno was as far away from any water source as you could get; there was nothing they could do other than wait for it to burn out.

"If this is the end of the bloody world, I sure as hell don't want to spend it in Sutton bloody Green!" commented the Fire Chief.

It took five more hours for the rubber fire to show any signs of abatement and several weeks for the acrid smell to leave the atmosphere. The next morning there was a thick caking of oily black droplets over everyone's windows. Fred, the window cleaner really earned his money that week.

Bonfire night itself, saw a divorce of the two camps but with a new mutual respect. Admittedly, we launched rockets at one another's bonfires but it was all in good fun. Kids brought their 'guys' to burn and parents brought baked potatoes and chestnuts. Jumping Jacks and Catherine Wheels prompted the mandatory "Oooohs and ahhhhs!" The magic of bonfire night was all that it was built up to be. Good old Guy Fawkes!

Chapter 30: Bronchitis

Bonfire Night had heralded the start of the smog season, where every one's chimney spewed out thick smoke to impregnate the November fog. Mum encouraged us to wear cowboy-style hankies over our faces when we ventured out in the sickly evening air. However, this proved to be little filter against the unique odoriferous sulphur-based smog.

Most traditional games had to be abandoned in smoggy weather because visibility often dropped to less than six-feet. However, one game that proved more enticing than ever was rosy apples. Where you would normally have to watch from a hundred feet away after ringing a doorbell, the curtain of smog meant that you could get away with hiding ten feet away. Each house saw us a little braver. Finally, we took the ultimate challenge: the Baggots.' Their backdoor faced mum and dad's backdoor and there was only ten feet between the houses.

I rang the illuminated bell and then rolled, commando-style, to the end of the shared portion of the front path. We had expected Horace senior or Horace junior to answer but, instead Nancy Baggot, the blind old lady was heard to answer the door. It had instantly turned from a harmless jolly wheeze, to a despicable trick!

"Can I help you?" Mrs Baggot asked. We lay silent on the ground riddled with guilt at our dastardly prank. Any other adult would have uttered, "Bloody kids!" to herself and slammed the door. However, smog was no mask to Nancy Baggot.

"Martin, did you want something?" she asked. I had not made a single sound, yet she seemed to be directing her voice specifically in my direction. I remembered how I had heard that blind people's hearing is often enhanced, to compensate for the loss of their sense of sight. However, this was uncanny. She had Superman's super hearing and, since neither of us could see, she had the definite advantage.

"Martin Wells, why did you ring my doorbell?" was her response to my silence. I held my breath but my heartbeat felt loud enough for her to hone in upon. I knew I was caught yet, shame held me to quietness.

"What's going on Nancy?" asked Horace Baggot senior.

"I thought that your lady friend was paying us a visit!" said Nancy, snidely.

"For God's sake, woman, will you give it a rest?" Horace retorted, reflecting that he was at the end of his tether in terms of suffering.

"Perhaps, you should ask *you know who*, to give it a rest!" blurted out all the insecurities of the blind woman.

"For the last time, why would I read the bloody thing out to you, if I wanted to keep it a secret, Nancy?" he reasoned.

"Because you're a cunning old fox, Horace Baggot," she retorted, without much regard for logic. My accidental love letter had obviously led to months of mistrust and animosity in the Baggot household.

"Everything okay, Nancy?" added mum's voice from our backdoor step.

"Your Martin rang my doorbell, Beryl!" said Nancy.

"Oh, I don't think so, Nancy. He knows about your handicap and he certainly would not do anything as wicked as that," she insisted. The whole speech carried a different message to different ears. To Nancy she was saying, *"How dare you accuse a member of my family of committing such a crime;"* to me she was saying, *"I know you are guilty of this great evil and you will be punished mercilessly."*

Perhaps Mrs Baggot's heightened senses heard some of the undertones that were aimed at me because she suddenly said, "You're right Beryl, and it could be any number of people. It might even be 'you know who!'" This smacked of irony because, unbeknownst to everyone but Whiskey, I was 'you know who!'

"Exactly!" agreed mum, oblivious to the reference. Mum went back inside.

"Exactly!" parroted Nancy Baggot, as though mum had been tricked into a revelation. "Goodnight Martin," was her final words before she shut the door. I did not respond verbally but I believe that my pulsating chest replied on my behalf.

"Now you are being ridiculous!" complained Horace's indignant voice from behind their backdoor. My

277

friends and I lay still for another thirty minutes before innocently entering the house.

"You didn't ring Mrs Baggot's doorbell earlier," mum asked, inviting me to lie.

"No," I obliged, maintaining casual eye contact.

No evil deed goes unpunished; my penance for the evening smog skulduggery was bronchitis. In fact, little Eric and I were both wheezing like Grandpa Eric. I was running a temperature and coughing up so much infected yellowy brown mucus, that school was off the agenda. The ultimate threat became a sudden reality and before we knew what had hit us, mum was wrapping Eric and I up in woollies and scarves and loading us into the back of Carl Wagstaff's Land Rover. If I had known where we were heading I would have asked for a blindfold, as well.

"Okay mum, Jim and I'll swing round to pick 'em up at about 4:30. Beryl says you're really kind to do this," said dad.

"Mmmm," Nana Lena replied, offering her cheek for dad to peck at. Dad kissed her, on command, and was duly presented with a five-pound note. He looked over at Wagstaff with embarrassment. However, it was obvious that Nana Lena wanted Jim to bear witness to her unbridled generosity. No sooner had the Land Rover left the driveway than our 'kind' grandmother showed her true colours.

"If you're too sick for school, you're too sick to talk!" she insisted.

She escorted us to a spare bedroom with a double bed. She laid sheet on top of the bed-cover and said, "You can both sleep on here!"

"Do we take our shoes off?" I asked, in what I thought was my politest voice.

.

278

"I said you're too sick to talk!" she screamed, accentuating her conviction with vicious slap across my leg. It was obviously a pre-planned move.

I grimaced silently and Eric looked as though he was about to cry. I gave him a reassuring glance and this calmed him.

"Tissues, waste-paper basket; use them!" she ordered, as she pointed out the items. I was in a genuine dilemma as to whether to use my manners and say "Thank You," or follow the strict code of silence. I decided against making any sound, which seemed to be the correct choice.

For the next couple of hours, Eric and I lay silently on the bed desperately battling the desire to hack up lumps of sputum. The grandfather clock on the landing made us consider every second. Relentlessly it ticked, like the Chinese water torture that Andrew had described to me on numerous occasions. Eventually, I slipped into a fever dream:

"Hickory dickory dock, the mouse ran up the clock," laughed Nana Lena. The clock door swung open and, sure enough, there was a rodent climbing up the clock's pendulum.

"Ahhh,' screamed Nana Lena, "it's a rat. Kill it Peter, kill it!" It was certainly too big to be a mouse but I then suddenly realized that it was not a rat; it was a hamster.

"It's Whiskey!" I exclaimed but nobody was hearing me. Andrew and dad were both there with double-barrelled shotguns. Nana Lena had now turned into Mrs Baggot but she had the same message, "Kill it, Peter, kill it!" Dad took aim and I threw myself in front of Whiskey fully expecting to feel the familiar sensation of gunshot in

my abdomen, however, there was no bang. The clock begar to chime.

To my relief, I was awakened by the ringing of the phone. I wondered whether it was dad, letting her know that he was coming back to rescue us. It was not.

"Oh Gladys, that's awful. Such a handsome man," we overheard her say. Then she came in to tell us some awful news. "Children, do you know who President Kennedy is?"

I nodded, reluctant to make a sound. Eric copied my gesture, even though he did not really know anything about the President of America.

"Well he's been killed!" she told us. "I have a friend, Gladys Doulton, coming around. She's very, very rich, so you must be on your best behaviour."

A few minutes later, we heard the visitor arrive and for the next twenty minutes, we heard Nana Lena's bellowing and sobbing, as the rich lady made consolatory noises.

"He was such a good man," whimpered Nana Lena's voice.

"I know, Lena, I know," replied Gladys Doulton. "He's the only one who could stand up to the Russians."

"Such a handsome man," added Lena.

"Died in his wife's arms," said Gladys Doulton.

"Oh, poor Jackie, such an elegant woman!" cried Nana Lena starting up again with the tears. It occurred to me that Nana Lena's upset only became real when she had an audience. Next, we heard them were uncorking the brandy and the weeping quickly turned to laughter. Cigarette smoke drifted into our bedroom, which agitated Eric's lungs. Suddenly, he was coughing up some serious dollops of snot wads. Luckily, the 'sound ban' had been temporarily relaxed, in deference to the visitor.

280

"Oh Gladys, you must come and meet our Peter's boys," she bragged, already forgetting her inconsolable grief over the dead president.

"Children, I would like you to meet, Miss Doulton," said Nana Lena, with no hint that she had brutally bullied us into enforced silence prior to her visitor's arrival.

"Hello Miss Doulton," I replied in my most charming manner

"Oh please, everybody calls me Gladys; what's your name? she replied. I caught a glimpse of Nana Lena who was giving me the vibe that I had better not call her Gladys.

"My name's Martin and this is my little brother, Eric," I told her.

"Named after my Eric, of course," Lena added.

"What delightful children, Lena," said Gladys, "and so well-mannered."

"Of course," said Lena, who had turned almost nice since her intake of Brandy. "I'm looking after them for Peter; they're both sick, you see."

"Lena, you truly are a saint," Gladys Doulton told her.

"Well, one does what one can," said Lena, adopting the royal third person.

"What are you giving them for dinner?" Gladys asked. This was a problem to which Nana Lena had obviously given no thought.

"What do you think they'll eat Gladys?" replied Lena, like we were exotic zoo animals.

"Mmmmm," pondered Gladys for a few seconds, then she answered, "Fish and Chips!"

"Yes!" Eric and I replied together. Things were looking up. Gladys headed off to the chip shop around the corner and returned with fish and chips for all, along with a couple of bottles of Hubbly Bubbly.

"It's been so long since I've had Fish and Chips," admitted Lena's brandy. Despite Gladys's richness, she did not have the airs and graces of the hoity-toity people in Nana Lena's normal circles. Lena's pretentiousness was a product of marriage rather than breeding. The food of the commoners was a welcome break from the caviar and vol-au-vents that she was condemned to enjoy. Eric and I gobbled down our dinner and then made ourselves as insignificant as could be, whilst Gladys and Nana Lena guzzled brandy so that our presence was less noticeable to them.

"Who will be the President now?" asked Lena.

"Probably his brother Bobby Kennedy," guessed Gladys.

"Do you think he'll make Jackie move out of the White House?" asked Lena, somewhat trivializing the assassination. I could see that Gladys, even in her inebriated state, was perturbed by Lena's superficiality and she tried to change the subject.

"Was Peter as well-behaved as these two?" inquired Gladys, smiling at us.

"No, he bloody wasn't!" she revealed, "the bugger was always jumping off things. I mean bloody walls, trees, buildings, anything!" My ears picked up at this. I had finally found a trait that I had inherited from my dad. I knew I had my Uncle Peter's *awkward streak,* Uncle Bennie's mischievous nature and my mum's ability to annoy my mother. However, it had never occurred to me that dad and I shared an innate talent to leap fearlessly from any height; we were like Spiderman.

"Was it Peter that had TB as a child?" asked Gladys.

"I think he might have," replied Lena.

"I thought he was in a sanatorium for two years," asserted Gladys.

"Oh yes, he was. People used to die of TB in those days Gladys," she said, suddenly remembering to adopt the sad face that should accompany such a story.

"Must have been worrying for you, Lena," said Gladys.

"Worrying.....yes, worrying," was Lena's response; the alcohol delayed her thought processes. It seemed inconceivable to me that the two-year long childhood event, that so haunted dad, was little more than a blurred memory for his mother. It led me to wonder whether my mum's evil mother had any recall of the famous 'coal house saga' - the very flagship of cruelty of her formative years.

For the next couple of hours, I was basically on my own, as Nana Lena and Gladys snored away the afternoon. Eric also took a long nap. I was sitting quietly reading my Justice League comic, when I witnessed a new phenomenon. Firstly, Gladys let loose a rip-roaring fart. Then, Nana Lena reciprocated with a booming trump, so loud that both visibly jumped in their sleep. This continued for a while, as if they were sleep-talking to each other, through their bottoms. It took me all my powers not to laugh. I was just wishing that Andrew had been there to witness the spectacle.

It was about four o'clock when they finally stirred. Gladys departed, leaving Nana Lena with a window of only thirty minutes, to victimize us before my dad was due to return. The post-brandy hangover did nothing to help her temperament. Gone was the adorable fish-and-chip-loving grandmother and back was that give-me-half-a-reason-and-I'll-knock-the-living-daylights-out-of-you evil guardian. Unfortunately, the challenge of remaining in her good books for another half-an-hour laid down the gauntlet to my 'awkward' alter ego. Suddenly the image of her and Gladys having a sleep-farting competition would not leave my mind.

"What are you staring at, impudent child? Nana Lena demanded.

"Nothing," was my reply, using all my willpower to stifle a fit of giggles.

"Well wipe that smirk off your face, or I'll wipe it off for you!" she insisted. This triggered an involuntary flood of laughter.

"Bang!" she thumped me hard across my temple. A bright flash went off in my head, accompanied by an odd taste in my mouth. It took me a few seconds to refocus but, when I did, her face was so close that I could see every make-up filled pore.

"I'm not your mother!" she taunted, spitting alcohol-flavoured saliva in my face. Mum's tempers seemed tame and rational by comparison. I heard Eric start to cough in the background. This caused a slight distraction. Luckily, dad arrived at this moment and I watched her mood revert to pleasant again.

"Did you hear about President Kennedy?" dad asked.

"Yes, Gladys Doulton came around," she responded.

"A terrible business," dad added.

"Gladys says he died in his wife's arms. She treated the kids to fish and chips," Lena explained, unable to dissociate the importance of these two events. I saw confusion register on dad's face as his mind entertained the vision of the President's widow buying fish and chips for her bereaved children.

"Fish and Chips and Hubbly Bubbly," said Eric, which clarified everything.

"Have they been okay?" dad asked, referring to our health.

"No trouble," she told him, interpreting his question as being about the level of hindrance we had caused for her.

"How are you feeling kids?" he asked us directly.

"Much better," I wheezed, "I should be ready for school tomorrow." I was convinced that it was better to risk the red sand bucket than another day at Nana Lena's house. I felt a bond with dad, knowing a little more what he had endured during his childhood. Perhaps the sanatorium saved his life in more than one way.

Chapter 31: Back to the Opticians

I did not go to school the next day because there was another facet of hell lined up. The aromatic cocktail of dusty seats impregnated with stale smoke, diesel fumes and an undercurrent of urine, placed me unmistakably on a PMT bus heading for my biannual eye test.

Mum had pulled out my wire-framed, eye-patched glasses and insisted that I wear them for the trip. She felt that I needed to do a couple of hours in them, before the inquisition at the hospital commenced. This turned out to be fortuitous because, when we getting on the bus, a voice from my past struck terror through my brain.

"You going to the hospital are you, love?" asked the bus driver, making his own assumptions about my gimpy glasses. I recognized the voice because, last time I had heard it, it was calling me a 'bloody hooligan!' The very same driver that had threatened to send the police to my house, was now flirting with my mother.

"Yes, one-and-a-half to Hartshill, please," replied mum.

"Don't worry duck, save your money. I've got a handicapped kid of my own at home," schmoozed the driver. I pondered whether all bus workers gave favours to visually challenged kids. Mum tucked her money back into her purse.

"Handicapped indeed?" I thought to myself.

"Thank you, but he's not a spastic; he's just got a lazy eye," mum responded, feeling obliged to give him a little conversation for his flirtations. Of course, the last thing I wanted was to have my face scrutinized by the man that had once wanted to put me in Borstal. I reasoned that my secret identity was protected, like Clark Kent, whilst I was wearing my glasses. However, I was nervous because I was wearing the same duffel coat, as I had on that faithful evening of the errant snowball.

When we arrived at the etherized ward of the eye doctor, we were greeted by the same technician as six-months previous. However, she had changed in a big way. Literally, she was massive; she was obviously in the second trimester of pregnancy.

"I remember you, its Martin, isn't it?" said the nurse. Pregnancy obviously suited her because she seemed far chirpier than our previous encounter. She then turned to mum, who was anticipating further conflict, "And Mrs Wells, how are you today?"

"I'm fine thanks," replied a relieved mum. "So when is the baby due?"

"What baby?" responded the technician, as though mum had just committed a serious faux-pas. Mum blushed, as the nurse held her straight face just long enough to make her feel uncomfortable, then she laughed.

"Oh, you nearly had me there," chuckled mum, relieved. It was the nurses turn to claim 'sense of humour' in this encounter.

"And here's the proud daddy," said the nurse, as the optician entered the room. It seems that the scenario that we had witnessed on our previous visit had been the catalyst to their relationship because I noticed that they were both wearing wedding rings. The doctor was indeed beaming with pride.

"Good Morning. Its 'fishy-in–the-tank boy, isn't it?" he quipped.

"This is Martin," said the technician, despite the fact that he already had my notes in his hand.

"Thank you, dear......, I mean nurse," he responded, this time without cynicism. He turned to mum asking, "Has he been wearing his glasses?"

"Of course," mum lied.

"Good," he responded, obviously knowing that she was lying. I prepared nervously to fake the 'fishy in the tank.' However, to my astonishment I did not have to pretend. Amazingly, the fish swam straight into the tank. Next, the cat was in its basket and the ultimate test came when I confirmed that the dog was finally in its kennel.

"Splendid," announced the doctor, "you've been such a good boy, wearing your spectacles, that your eye isn't lazy anymore."

"Does that mean he doesn't need the plaster anymore?" asked a bewildered mum.

"Better than that, he doesn't need glasses anymore! Look!" he insisted, grabbing my head and turning it to my mum, without warning, "No squint!" He turned my head toward the nurse and repeated, "No squint!"

Mum and I were agog at the miracle cure. I thought back to the beginning of the month when gunpowder had temporarily blinded me and wondered whether it was that which had rectified the wandering eye. It seemed unlikely. Then it hit me, like a lightning bolt. Straight after Nana Lena's punch to the head everything started to look more three-dimensional. I remembered how clear and frightening her distorted face had suddenly appeared. I considered the ironies: Tricking an old blind lady, by ringing her doorbell and hiding in the smog had led to me being punished with bronchitis, which forced me to spend a day with the wicked grandmother, whose sadistic behaviour had saved me from a life of squinting, two-dimensional vision and endless ridicule. As Andrew often quoted, "God moves in mysterious ways."

If it were God controlling my life, he had one more sting in his tale. We had a ceremonial discarding of the old glasses before I left the opticians, for the last time. However, when the Penkhull Circular, pulled up at the bus stop, it was the same driver. Unfortunately, God or fate had contrived to rob me of my disguise.

"Take a good look at this face and tell me if you see anything different," said mum, picking up on the previous flirtation. She was speaking with pride but could not have created a more difficult predicament for me.

"Let me see, there's something different," the driver played along. I stared at the ground dying for the moment to end.

"Come on Martin, show him your big blue eyes," mum insisted. I could not believe it; she was now telling him my name- the same name that I had used on that haunting February evening. I was about to be discovered and probably arrested.

289

"I have it!" declared the bus driver. I felt faint with trepidation, as my secret identity was about to be revealed and I was about to be joining Pablo and his pals at Borstal. "It's the glasses! He's not wearing glasses."

"That's it!" replied mum, "he doesn't have to wear them anymore." Amazingly, he still did not recognize me.

"That'll be sixpence, please," said the bus driver, obviously unwilling to waive the fare, now that I no longer looked like a spastic. Mum seemed offended but I was just delighted to have survived the ordeal.

Chapter 32: Let's Twist Again!

December had a smell of its own. The muster of old Christmas decorations, fastidiously packed and unpacked year after day, mingled with the pine fragrances from a Christmas tree. There were two separate time frames for Christmas: School mayhem started on December the first, whereas mum and dad refused to officially acknowledge the season until the twenty third of the month.

"Decorations should go up two days before Christmas day," was the Dickensian rule in our house. It was about the only thing they really agreed upon.

The top agenda at school was the casting for the Christmas plays. Andrew was going to be a shepherd in their traditional nativity play but Mr. Locket had combined forces with Mrs Forsythe to create an ambitious pantomime extravaganza - Cinderella, no less!

"Ian McKay, how would you like to be Prince Charming?" Mrs Forsythe asked, resurrecting her old favouritism.

"Not really, Mrs Forsythe," he replied.

"Okay Martin Wells, I think you'd make a splendid Prince Charming. What do you think?" she asked.

"Not really, Mrs Forsythe," I replied, carefully choosing the exact same tone as Ian's rejection.

"Great that's settled," she insisted. Either, she did not hear me correctly or she was losing patience with the selection system. Either way, it was fruitless to protest. I was now the leading man in the Christmas play.

"Okay girls, who wants to be Cinderella?" she asked. There was not the same reluctance from the girls and fifteen hands shot up.

"Please God, don't let it be Yvonne Clamp," I prayed. God seemed to be looking out for me a little more, lately and so I was really hoping that he would come through on this one. *"Not Yvonne Clamp, not Yvonne Clamp!"*

"Sally Doyle" announced the voice of God, through the earthly vessel of Mrs Forsythe, "Splendid, splendid!"

"Splendid!" my subconscious echoed. It made perfect sense to me that the prettiest girl should be Cinderella, but teachers did not always work from the book of logic. I remembered the Paul Moore football team fiasco and thanked my lucky stars that Mr. Barton was not involved in the casting.

"What about the Ugly Sisters?" Mrs Forsythe asked. Ruth Parsons and Yvonne Clamp were the only two girls to volunteer for these parts.

"They seem to know their place," I thought.

Mr. Locket felt obliged to soften the blow by stating, "How funny that the two most beautiful girls in the class want to be the Ugly Sisters," but his words sounded so phony that you could see that he regretted them the second they left his mouth. Penelope Evans got the coveted Fairy Godmother role and Ivy Morrison had to settle for being the Wicked Stepmother. We rehearsed every day for the next two weeks in Mrs Clark's music room, while the rest of the class worked on props and decorations. For some reason, I was embarrassed to tell my mum for a few days, thinking that she might be annoyed with me. However, I had to have a costume and so I eventually let the cat out of the bag. I chose a Thursday evening when Kate Dawson was there.

"I'm Prince Charming in the Christmas show,' I blurted out. It seemed that my timing was correct because mum visibly swelled with pride.

"Oh, that's wonderful dear," mum replied.

"I'm supposed to have a costume," I uttered, waiting for a reaction. I had already been hearing what a 'lean' Christmas to expect and now I was making further demands on the meagre family budget.

"How long have you known about this?" mum asked. I thought I detected a thread of anger but felt somewhat protected by Kate's presence.

"A week," I answered. There was a silent pause for a split second, as mum drew a breath.

Then she said, "Oh well, we still have plenty of time. So, we will need a white frilly shirt and I've got some pale blue satin that I can turn into knickerbockers.

"You can borrow a pair of my virgin socks," said Kate. They both looked at one another and laughed for some reason. "And I've got those old blue velvet curtains. You can cut one up. It'll make a perfect prince's cloak." I had apparently worried for nothing. Mum and Kate were thrilled to help.

Walking home was never fun on the cold December evenings. That was, until Alan Shaw had the brainwave, that we should try carol-singing.

"Good King Wenceslas looked out on the feast of Steven," we belted out in unison. At this point in the song, we would 'legitimately' ring the doorbell, and continue the next line, "Though the snow lay round about, deep and crisp and even." It was the easiest of all carols to sing because of the short staccato style. Nine out of ten people would either refuse to answer the door or they would say, "Come back nearer Christmas." However, that tenth person, usually an old lady entranced by our cuteness, would cough up money. The couple of nights Alan and I averaged three shillings each. Unfortunately, Alan had to brag to everyone else and there was suddenly blanket bombardment of all the houses on the route from Marston Road to home. As the competition grew, the funds dried up.

Graham Parsons, the Aussie misfit, had left me alone since the summer. In fact, despite losing the fight that day, I had apparently earned some respect. Perhaps, it was my ducking and weaving, or maybe it was merely my willingness to 'have a go.' However, my role opposite Sally Doyle in the Christmas pantomime, had resurrected an old jealousy in him and he was once again after my blood.

"I'm coming carol-singing with you tonight," he told me and Alan.

"We've stopped doing carols," said Colin Shaw, who was also one of Parsons' previous victims.

"Well, you'd better start again!" insisted the antipodean ex-boxing champion.

"You'll have to catch us first!" yelled Shaw, taking off in a sprint. I instinctively ran with Colin. For all his strength, there was no way that Graham Parsons could keep up with us. At the end of the road we stopped and looked back.

The bully was walking briskly toward us shouting, "Wait for me, you buggers!" We waited alright, until he was thirty feet away and then we shot off again to the end of the next street.

"Sod off, Parsnips," shouted Colin, from a safe distance. We half expected him to give up but he just kept on coming.

"I'll kill the pair of you Pommie bastards," yelled our increasingly frustrated pursuer.

"You'll have to catch us first," I goaded, potentially signing my own death warrant. Time after time we lured him away from his own turf and toward our estate, with our tortoise and hare tactics. If only we had remembered that the tortoise won at the end of this fable. Indeed, as we got closer to home, we began to panic that he might find out where we lived, which would have been disastrous. It was not a well thought out plan. Finally, we reached Berwick Road, and our tenacious assailant was still on our tale. Mum had often had to remind me to "Look the way you're walking," and this would have been good advice at this juncture because, in trying to keep one eye on one bully, we inadvertently ploughed backwards into another –Doug Pitt.

"Sorry Doug," came our instinctive grovelling.

"What the bloody hell are you up to?" asked Doug Pitt, punching his fist. I was hoping that he would recognize me from our day of tire bowling together.

However, it was apparent that he had no long-term memory - the kindred spirit we had shared, just four weeks earlier, was completely erased.

"There's a boy after us. He reckons he's the hardest kid in the city," I told him.

"Oh, he does, does he?" said Doug, taking the bait. At this moment, Graham Parsons turned the corner.

"Graham, this is Doug," said Colin, "He wants to fight you."

"What are you staring at?" demanded Doug as his precursor to the onslaught. Sure enough, Parsnips was captivated by the brown patches on the face of his opponent.

Then, pure impulse drove the Australian to utter five words you should never say to Doug Pitt: "Ginger, freckled, freak, Pommie bastard!"

We did not hang around to see the results but there were slapping and slamming noises as we made our escape. We never discovered the outcome of this international brawl but I was pleased to see that Parsnips did not turn up for school for the rest of the term. It was not particularly unusual for the boy to miss several weeks at a time but I had a nagging feeling that Doug Pitt may have killed him.

I would normally have spent time fretting about this potential murder but another distraction arrived, in the form of a love letter. It was in the same style as before and read:

> *Dear Martin,*
> *I can't wait for our first kiss, my darling. I love you. Simply, love you.*

Forever yours,

Guess Who?
It was shorter than the last one, but surely written by the same hand. It had the strong pong of Lavender, a similar eloquence, and it was S.W.A.L.K.-ed again. I considered the clues. For instance, we had obviously never kissed. This eliminated the prime suspect, Ivy Morrison, along with Jane Dawson, who had been more of a long shot. I really hoped that it was not a cruel hoax by Jimmy Drinkwater or Andrew. Surely, if they had written the previous letter back in May, they would have tried to tease some response from me long before now. I had purposely told nobody about the letter, except Horace Baggot Senior, who had inexplicably felt the need to read it to his blind wife. My biggest fear of all was that David Foot, the sex maniac, had some perverse hand in it but it was irrational to consider that he could write with such passion and sophistication.

On the Saturday before the end of school Andrew and I were whisked out to buy some fashionable clothes. Apparently, Dr McDermott's daughter was home from boarding school for the hols and she was throwing a Christmas Party, at Inglewood Hall. We were invited, meaning another chunk of the meagre Christmas budget was to be siphoned off, to make us appear less like orphans. Andrew bought a black nylon polo neck sweater and I got a white one. These were the only trendy clothes that we had ever owned. Dad enticed Grandpa Eric and Nana Lena into delivering us in the Rolls Royce. They were happy to perform the service, just so Nana Lena could phone all her friends and drop the words Inglewood Hall into the conversation.

I felt a certain parallel with the Cinderella story that was currently dominating my life, as our 'carriage' dropped my brother and me at the 'ball.' Our chaperons then took off on a pub crawl around Leek. Of course, I was familiar with the house but it was no longer the 'home' that we had enjoyed over the summer. The massive living room was packed with teenagers dancing to Beatles and Dusty Springfield songs. Coloured lights added to the ambiance and our high-fashion clothes fitted in perfectly.

The hostess of the party, Sarah McDermott, noticed that Andrew and I were looking a little lost in the corner and so she insisted that we dance with her and her friend, Sasha. I battled my shyness and tried to emulate their dancing technique. I had never attempted any form of dance; as far as I could see, it was just a matter of rocking, whilst alternating one arm in front and one arm behind your body. Sasha had back-combed hair and huge false eye-lashes, like Dusty Springfield. She wore a black-and-white checked woolen trouser suit. Her dedicated fashion sense gave no consideration to the heating effect of a collection of human bodies. Soon body thermal units were accruing, causing her to sweat profusely.

"Close your eyes and I'll kiss you, tomorrow I'll miss you," sang Sasha, the perspiring trend-setter. There was something empowering about being accepted by these 'children of breeding.'

The party games were more sophisticated than usual. My favourite was one called 'Killer.'

"Brilliant in its simplicity," Andrew and I agreed. This phrase seemed to impress our new peers. We sat in a circle on the floor and the simple rules where explained.

298

Everyone was dealt a turned down playing card, and a lit candle was placed in front of them. The person with the Ace of Spades was the 'killer' and they killed people by winking at them, surreptitiously. If the killer winked at you then you had to wait ten seconds and then "die," by turning over your card and blowing out your candle. Most victims added their own flourish to the death. The game became more intense as the room darkened. If you suspected that someone was the killer, you could nominate them. However, someone had to second your nomination before the suspect was forced to turn over their card. If wrong, the seconder's flame was extinguished. A clever killer would throw in red herrings by nominating others. There was so much eye contact that you hardly dared to blink, in fear of sending the wrong message.

On the fourth occasion of playing I could hardly contain myself. I nonchalantly checked my card, only to discover that I had the ace!

"Act casual," I told myself, as my adrenal glands sent me a conflicting signal. Whilst the 'fight or flight' options that the sudden surge of hormone was offering were tempting, the only way to win this game was a calm, collected approach.

I feigned indifference to my card, then I 'took out' Andrew, knowing that he would be the most likely to want to expose me. At first, he shrugged at me in a what-are-you-doing gesture, but ten seconds later he died like a gentleman. I nominated Sasha, as though I had seen something, and took advantage of the distraction by winking at three boys in rapid succession. Sure enough, after a suitable delay their candles went out. Next, something weird happened: a girl that I had not even winked at died anyway. I guessed that somebody else must have accidentally killed her.

Sarah then announced "I nominate Sasha!" Everyone looked to me, to see if I was willing to back my first hint by seconding the nomination. This was a clever ploy because it threw transparency on my 'red herring.' I was blushing by now, casting further suspicion upon myself.

I countered with an instinctive retort, "I nominate Sarah!" All eyes, except her own, swung in her direction and I took advantage by killing her with an ultra-fast wink. At first, I was not sure whether she had seen me but, a few seconds later, she launched into a candle-snuffing display of Jimmy Drinkwater proportions. The next few minutes were intense with everyone staring for winkers. As the tension reached crescendo I decided to strike. I winked at a girl opposite. At first, I thought that I had 'muffed it,' as I judged that the girl next to her had also seen me. My cover was surely blown? However, amazingly both girls interpreted that I was directing my wink at them and they died simultaneously. This created enough disruption for me to pick off several others with a machine-gun style eye-batting rampage. Only three candles remained.

Then Robert McDermott said, "I nominate Martin!" He was looking to the girl next to me to second him. I could see that she was drawing breath to second him so I killed her, licked my finger and thumb and stylishly pinched out her candle.

"I win!" I declared smugly turning over my ace. Rapturous applause broke out. In my own circle of friends, I would, no doubt be accused of cheating but these were people of honour. I felt that, at least until the 'ball' was over, I belonged to this upper echelon. I realized why Nana Lena wanted so badly to be part of this class. I also understood where she was going wrong. These people were not snobs. They did not look down on others -they gave them the benefit of the doubt. They embraced differences rather than resenting them. Admittedly, they were somewhat protected from the realities of the common world but they judged people on their merits rather than social standing.

Next, we moved to a game involving a single candle, which was passed from one person to another. The flame-bearer had to tell their favourite story. I was dreading my turn but this was unfounded because it soon became apparent that there were no rules and everyone's story was validated with cheers and laughter.

Podmore the assassin's younger brother went first. "When I first tried to milk a cow," he started. My ears picked up because I had a serious empathy with this story. "Well, I was pulling and tugging and getting nowhere, when dad said, 'That's a bull son!'" Laughter erupted. He passed the candle to Sasha.

"My favourite story is *Wuthering Heights* where Cathy falls in love with a stable boy, Heathcliffe - their love is destroyed by pride."

"Ah……..ahhh," was the chorus of girl's voices. The boys clapped politely.

A red-headed boy told a funny joke about a parrot and a postman which had us all giggling for ages.

Then Andrew received the flame; he did the Wells family proud, with his chilling rendition of "The Severed hand." He had told the 999ers this story several times under torchlight in the shed and so, even knowing the finale, it still frightened me. At the end of the story the hand comes to life and strangles a man. By starting with his hand far away from the candle and slowly bringing it closer he cast a shadow of a hand that grew to about ten feet, making a couple of girls scream. Then, at the critical moment, he blew out the candle throwing the room into pitch black darkness.

"Ahhhh.........aaahhhhhhhhhh," everyone joined in the screaming. The hysteria was infectious and the terror-driven cacophony caused the drunken adults to burst in from the kitchen. They threw on the lights as if they were expecting to find a bloodbath.

"Its okay, daddy," reassured Sarah the hostess, Andrew was just telling a scary story. You could not help but hear the admiration in her voice as she said my brother's name. The adults staggered out again and the candle was relit.

Sarah stood up and performed a hilarious soliloquy, acting out the lyrics to Leslie Gore's song, "It's my party!"

"Nobody knows where my Johnny has gone!" she decreed with 'Hamlet-like' delivery. She feigned bemusement, staring wide-eyed around the room. Her acting was brilliant and it drew raucous laughter from everyone. Then she tapped her temple, as though a she had just had a brainwave. "But Judy left the same time!"

"Oooooohhhh," the audience obliged. It truly was a captivating and hysterical performance.

"Why was he holding her hand?" Sarah further demanded.

"Good question!" shouted Podmore the younger, tapping into the crowd's ebullience with his heckle.

Sarah handled it brilliantly. She paused, as though she was offended, reducing the audience to pin-drop silence, and then suddenly declared, "Well, at least he didn't try to milk a bull!" Spontaneous applause and laughter broke out.

"This girl is funnier than Barry Pratt, at his best!" I thought.

"Why was he holding her hand," she reiterated, "when he's supposed to be mine!"

We all knew the chorus and the anticipation of how ludicrous it was going to sound tickled everyone. Sarah's delivery did not disappoint:

"It's my party," she whined, as though she was a complete brat, "and I'll cry if I want to!"

"Boo hoo....ooo," interrupted young Podmore, obviously more thick-skinned than we imagined.

Again, her glance silenced the group, as we waited for an equally brilliant retort. The pause became uncomfortably long and then she drew breath and reiterated, "I least I didn't try to milk a bull!"

There was uproar!

"Brilliant in its simplicity," I told myself.

Next, we played games that were within my realm of knowledge, namely pass the parcel and musical chairs. However, the prizes were not just the usual bag of Maltesers or tube of Smarties. There was a watch, a bracelet, a Majestic yo-yo, a Compendium of Games and a Beano Annual. Any would have served as adequate main Christmas gifts in my world, not just casual give-aways. Unfortunately, I did not manage to win anything.

The final challenge was a twisting competition. Sasha and I were hopeless. She seemed unwilling to give her sweat glands any more reason to embarrass her; I had no clue how to twist. In fact, we were the first to get the dreaded, yet welcome, tap on the shoulder. Still, we were sportingly clapped off the dance floor. On the other hand, Andrew was again paired with the hostess, who had obviously practiced long and hard for this contest. He was a little stiff at first but soon it was, *"Round and round and*

303

up and down we go again," under the direction of Chubby Checker. Amazingly, they won the competition and he got an amazing prize: It was a miniature bagatelle game. I was proud and jealous at the same time.

The night ended as it began - dancing to the Beatles. Andrew got his first kiss ever, some nine months after I had rescued him from the lips of Jane Dawson. Sarah McDermott was an impressive conquest and he did not have to try. In fact, he had no choice in the venture. She grabbed his hand, dragged him into the corner and struck like a Praying Mantis. This was the signal for all the couples to ratchet up their game. Sasha decided to make me her 'Heathcliffe,' despite the fact, that I was three years her younger. It was a pleasant kiss but it seemed to go on longer than necessary. I think that Sasha was more interested in her friends witnessing us kissing, than the actual kiss itself. I reciprocated, happy to become part of her embellished story, back in the dorm-rooms of her boarding school. Furthermore, it was extra practice, in case I ever found myself snogging Sally Doyle.

Our Cinderella evening did not end with the clock striking twelve. However, Andrew and I were forced to make a rapid exit, at 11:15pm., when the blue Rolls Royce arrived and a loud, mink-coated drunk spilled out.

"Inglewood Hall!" was the only coherent phrase we heard. Andrew and I calculated that every second she was there would be an embarrassment in front of our newfound friends.

"Thank you," we shouted to the McDermott family, as we leaped into the Rolls.

"Have you children had a nice time?" asked the more coherent Grandpa Eric, as he took off down the long driveway.

304

"Great," said Andrew. He seemed distant, probably mentally working on some embellishments his own romantic tale.

"It was the best day of my life," I determined.

"Wonderful," said Grandpa Eric, delighted to have been part of the experience.

"I should bloody well hope so," agreed Nana Lena. "Not many children get to go to a banquet at Inglewood Hall, you know!"

"She just doesn't get it," I told myself.

It truly was the perfect evening.

Chapter 34: Cinderella

The blending odours of candle wax and damp mould impregnated anything that entered Beechwood Heights Church Hall, which was often used for special events: Annual Bring and Buy Sale; Prize Giving; the Harvest Festival; and most importantly the Christmas Show.

The rehearsals at school had gone quite well. Ideally, we wanted to get into costume and use the props but Mrs Forsythe made it clear that this would not happen until the dress rehearsal - this would be the morning of the show. Until then, we were expected to pretend, which was most frustrating for everyone. It seemed that all teachers derived some perverse pleasure from making children wait.

"You shall go to the ball," decreed Penelope 'Fairy Godmother' Evans, waving an imaginary wand. Cinderella, who would on the night be wearing a peasant cloak over her ball gown, was supposed to put down her imaginary scrubbing brush, spin three times and discard the make-believe cloak. It was hard to visualize.

The ball scene was a little more tangible because Miss Devonport, Mrs Forsythe's best friend from the zoo trip, had come in to teach us to waltz. Mrs Clark played an old-fashioned piano, called a harpsichord, which sounded just like the authentic music of the day. At first, we were shambolic, until Miss Devonport explained that, "If you can count to three, you can waltz!" Sally Doyle had taken ballet lessons so she was a natural. I soon worked it out once I had heard the counting rule which was '*Brilliant in its simplicity*.' Meanwhile, Mr. Locket's group was busy turning a trolley onto a magnificent carriage. It was truly going to be a spectacle.

On the eve of the show, I could tell that mum was working up to a bad mood; Kate had cancelled the hair appointment at the last minute. I decided to keep a low profile. I rehearsed with Whiskey in the shed. My hamster friend seemed to be particularly attentive. Mrs Forsythe had emphasized that I should 'project' my voice so that the audience at the back of the hall would be able to hear.

"Whoever this slipper fits, I shall marry!" I declared. Whiskey approved, as I picked up an imaginary slipper and placed it on an imaginary velvet cushion held by my imaginary footman.

"Martin, are you okay in there?" came the unexpected voice of Mrs Baggot, next door. Obviously, the combination of my over-projected acting and her intensified sense of hearing, gave her cause for alarm.

I opened the shed door and explained, "I'm just practicing my acting Mrs Baggot." Luckily, she could not see me blushing.

"Who's there, dear," old Horace added to the conversation.

"Not who you were expecting," snapped Nancy.

"Drop it, Nancy!" he snapped back. I felt terrible that I had inadvertently created, what was turning into a lifetime of conflict between the neighbours.

"Everything okay?" dad's voice added to the backdoor conversation.

"Fine Pete," said Horace.

"Why don't you ask your wife?" the blind lady piped up.

"What do you mean?" asked dad, genuinely confused.

"Ask 'you know who' where the 'usual place' is," Nancy elaborated. It suddenly dawned on me that Mrs Baggot suspected that my mum was, 'you know who' from my accidental love letter. I knew that the only decent thing to do at this point was to confess everything. However, it was all too embarrassing, and I had left it far too long. So, I decided to keep it between me and my hamster. I could hear mum and dad arguing as I projected quietly, in the shed. Surely, dad could not suspect that mum and engaged in anything untoward.

"Hanky panky," I heard her shout, "with Horace Baggot?" I grimaced as I heard the slap from my shed sanctuary. As its usual recipient, I felt an empathetic tingle in my left cheek. Sure enough, that side of dad's face was glowing red when he slammed the backdoor and headed off, presumably for his regular Thursday with his friends at the Hospital Club.

"*Thanks dad,*" I thought sarcastically, knowing that I would now be the main target. My first thought was to stay in the shed until bedtime. However, lately I had taken to hastening the inevitable. "*It can't end till it's begun!*" was my philosophy. This way, I at least reclaimed some control. So, I fed Whiskey and then went into the house ready to take my beating. Andrew and Eric were playing in the kitchen and I ignored their warning glances as I entered the living room. Mum had obviously been crying.

"What do you want?" she predictably responded, with a mixture of sadness and rage.

I grabbed her hand, and said "Sorry mum." Of course, she had no idea that I had reason to be sorry - that I was the sole cause of everyone's hostility that evening. However, the problem was no longer anything to do with hanky panky or Mrs Baggot.

"Your dad's such a bully!" she told me. It seemed an odd comment because she was obviously the abusive one. "Are you ready for your play tomorrow?"

"I think so," I told her. I was glad that she had decided to change the subject. But she could not let it drop, after all.

"You see, his mother was a dreadful bully - that's why he's a bully!" she confided. I had certainly been the victim of Nana Lena's cruel hand but I had never seen dad act like that."

"Talk about pot calling kettle black!" I silently said to myself, quoting one of Andrew's favourite sayings. I was speechless but my body language must have registered disbelief.

Tears trickled down her face as she opened up to me, "Oh I know what you're thinking; you think I'm the cruel one. But your father's an emotional bully! My entire childhood, I was abused by a heartless mother, while my father looked the other way." It was uncanny to me because I felt that she was describing my life.

"Sorry mum," I empathized.

"Sorry, why are you sorry? It's not your problem," she told me. Dangerous as it was, especially since dad had left the building, my *awkward streak* compelled me to 'grasp the nettle.'

"Mum," I braved.

"What is it?" she dared me to continue at my own peril.

"I know how grandma hurt you," I stated with all sincerity. This was a taboo subject and I knew I had crossed the line. I awaited a slap.

"What are you talking about, you never met the woman?" she barked. All wisdom was telling me to back off but my awkwardness ploughed right on.

"I know how much she hurt you!" I repeated

"How could you possibly know?" her possessed voice demanded, as she raised her right hand.

"Because ....because, you bully me!" I shouted.

"I bully you?" she screamed, grabbing my ear and dragging me through the kitchen, then outhouse, and through the back door. "How about I lock you in the coal house, awkward little boy, then we'll see who's a bully?" Her statement defied logic.

"Ahhhhhhhh...hhhhhhhhh!" I screamed, in fear and pain. For some reason, the idea of being locked in the coal house terrified me. Admittedly, I had hidden there in the past, playing hide-and-seek, without apprehension. But knowing that this was mum's most horrific childhood memory, which she was now planning to inflict on me, was too much to bear. However, as she had one hand on the latch, and the other still wrenching at my ear, the most unlikely of heroes came to my rescue.

"Beryl, let the boy go!" insisted Sparky Ears Johnson.

"Get off my property, you interfering old hag!" shouted mum.

"I'm not budging till you let the boy go!" Sparky Ears commanded. "He's a good boy, Beryl, let him go!"

Miraculously, our neighbour's words seemed to penetrate; the spell was broken. Mum loosened her ear-clench and I scampered back in the house clutching my throbbing red lug-hole. It was extraordinary that Mrs Johnson had ignored her own personal safety to save me. What is more, she thought that I was a 'good boy,' despite me castigating her, long as I could remember.

Andrew grabbed my sleeve, and escorted Eric and me to the bedroom. My heart pounded mercilessly in my chest whilst I listened for mum's inevitable footsteps on the stairs. It was almost an hour before she finally came up, and I literally prayed that she had reached the apology stage of the conflict. She gave a short speech:

"Martin, you are right! I've turned into my mother; your dad has become my father; and you have become me. I'm sorry; it will end tonight but I need you to promise to stop being so awkward. Goodnight, God bless, see you tomorrow. I love you."

"I love you, mum," I replied. I felt that it may have been a cathartic moment. At least it was over for the month and the rest of Christmas could be enjoyed by all. Later, I heard a drunken dad come in and they were both laughing and joking.

"Oh Horace! You're irresistible" mum joked.

"Come here, Nancy," he replied. Then it went quiet.

The next morning, at breakfast, everyone was chirpy. I chomped down three Weetabix and gathered my outfit for the dress rehearsal into my duffel bag. Just as we were leaving for school mum wished us, "Good luck in the show, boys." Then she turned to me and said, "I meant what I said last night, you know." I was not expecting miracles but it offered some hope. At least I was more confident that I might reach 1964.

The caretaker was putting out chairs when we arrived at the musty church hall. We were ushered into a tiny back room where we were expected to change in front of the girls. This was a little embarrassing because I had to get down to my underwear, to don my knickerbockers and frilly blouse. I was worried that the costume looked a little feminine, but luckily, I had my royal blue velvet cloak to assert my masculinity. I need not have worried because the girls were too involved in putting on make-up, perfume and lipstick to notice my state of undress.

The first excitement was group photos for the Evening Sentinel. Andrew's nativity play was attracting attention because they borrowed Tina Carolla's new baby sister to play the new born Jesus. It seemed a little sacrilegious to me, to use a girl for this part but you could not really tell. However, it caused an annoying distraction, as every girl in the school wanted to hold it.

Our rehearsal started splendidly. Mr. Locket had mounted a giant pumpkin onto a kid's trolley so that it could be pulled off the stage at the same time as the magnificent carriage was rolled into its place. Mrs Forsythe flashed the lights to add a magical effect. The four mice removed their little rounded mouse ears and replaced them with over-sized horse ears, in one coordinated moment. The whole transformation occurred in less than ten seconds, whilst Sally Doyle pirouetted from peasant girl to princess, all at the wave of Penelope Evans' wand.

Yvonne Clamp and Ruth Parsons took more effort than was necessary to uglify. Yvonne Clamp must have been studying the Hunchback of Notre Dame, judging by stance, and she adopted a matching slurpy voice. Ruth Parsons had taken to wobbling her head and trying to talk like a man.

"Stop!" insisted Mrs Forsythe, bemused by their sudden personality changes.

"Yvonne, what on earth are you doing?"

"A funny voice, mish" she retorted.

"It's not Mish, its Mishes," said Mrs Forsythe, much to our amusement. She froze us with the glare. "Stand up straight, girl! And lose the stupid voice! Now, Ruth Parsons, this Pantomime is called Cinderella, not Little Noddy!" We laughed again.

"Sorry Mrs Forsythe," she rasped, thinking she would still keep the male voice.

"Good grief, girl!" The frustrated teacher puffed with exasperation, "You're not Louis Armstrong! You'll be pulling a trumpet out next! Listen, everybody: No funny voices; no funny walks. Does everybody understand?"

"Yes, Mrs Forsythe," we all grunted.

Martin Butcher was the frog, turned footman, and he had no talking part. All he had to do was hold out a cushion that would eventually carry the discarded glass slipper. Unfortunately, he was the epitome of stage-fright and I seriously wondered whether he would be able to hold it together, once the audience arrived.

A harpsichord cord signalled that we take our positions for the dance. I bowed and Sally Doyle curtsied, holding out her hand. I took her delicate hand and lightly brushed my lips across her knuckles, just as Miss Davenport had trained us, and that was an unforgettable moment. For, as I caressed her hand, an unmistakable stimulus entered my nostrils: *"Lavender!"* I must have blushed a hundred shades of red, as I discovered that my dream girl was also my secret admirer. I swung my cloak across my face to cover my redness.

"Stop!" ordered Mrs Forsythe, "Martin, what are you doing?"

"Nothing, Miss.......errr...Mrs Forsythe," I stammered.

"You're Prince Charming, not Batman," she quipped. Everybody laughed. This did not help my coloration.

Ivy Morrison felt obliged to point it out, just in case anyone was colour-blind, by shouting, "Martin's gone red!" I had so many racing thoughts but the professional in me took over and I gathered my poise.

At the end of the practice Mrs Forsythe gave us a pep talk, "Dress rehearsals are traditionally abysmal. Who knows what abysmal means?" She never missed a teaching moment.

"Is it bad?" guessed Ian McKay, who's only job was to ring out twelve chimes on the glockenspiel but had stopped at nine for some reason.

"Well it's not good," she clarified, "but hopefully, we have ironed out all the faults and this afternoon's performance will be flawless."

As the church hall filled up I noticed that mum had brought Kate Dawson with her.

"She probably wants to keep an eye on her virgin socks," I thought. I peeked out through the door as they watched Andrew's nativity play. My brother was a pretty convincing shepherd and the performance would have been flawless if 'Jesus' Carolla could have just held off the crying for one extra minute. I think she was startled by the 'wise man' bearing Frankincense.

Next came our turn. The scene began with Cinders on her knees with a scrubbing brush and the

Wicked Stepmother marched in, projecting a little too well.

"When you've finished scrubbing the floor, you will wash the dishes and cook the dinner!" she yelled. I could see Ivy's mom bristle with pride as her bratty daughter lived up to her type-casting.

"Yes stepmother," said Cinderella, meekly by comparison.

"Project!" prompted Mrs Forsythe, in an irate whisper, from the aisles.

"Yes stepmother!" Cinderella repeated.

In burst the two Ugly Sisters, launching confidently into their lines.

"I'm going to dance with the Prince," insisted Yvonne Clamp. She, 'accidentally on purpose,' kicked Cinderella's bucket and acted as though she was about to fall over, "Get out of my way, stupid girl!"

"I hope that you dance better than you can walk!" said Ruth Parsons' character. Ruth was rewarded by a gratuitous laugh from the audience.

"Hee hee," Cinderella laughed, exaggerating her acting, by waving her hand in front of her mouth.

"What are you laughing at, stupid girl!" said Ugly Yvonne.

"Nothing," the cowering Cinderella replied.

"Only crazy people laugh at nothing. No wonder you aren't invited to the ball," stated Ugly Ruth. Again, a polite ripple of laughter emerged from the onlookers. This seemed to empower her enough to set off the head-nodding.

"Don't nod!" Mrs Forsythe barked from the side-lines, no longer making any effort to whisper. Ruth froze, as did everyone on the stage.

315

After a long embarrassing silence, Sally Doyle felt obliged to move things along with an ad lib: "I want to go to the ball!" she said in a timid voice.

This drew an "Ahhh" from the mothers in the audience. Then all eyes looked to the Wicked Stepmother for a response.

"Well you can't!" projected Ivy Morrison, who then proceeded to storm off the stage. The Ugly Sisters had no response to this unrehearsed section and, after a couple of shrugs to each other, decided to shuffle off sideways, much to the amusement of the audience. About ten lines were abandoned in this action but Mrs Forsythe decided that now was the time for the eager Fairy Godmother to appear.

"Why are you crying Cinderella?" she asked the bemused Sally Doyle. However, Sally was a professional and quickly picked up the cue.

"I'm sad because everybody's going to the ball except me," she whimpered.

"You shall go to the ball!" decided the fairy Godmother, raising her wand prematurely. This triggered a panic in mice/horses who were not yet on the stage.

"Who are you?" Cinderella finally asked, trying to return to the correct sequence of lines.

"Why, I'm your fairy godmother, my dear," Penelope added. The mice shuffled on, pulling the truck with the giant pumpkin. They were led by a reluctant Martin Butcher whose bottom lip was quivering quite noticeably.

"All I have, are these tattered clothes, fairy godmother," declared Cinderella.

"You shall go to the ball!" announced Penelope, waving her wand and setting off the sequence of events that we had so successfully rehearsed earlier. The flickering lights heralded the complete metamorphosis of the pumpkin, mice, frog and Cinderella's clothes and we were back on track. The audience applauded this magical transformation.

As Cinderella sat in the carriage, being pulled off stage, her fairy Godmother announced a very belated restriction to the evening. "You must leave before the stroke of midnight." Ian McKay was already making practice waves with the glockenspiel hammer, in anticipation.

Next was my first scene. The ball was the well-rehearsed part of show and we were confident that we would not let down Miss Davenport. She was a taskmaster and we were well-drilled. The audience "ahhh....ed" when I caressed my secret correspondent's hand, making me blush. Once again, the aroma of lavender confirmed my suspicions; there was definite chemistry.

As the waltz progressed a few flaws crept into the performance; Barry Cooper must have forgotten the 3-rule and seemed to be moving to a pattern of five beats to the bar. Sandra Adams suddenly opted for a clockwise rotation, whilst we were all spinning anti-clockwise. However, everyone managed to resolve their faux-pas' without total catastrophe. The bow at the end of the dance was the cue for Ian to commence the glockenspiel countdown.

"Dong!" rang out the first note.

"Oh no! I must leave!" cried Cinders.

"Dong! ...Dong!..Dong!" went the next three chimes, accelerating exponentially.

"No, don't leave yet!" I rushed, trying to stay with the pace.

"Dong!" continued Ian McKay. I could see that every member of the cast, including myself, was silently mouthing a six – as was half the audience.

"I have to leave!" said Cinderella. She was under strict instructions to be out of there by ten chimes.

"Dong! Dong! Dong!" came the next three seconds, at machine gun speed. I knew that I had to fire in my next line quickly.

"Wait! What's your name?" I asked.

"Dong!" rang ten, and Cinderella was gone.

Ian McKay slowed down eleven and twelve, "Dong..............Dong!" to dramatic effect. Then all eyes turned to me. I walked demonstratively over to the spot where Cinderella usually kicked off her 'glass slipper.' For the last few rehearsals we had used her black slip-on plimsoll. However, for the real event she was wearing her pink ballet shoes which were firmly tied on with pink ribbon. Unfortunately, when I reached the place where the discarded slipper was supposed to lay, there was nothing! Apparently, she had tried to kick off the slipper but, when it remained firmly attached to her foot, she panicked and bolted.

At first, I stood in disbelief but I did not panic. I instinctively leaned forward and picked up an imaginary slipper off the ground and summoned over the nervous-looking Martin Butcher, with his red velvet cushion.

I placed the imaginary slipper on the cushion and announced, "Whoever this slipper fits, I shall marry!" The audience seemed to be comfortable with the cover up and they were respectfully quiet.

Then, Barry Cooper piped up, "He's going to marry the Invisible Man!" The audience cracked up.

Meanwhile, backstage the mishap with the slipper was being taken very seriously. To Mrs Forsythe

the slipper was a pivotal part of the Cinderella story and she was determined that it should be on that cushion. So off went all the lights, causing some of the girls to scream, as though there had been a murder-in-the-dark and, when they came back on again, there sat a black slip-on plimsoll on the footman's cushion. Martin Butcher was like a hare frozen in the headlights.

At a loss, I picked up the plimsoll and reiterated, "Whoever this slipper fits, I shall marry!" The laughter was truly hysterical by this point and I was probably more scarlet than the cushion. However, the agony of Act Two was not yet over because, backstage they had finally prized the reluctant shoe from Cinderella's foot. The lights went off again, causing more screams than ever, and they came back on to show a ballet shoe, finally in its rightful position on the cushion.

For a third time, I picked up the offending slipper and projected, "Whoever this slipper fits, I shall marry!" The crowd broke out into whistles and spontaneous applause.

Before Act Three could commence there was some ego repair work to be done. Martin Butcher, who was going to have to follow me around with a slipper on a cushion was having a whiny moment and refusing to go back out there. Anton Zeleski was drafted in as his understudy. Sally Doyle was also pretty distraught about the shoe fumble. I suspect that Mrs Forsythe had been adding to her feelings of guilt.

I went over to try and offer consolation. "Good acting," was all I could think to say.

She half-smiled and said, "Sorry!"

"Sorry?" I responded, like I did not know what she was talking about.

"About the slipper; it wouldn't come off," she said

"I don't think anybody noticed," I lied, maintaining eye-contact.

"Really?" she said, a little incredulously. The eye contact trick seemed to reassure her. It occurred to me that acting and lying were pretty much the same skill.

"It's a great show," I acted, convincingly.

"Act Three, children; chop, chop!" Mrs Forsythe announced, clapping her hands, like all teachers do.

Act Three went off without a hitch. Admittedly, the comedy scenes, where the Ugly Sisters tried on the slipper, received less laughs than the Act Two's serious bit. However, the play finished, like the Cinderella story: happy ever after.

Mum and Kate Dawson met Andrew and me outside and fawned about how much they enjoyed our show. I saw Sally Doyle's mum heaping similar praise onto her daughter. We were just about to leave when Sally Doyle suddenly raced over, kissed me on the cheek, and ran off again.

"Sublime," I thought to myself. Andrew had taught me that this word described the best sensation ever - better than 'wonderful,' 'perfect' or 'magnificent.' This quick peck on my blushing cheek was a hundred times better than all my three previous kisses; better than scoring a goal for the school team; better than earning a Merit Badge; better than a long adventure with Teddy and Panda.

"Well I never," said mum.

"Can't blame her Beryl - he is charming!" said Kate.

"Prince Charming," laughed mum. I had a feeling that Kate had tucked a couple of Babychams into her handbag for the interval because they were both launched into the Thursday Night giggles.

That evening, I re-prioritized my account of the play, as I recalled it for Whiskey. Surprisingly, I did not harp on the embarrassing slipper incident, although I did tell him about Barry Cooper's Invisible Man joke. However, I gave detail, and a little embroidery, to the passionate embrace. I confessed that this lavender-flavoured caress was the most sublime moment of my life. I took out my two love letters and read them for the fiftieth time. I told my little rodent friend that it was going to be the best Christmas ever.

Eric was so excited that Santa Claus was on his way. Of course, Andrew had already found all of our presents under mum and dad's bed but we still acted surprised. Andrew got a camera and developing kit, which instantly sprung photography to number one on his hobbies list. I got a game where you could ask a robot questions and then he would spin and point to the right answer. I also got a Compendium of Games and Kenneth Wolstenholme's Football Annual.

Christmas dinner was excellent. Grandpa Eric had made an eleventh-hour donation, which was promptly translated into a whole chicken, roast potatoes, carrots, sprouts, stuffing, copious gravy, Christmas pudding and custard - not to mention a seven-pint can of beer, which exploded all over the kitchen floor, as dad opened it with a screwdriver and hammer. For the rest of the year our house smelled like the Berwick Arms.

New Year's Eve soon rolled around, bringing 1963 to an end. It was hard to believe that a whole year had passed since I had sat in the same shed with Whiskey, reviewing 1962 and pondering whether winter would bring any snow. There had been no hint that we would go on to enjoy the coldest winter ever. My *awkward streak* had brought me so many new agonizing secrets; secrets that only Whiskey would ever hear (at least for the next fifty years). I confided in my hamster that I had never anticipated being shot, vandalizing a moving bus or almost derailing a train. Then, there were the dreaded chilblains! I had fought with bullies, possibly, inadvertently arranging for one to murder the other. I had twice placed myself at the mercy of perverts and lived to tell the tale. I had saved Doodle from certain death. My mum had put a curse on a real-life gypsy prostitute. My accidental love letter had destroyed the marriage of our nice neighbours. On the other hand, our horrible neighbour had turned out to be my personal saviour. The relationship between my *'awkward streak'* and mum's 'temper cycles' had led to progressively worsening conflicts over the year. However, we had both pledged to eliminate these personality flaws, which offered some hope and solace. I had made my acting debut and nurtured my lying skills. I had witnessed at least a couple of miracles. Either a firework or wicked grandmother had fixed my lazy eye and I could finally get the 'doggy in the kennel!' Best of all, I had kissed four girls, including my true love, Sally Doyle.

I gave my love letters one final airing for the year and then hid them in my left Wellington boot. A cocktail of rubber, lavender, hamster, and creosote fumes consolidated my memory banks. There was no way of knowing what smells and memories 1964 would offer but I was excited to know that it was to be a leap year. I could hardly wait for the upcoming Tokyo Olympics. Andrew told me that The Beatles were planning to go to America and I wondered whether they would like them as much as we did.

I contemplated dad's words, "Show me a boy of seven and I'll show you the man." Seven seemed to be in the distant past. After all, I was only a few weeks off becoming a nine-year-old. Whiskey cast me a knowing glance then he curled up for his final snooze of 1963 – a most sublime and memorable year.

The End

Printed in Great Britain
by Amazon